FORT STARLIGHT

FORT STARLIGHT

a novel

Claudia Zuluaga

Engine Books
Indianapolis

Engine Books
PO Box 44167
Indianapolis, IN 46244
enginebooks.org

Also available in Hardcover and eBook formats from Engine Books.

Printed in the United States of America

10   9   8   7   6   5   4   3   2   1

ISBN: 978-1-938126-13-0

Library of Congress Control Number: 2013935827

To Christian, Pilar, and the sweet surprise of Wesley

She had neither rest nor peace until she secretly set forth and went out into the wide world, hoping to find her brothers and to set them free, whatever it might cost. She took nothing with her but a little ring as a remembrance from her parents, a loaf of bread for hunger, a little jug of water for thirst, and a little chair for when she got tired.

—Jacob and Wilhelm Grimm, *The Seven Ravens*

The Autumn Before

PAST THE BEACH HOUSES built on stilts in the sand, past the ocean highway that runs along Erne City, past an inlet that is a shade lighter than the ocean, past more houses, past small streets, past the Florida turnpike, past dark clusters of trees, two North American blackbirds, male and female, fly west over the southeastern shore of the Florida peninsula.

They fly over a dead armadillo in the middle of a roadway, flattened by a semi-truck's tires the week before, smashed grey shell, sticky black blood on the asphalt. They fly further west, until there are no more houses and few streets. They cross over the Starlight River, home to snapping turtles and army-green alligators. They pass flat fields, where shrubs grow in sharp, sparse grass.

They fly past an old Seminole burial ground, where, two centuries before, the last matriarch of a small tribe mourned for twelve new moons, her long gray hair disheveled, as custom dictated. Her husband had been buried with great care: his cheeks painted with broad stripes, his feet pointed east, his bow tucked under his arm.

The birds fly over earth that hides the fossilized skulls and teeth of mastodons, miniature horses, glyptodonts. This ground has been covered in ice, in ocean, in ice again. They fly until there is nothing but trees and swamp and trees and swamp, where there will be plenty of lizards and meaty insects to eat.

The land is part of Starlight County, but the place itself has no name yet. The map on the plans simply says *wetlands*, and it feels primordial, a place where anything dripping and new could step up out of the muck and begin its existence. In the afternoons, when the rain comes, small tornadoes move across these fields, two and three together. The earth smells both fresh and rotten. Families of dull-colored catfish have, in their isolation, grown bigger and blinder than any others in the state.

There will be a town here. The plans are confidential. Aside from a supermarket built off the turnpike, it looks like nothing, but a deal between the state of Florida and four different developers is in the works. Nobody else knows what will become of these seven square miles of muddy rivers, scrubby trees, swamp, the forest hammock. Or how soon it will begin.

The blackbirds land at the top of the tallest tree, in the middle of a dense wood. The tree is a live oak, four hundred and sixty-three years old. The branches are serpentine, strong, and draped in curling Spanish moss. In 1979, a bolt of lightning started a fire, burning many of the surrounding trees down to the mud, but the live oak was untouched.

A man, the only man for miles, walks through the grass, into the forest, and keeps going until he stops at the tree. He is going to build a home here, once he figures out how best to do it. He takes photographs of the tree from different angles, wraps a tape measure around the thickest part of the trunk, and writes the measurement in a tiny spiral-bound notebook that fits into his back pocket. He measures the thickness of the lowest branches, writes these figures down. Finally, he crouches, mops his brow, and closes his eyes.

The birds look out at the bright sky, at the expanse of damp, dark green. They spy a creek below and concentrate on the insects that hover just above it. The sun breaks through the trees in narrow beams, shining white gold on the surface of the water.

They lift, noiselessly, from the branch and fly down.

With one swoop, the female opens her beak, almost snapping it shut on the thorax of a dragonfly. But the dragonfly is too fast, and gets away.

ONE

"THAT'S A BIG ONE." The girl, Lily, turns the steering wheel and drives around the dark turtle crawling across the fresh black asphalt.

Ida Overdorff grips her head and watches the animal creeping along. The pain is mostly in her right temple. She can taste the beer from the night before. Since she overslept this morning and almost missed her flight, so focused on the part of her life that has not yet begun, she crossed eight states without even a sip of water.

In this bizarre emptiness of the Florida wilderness, the future has stepped to the side, forcing Ida to wait just a little longer.

Ida experiences the drive as if it were a dream; this is a place with no bearing on all that will come next. It feels like a dream. The wet heat of Florida in July cannot possibly be real. Neither can the haze rising from the black street. Or the turtle, crawling across the road like a broken toy running out of batteries. There is no reason to take any of it in. She'll be leaving again before any detail can leave an impression.

It is too bright, the colors too sharp. Even Lily, Ken Cantwell's teenage daughter, looks unreal, with her chunky pink forearms resting on the steering wheel, her glittery lip gloss, bright blue eyes, and red-gold hair. Lily is driving Ida through the empty streets of Fort Starlight to see the plot of land Ida bought through an ad in the back of *Rolling Stone* the summer after she graduated from high school.

Lily accelerates.

Ida grips her forehead. When she looks at the sky, she sees seagulls. "How close is the ocean?" she asks.

Lily points to the horizon. "That way. About fifteen miles. I hardly ever go. Too far. May as well not be there."

WHEN IDA WALKED INTO his office two hours before, the look in Ken Cantwell's eyes—she still isn't sure if it was alarm or simply surprise—didn't reassure her. On the phone, Ken suggested that signing the paperwork in person might eliminate layers of bureaucracy, that her remote location would mean weeks of delay.

She bought a one-way plane ticket, figuring she could take a cheap, slow Greyhound back, and flew in an airplane for the first time in her life. What surprised her was that the morning in New York was grey and damp, but the weather above the clouds was perfect and bright.

When she introduced herself, Ken put his hand under his polo shirt, scratched at his paunch, frowned. Before saying a word, he picked up a telephone and pressed a few buttons. Ida watched his thick chest rise and fall. He was listening to something; she could hear a woman's voice coming through the receiver. She looked around and saw scattered Styrofoam cups, stained at the edges with coffee. Half a chocolate donut on a napkin. An open dopp kit sat on the desk-top copier; a can of shaving cream, crusted at the opening, peeked out.

Ken placed the phone down and looked at her sideways.

"I'm kind of in the middle of something. Maybe we could do this some other time?"

"I flew here this morning," said Ida. "I'm the one from upstate New York, remember? Ida? We talked last Tuesday. I don't have anywhere to go. I just want the check and then I'll head back to New York tonight."

Not back upstate, where she'd lived her whole life, but the city. And once she got there, she'd go to the 24-hour McDonald's in Times Square, find the old man she'd seen working at three in the morning just a day ago, the one who had been wiping spilled Cokes, scraping gum from under the tables, pushing a wet mop across the polished concrete floor. She would give him five fresh hundred dollar bills. She could see him, shuffling home as the sun began to rise, taking off the McDonald's visor as he walked into the single rented room he probably shared, in a crummy apartment in an outer borough, hiding the bills between his mattress and sheet. If he had a sheet. She remembered how his expression didn't change as he worked, even when the drunken frat boy knocked over his strawberry shake, stepped in it, and walked the sticky pink footprint all the way to the door.

Five hundred dollars. Probably would be gone in a blink, but what he did with the money didn't matter. Everybody needed a windfall once in a while. She'd done nothing to deserve what she was about to get.

Ken pointed to a black folding chair. She sat down in it and rubbed her bare forearms; the office was freezing.

He picked up the phone again, and nestled it between his shoulder and his ear so that his hands would be free to type. Once in a while, he'd press a number on the phone and then he'd type some more.

She listened to the hum of the air conditioning, eying the half donut. If it were offered, she would eat it no matter how long it had been sitting there. She also had to pee, but she couldn't see a bathroom in the office. No door to anywhere but the outside.

She cleared her throat, knowing it sounded obnoxious.

Ida hadn't thought about the land even once in the six years since she bought it, until a month ago, when she got the letter from Ken Cantwell's office. Her quarter acre was worth three times her initial investment, the letter said, but since land values had plateaued, she should consider selling it as soon as possible through the agency acting on behalf of an investor. Money. Except for right now—with three weeks of paychecks saved up, and her apartment vacated with her rent overdue—Ida rarely had more than a few hundred bucks at any one time.

Ken held his hand up as if to say, 'wait just another second,' but five long minutes ticked by before he put the phone down and stood up.

"I'm having one hell of a crazy day," he inhaled and exhaled, loudly, as though it were an effort to breathe. "So…do you want to see it, before you sell it?"

"See what?"

He pointed to a blueprint map of the town, tacked to the wall.

"The land. The land you're selling. It's officially yours until the paperwork goes through all the way, so I figure if you're here, you may as well."

"Huh," she said, squeezing her thighs together.

"You're kind of young to be a landowner."

"I guess," she said. "I'm twenty-four."

"And you bought it when you were just a kid. That was a grown up thing to do, don't you think?"

She shrugged. "I guess."

She didn't tell him that, at the time, buying the land had been the only way she could resist blowing the thousand dollars on an unsatisfying shopping spree or throwing it into the fire that was her family's constant need. The phone shut off, the power shut off, the family Chevy, up on blocks on the muddy lawn.

"They aren't making any more land," said Ken. "The economic future of this whole country is in new towns."

He scratched his stomach, his nails making a scritching sound over the fabric of his shirt. He walked to the blueprint map on the wall and traced his finger along until he found her lot. "Well there you are," he said, and finally grinned at her. His eyes were watercolor blue.

"Okay, I've seen it. So when will I get the check?"

"No, no," he laughed. "See it in person. My daughter, Lily, can take you over there." He pointed outside, where the young, chubby girl stood, leaning against the storefront glass.

"Sure, I guess."

Ken went over what needed to happen before the sale was complete. She half listened; the specifics did not hold her attention, but the overall gist was that everything would most likely be set by tomorrow. A few things still needed to be double-checked and notarized. She would have to stay in a hotel tonight. Fine. Whatever she had to do. She nodded.

"Is there a bathroom nearby?"

"There's a big one at the Karr's supermarket down the plaza," he said, pointing. "But there's a closer one just two doors down. Here's the key. I'll get you and Lily a smaller map while you're in there."

The strip-mall bathroom was white and windowless. Ida turned the light off before turning the knob, and the heavy door and rubber threshold blocked the sunlight completely. For a moment, she stood in a square of perfect darkness. She felt around on the wall until she found the light switch.

Ken handed her a photocopy of a section of the map, folded in two, and held the door for her. Lily stood outside, bored, tossing the car keys in the air and catching them.

"Lil," he said. "Take her out to Ring and Marine." He turned to Ida. "It's a corner lot."

"Noooo," Lily said, her voice a whine. "Please tell me you aren't asking me that now. I've just been waiting here to tell you that I have to go. I was trying to be nice and not interrupt."

"Go where? You're at work. You can't go."

"Go home. I don't *feel* good," she said.

"You don't feel *well*."

Lily stared at him blankly.

"Here's the deal. If you still don't feel well after you take her, then you can go home early."

THE FLOOR OF THE car is covered in sand, crumpled tissues, empty soda cans. Lily hasn't talked much during the drive over, though she intermittently hums along to the Top 40 radio station. A thick chunk of her hair blows into her mouth and she gags, coughs, and pulls it out, tucking it authoritatively behind her ear, as though it had better not piss her off again.

"I wish we never moved here," says Lily. "This place sucks."

Ida doesn't have the energy to respond. She remembers the half bag of Skittles still in her purse from the day before and reaches in with her right hand, poking her fingers into the bag to pull some out. She doesn't want to share. The sugar and citric acid go straight to her bloodstream, like a bright light has been turned on in her head.

There are fewer and fewer cars as Lily drives them onto smaller roads. Outside of the car's windows are open fields, dotted every once in a long while with a squat, rectangular house. Wooden telephone poles line both sides of the streets. A big, ungainly bird, perched on top of one of the poles, scans the land below.

"We're on Ring Road and that's Marine up there, I think," Lily points at the map. "That's probably your land over on that corner, or maybe the one right after. I'm bad with maps. Specially when the streets don't have anything on them. You figure it out."

Ida takes the map and holds it in her hands. The red and black lines blur together. This is real. This is not a dream. For that whole six years, from 1991, an official piece of paperwork with her name on it sat filed away in some official drawer. It is now 1997 and she owns something: an actual piece of the actual earth. She has never even bothered picturing it.

A yellow pick-up truck speeds by, music blaring. Lily slows down and sticks her head out of the window.

"Jason! Whoooo!" She shouts and honks the horn. The yellow truck stops and reverses until the two drivers' windows are next to each other.

Inside the truck are two burly teenaged boys and, between them, a twiggy, red-haired, teenaged girl with an unimpressed expression.

Lily and the boys call to each other across their cars.

"What up?"

"What up?"

The red-haired girl stretches and yawns and turns the music up higher.

"Come hang out," the bigger boy calls to Lily. He revs the engine. His eyes are small, his lips puffy. He has a red beer can in his hand. "I been looking for you. We're gonna head back to Valponia and see a movie. Some 3-D shit."

"Can't," Lily shrugs, gesturing at Ida with a tilt of her head, and this subtle dismissive move ordinarily would piss Ida off, but she doesn't have the energy for it.

"Come on. At least for a couple minutes."

"Gimme a sec." Lily turns to Ida. "Listen, I'm going to drop you off for a little bit so you can look at your very own piece of property. I swear I'll come right back and get you. Like in five minutes."

"It's right over there. I'll walk." Ida steps out and slams the door.

"I swear I won't be gone for more than, like, a couple minutes. I just want to talk to my friends." Lily smiles like a six-year-old hoping for another cookie. "I'll meet you here. Don't forget. Right here," she calls. She revs the engine and speeds down the road. The truck follows.

Ida is glad to be away from her.

There are no sidewalks anywhere. The lush black asphalt of the newly poured street is soft and smooth under her feet and gives slightly with each step.

As she walks, she wipes her forehead with the sleeve of her t-shirt. How could anyone get used to this heat? Ida's mouth fills with saliva; a wave of hot nausea moves through her body. Stupid. She should have walked down the plaza to the grocery for a bottle of water when she had the chance.

She steps over a dead snake, its middle flattened by a tire's tracks. She sees another.

And then another. The biggest yet. About as long as she is tall.

The land at the corner of Ring and Marine has a small house on it. Ida unfolds the map section that Ken gave her, and checks the lot number again. Yes. Definitely here. Off to the left and winding back is a canal, just like on the map. The ranch-style house is new, coated in beige stucco, and looks as if it is waiting for someone, its two front windows like watching eyes.

She approaches the house and knocks at the door. The sound echoes and she tries the knob. It opens. Inside, the house is empty, unfinished, with short wires hanging from the ceiling. The house gives off a dry, acidic smell, like the pages of a new notebook. The concrete floor is covered in a powdery white film. On the right is a living room, but half of one wall is missing, with a blue tarp sealing it off from the outdoors. Strips of silver duct tape hold the bottom in place, but there are gaps. She walks over to the tarp, puts her hand in front of it, watching it moving in and out. The blue reaches toward her hand, the blue pulls back.

On the left is the kitchen, with just a steel slop-sink and *x* marks on the wall, denoting where a refrigerator, stove, and dishwasher will someday be.

Ida regards all of the effort with a little solemnity. So much work. If the world were made up only of people like her, there are some things that just wouldn't happen. Built shelters, for one thing. She eyes the straight walls, the even floor. A world made up only of Idas would be a world of people living in caves. No cars, no telephones, no scientific wondering about the stars and the heavens and the role of the sun. It would be a flat earth. Maybe there would be some useful things, but she can't think of any right now.

Down a small corridor she finds two bedrooms and a small, windowless bathroom. Her breathing quickens as she peers into each of the rooms, half expecting to find someone standing in one of them.

In the kitchen Ida tries the light switch. There is a quiet buzzing sound, but the light doesn't come on. She looks up at the fixture: no bulb. She turns on the sink faucet. A thin trickle of brown water begins, then clears and strengthens. She leans in and drinks from the faucet. It tastes of sulfur, but she drinks until she can feel the water sloshing around in her empty stomach.

When she looks out the kitchen window at the back of the house, she sees the canal, the dark water sparkling in the sun. A green lizard sits on the outside windowsill, jerking its head back and forth.

It makes no sense. If this is her land, the letter should have mentioned that a house had already been built on it.

She walks out of the house and shuts the door behind her. There is another house, off in the distance. A car is parked in front of it, though it is far enough away that she can't make out the color.

Ida can't remember exactly where Lily left her. Everything looks pretty much the same. Her armpits and the backs of her knees are wet.

She stands still in the heat, holding her hand up over her eyes like a visor, watching. Lily will see her. How could she miss her?

The sulfury water rises in Ida's throat. She longs for a cold tile floor to rest her cheek against. She remembers the first bottle of beer Linda pushed into her hand the night before, how the condensation had dripped down her bare wrist, how good it had seemed: a perfect gateway to the next part of life, this colossal hangover a rite of passage.

Sweat rolls into her eye, stinging. She could easily die in a place like this. She hears her heart beating in her ear and feels the sun burning her nose and the tops of her cheeks.

Ida stares at the asphalt, counting a minute, another minute, then more and more minutes, because if she concentrates on the numbers, she can distract herself from the real question: what if Lily doesn't come back? She has no idea which way civilization might be, but she doubts it is within walking distance. *Now,* she mutters, *Come now. Fucking please NOW.* When the truck finally comes into view, she is convinced she has willed it there.

Lily's eyes are bloodshot.

"What the hell took you so long?" Ida says as she steps in. "I've been waiting for you for an hour." She doesn't know if it was an hour. Maybe it was two hours, maybe twenty minutes.

"Please don't tell my dad I left you," Lily pleads. She giggles stupidly for a few minutes, and then turns the radio on, singing along quietly to a heavy metal ballad, each line a second behind the actual song. Ida shakes her head. She rolls her window down and closes her eyes, letting the air dry the sweat from her face.

KEN GREETS IDA WITH a light slap on her shoulder.

"You'll be happy to hear that I personally delivered a copy of the property information over to the right people. Just a few minutes ago. They told me they'd get it all done by the end of the week."

"Oh," she says, frowning. "Earlier I think you told me a day or two."

"I mean completely done. Over and out."

"So I'll definitely get a check?" Ida says, her hand on her hip. The coffee cups are gone, the dopp kit put away somewhere.

"No doubt. You'll have to sign a few more documents first, but they will hand it over right after you do."

"Huh," she says. "I'm not sure what to do."

"There's a motel right at the other end of the plaza. I think they're running a pretty good special, too. You can just hang out until then and you'll get your check on Friday and you'll be done."

He opens the door and points a thick finger to the left.

"Right there," he says. "That pink building."

It looks nice, with potted palms out front.

"I hadn't really budgeted for that."

"Well what did you think you'd do, then, little lady?" he says, incredulous.

Ida shrugs. She looks down at Ken's bright white running shoes.

She says, "There's a house on my lot. It's not really finished being built, but the power is on. There's water in the pipes."

"No," he shakes his head. "Couldn't be. Sweetheart, you must have been looking at the wrong lot. Maybe a half a mile from there, there's a house that I think was getting built. One of the demo models for the housing community that's coming. Also a couple spec houses that already got bought and built. Not near Ring and Marine, though. Are you sure you went to the right place?"

Ida nods.

"It all looks the same out there." He smiles as though there is nothing left to say about the matter, so she doesn't insist. She can bring it up on Friday.

"Want one of these?" he asks, holding out a bag of donuts.

"Good God, yes," she says, and she picks one: glazed blueberry. She takes a big bite and smiles at him as she chews. She is way too easy, she knows. She waves goodbye and throws her duffel over her shoulder, walking toward the motel.

The lobby has a skylight that lets in the heat and brightness of the sun. On every surface is an arrangement of artificial tropical flowers. No one is at the front desk. A sign lists the special Ken mentioned: $60 a night with a continental breakfast.

"Can I help you?" A bald man comes out of the lobby restroom, wiping his hands on his pants. "You're not with the state, are you?"

"Nope," she says. "I'm just…a regular person." One who has never stayed in a hotel before.

"I didn't think so," he says, going through the gate to the lobby desk. "Too young. Florida planners and developers are really the only guests we've ever gotten. So far."

Ida nods, noticing a telephone on the wall marked *Courtesy Phone* and a laminated list of numbers next to it. *Star County Car Service gets you around lightning fast.*

"How many nights will you be with us?" he says, typing on the keyboard behind the desk.

"Uh," she says, counting. "Four."

"Check out Friday morning, then?"

She nods, thinking excitedly about the cable TV, the bath she'll get to take, the air conditioning she will turn on full blast while she sleeps naked under a thick comforter. Tiny bottles of shampoo.

The man mumbles as he pecks at the keyboard with one forefinger. He is about to tell her a dollar total. It will cost a lot of what she has to make it to Friday, not even including food. She doesn't like how much lighter her roll of cash has gotten in the day and a half since she left her apartment, when she'd locked it up and slipped the key under the door without even a note to the landlord.

She has an idea that makes her uneasy: she can stay in the strange, unfinished house and not spend any money on a hotel.

"Is this going to be cash or a credit card?" he asks.

She'll have the money, in case anything goes wrong.

"You know what," she says, "I think I've changed my mind."

She can deal with sleeping on the floor. She will survive. And it is her right, anyway; since the land is hers, the house is also hers. That is how these things work, she is certain. She writes the car service number on the palm of her hand and walks to the supermarket.

She has never seen a store like it. Massive. Bright stainless steel carts, tanks of live seafood. The produce is brightly colored and piled high along the mirrored walls. The automatic mister comes on, giving the broccoli and asparagus bundles an ethereal shine. It is an amusement park of food, nothing like the dingy, unappetizing Food-Town in Aster, with its piles of graying lettuce.

The back of the store has a housewares section selling ice cream makers, mushroom brushes, alarm clocks, striped beach towels. On the walk over, she comprised a list, but hadn't counted on being able to find cheap, thin chair cushions she could sleep on. She grabs a flat sheet, a pillow, a paperback book, a cooler. She buys enough food for a few days: crackers and fruit and chocolate and potato chips and popcorn, fried chicken and tuna salad from the delicatessen, which she will nestle in the cooler once she fills it with ice.

A stock boy follows her as she moves from aisle to aisle; she sees him peeking around the corners, his mouth open, his brow furrowed as if she is something he needs to figure out. He is wiry and redheaded. Eighteen, tops. She isn't sure at first that he is following her, but there he is again by the pyramid of oranges. And again by the toilet paper.

One side of his mouth curves up in a smart-ass smile. He leans against the shelf and she feels pleasantly eaten up as he looks at her. It doesn't happen often. She stands there, letting him look for a minute, sucking in her stomach, wondering what the magic is about. He slinks away, disappearing behind a row of crayons and coloring books.

Ida grabs a bottle of pear-scented shampoo, a hairbrush, a new toothbrush, bottles of water, toilet paper, a ceramic dish, two drinking glasses, a fork, knife, and spoon, a sponge, a tiny bottle of dish liquid, bubblegum, a disposable camera. A bag of ice. All of it costs just under sixty dollars. At the cash register, she turns back and sees the stock boy again, standing in the middle of an aisle. He holds up his price gun and aims it at her.

Pow, he mouths.

She laughs. Maybe he can see her future. Maybe courage and optimism are radiating from her. Maybe they combined to create a potent new pheromone that cancels out the layer of grunge left over from her long journey.

Ida calls the car service from a pay phone outside. Night is coming on. She waits, watching moths buzzing under the lights. A light wind smells of salt and wood, clean and dark. Maybe the ocean is closer than Lily said. Her ponytail floats up and falls back down, as though someone lifted it and let go. She is anxious to see the house again. Had it really been there?

The driver helps her put her things in the trunk and then drives them away from town through the darkening streets. They pass a gas station, not yet open.

"Heard they're gonna connect the highway here," he says. "I don't know when."

They don't pass a single car. Several times, he opens a small map and drags his finger along its roads. He is old, maybe too old to be working. He is probably somebody's great-grandfather.

He says, "I've never been exactly right here. I didn't know there was any houses except for the ones near that grocery."

"Damn," Ida whispers to herself. She forgot to buy light bulbs; the house will be dark.

Half of the sky holds the sunset and is pink and gold. The other side is smoky blue, the shadows of the power lines long.

He has gone too far and turns around. "I'm not charging with a meter, don't worry."

He gets lost again, driving on a dirt road when the asphalt ends. Once he realizes the asphalt isn't going to start back up, he puts the car in reverse, sandy dirt rising up in a cloud around them. It gets darker. He drives more slowly.

Finally, the car's headlights light up a house.

"That's it," she says, recognizing the blue tarp.

Keeping the car running, he opens the trunk and helps drag her Karr's bags to the front stoop.

"I don't have a phone, but you think you can come back and get me on Friday? Three o'clock? I need to go back to where you picked me up then."

"I can do that. Sure," he nods and gets back in the dusty sedan.

"You'll remember where it is?"

"Sure I will," he says, and nods goodbye to her. When the taillights disappear in the distance, there is no other light. She wants to feel triumphant—everything is happening almost exactly as she'd hoped—but when she opens the door to the dark house, she isn't sure.

She eats a fried chicken breast all the way down to the bones and cartilage. She stuffs her mouth full of cool grapes. She fills her glass with water and ice, and sips it. After, she feels around for the bag containing the chair cushions, and she sets them down on the floor, curls up on her side, and hopes that sleep will come. A cricket chirps, too close to be outside. She tries not to think about snakes. She looks out the window and sees the half moon, shrouded in a thin cloud. She moves her arm in front of her face and it looks like a smooth, white bone.

TWO

THE RAIN AND WINDS kick up. The tarp sucks in and sucks out. Ida heard this noise the night before, in the dark, but couldn't figure out what it was. The house is breathing. Respiration: automatic, rhythmic. Ida stares at the tarp, counting the seconds between breaths and matching them with her own. She wonders if and when the builders will come back to finish. Hopefully not before Friday.

She survived. In the bright sun of the morning, she finds mosquito bites all over her arms and legs, one on her chin. All of the humidity and sweating, even the mosquitoes, pulled the last of the toxicity out of her. So much happened in just a few days: the rushing, the packing, the momentum of leaving everything that was nothing to lose and would not miss her anyway. For the first time, her body pulses with energetic confidence.

She has three nights to go, but she will make it, even without light bulbs or cross-ventilation. There aren't any screens in the windows, and she isn't about to invite more mosquitoes in. Today, she doesn't have to go outside at all. She can stay here all day, read her book, and take a cold bath in the virgin tub. The rooms are perfect boxes, the corners crisp, and she is protected. The back corner of the house is the tarp, blue and alive. The house is breathing.

❀

SHE WALKS INTO THE kitchen and looks out the back window at the field that leads to the canals. A sleek white egret steps gingerly across the muddy banks, its legs so thin that she can barely make them out, as though it is floating along in the air, a small, low-lying cloud.

This house will be someone's happy beginning. Ida looks at the spot where the stove will go and imagines someone standing there, pushing scrambled eggs around with a spatula, popping the toast down for another round, talking to someone in the next room. Other houses will soon be built on the lots on Ken's map, and there will be neighbors for friends, and they can take turns making dinner for each other. A dozen times, she touches her cheek to the powdery sheetrock, letting it give her a soft kiss.

Thank God she bought the book. *The Luck Unicorn.* Mysterious stenciled unicorns were appearing on people's front doors. The blue chalk ones brought good luck to the people inside, but the red chalk ones brought the obliteration of everything good in their lives: newborn babies contracted deadly infections, furnaces exploded, damaging secrets were brought to light. The part of the book that she can't quite swallow is that it is told in the voice of a six-year-old, a six-year-old with a far better vocabulary than even Ida has, and what seems to be unlimited freedom for roaming the streets, alone, late at night, as she tries to find out who is responsible for the stencils. Ida stops reading when what she suspected would happen does happen: the six-year-old comes home just before sunrise, only to find a red stencil on her own door.

The sun is setting. Ida closes the book and thinks about the stock boy in the supermarket, the raw look he gave her, how long they locked eyes.

As it gets darker, she imagines going into Karr's at closing time and slipping inside. No one will know she is there and the employees, except for him, will exit through the back door while she wanders the dim aisles. He will sense her. The door will be locked and the lights will go out and she will hear the sound of his breathing. She will stand still, waiting for him to find her in the dark. A rough, warm hand on the cool skin at the back of her neck.

FORT STARLIGHT

✻

THE NEXT MORNING IS Wednesday, halfway through, just two days away from the check. It is almost nine o'clock when she wakes. If she were still in Aster, she'd be leaving for work at the Aster Community Center, setting up crafts tables for adult day-campers, with glue sticks and glitter and markers and paints. It was the only job she'd ever quit and given any notice. They were autistic or had Down's Syndrome, and one who didn't fit in at all was just plain blind. They all needed something to do. She brought them to matinees at the Aster movie theater, took a chartered bus to the zoo two towns away, danced the hokey-pokey and the alley-cat when the weather was terrible.

Ida splashes water on her face and tugs on her t-shirt and shorts. She wonders if anybody misses her. She opens the door to the bright sun and closes it again. She goes to the bathroom and brushes her teeth.

Three minutes have passed since she first opened her eyes. She should have bought more books. She sits on the floor with a handful of crackers and opens *The Luck Unicorn*. The six-year-old has decided to wipe away the red chalk unicorn stencil. No need for her mother to find it and panic. She watches her mother drink coffee and fry eggs, and is relieved to see no signs of imminent disaster. The house does not burn down from a rebel flame on the stove. Nobody chokes. Together, they pack her bag and go out to wait for the school bus.

How this child makes it through every day not sleeping, Ida has no idea, but when the book is three-quarters finished, she closes it. Better to save the rest for later.

Ida presses her feet together, closes her eyes, inhales very slowly, exhales, tries to meditate, concentrating on the mantra of *soon, soon, soon*, but she can't do it. Her limbs are too charged, like she is full of caffeine. She looks at her Timex and does the math. Fifty-three and one half hours of this. She looks out the kitchen window and sees a fading rainbow so high and wide that she can't see either end. She pushes her feet into her canvas tennis shoes, grabs a bottle of water and twenty dollars, and walks out the front door. Maybe she'll find that the supermarket isn't so far, and she can buy herself a few more books.

The grass is damp on her ankles. She turns right.

Stubby trees, soggy, dark canals, fields of buzzing grass. This is not how Ida pictured Florida. No plastic flamingos, conch shells, tourists in loud shirts. Nobody ever imagines anything but the coast, and she hasn't seen a speck of coastline. The place looks thirsty and rough, like something from a National Geographic safari show.

Ida walks with sweaty determination, not turning into any of the streets she passes, walking straight until the road ends in sandy dirt. Across a long field, beyond a stand of trees, she can make out two houses. She wants to see them up close, to see if anyone lives in them, but the yellow-green grass prohibits her shortcut. It has to be full of snakes.

She backtracks and makes the first left. The sun is getting serious now and she has no sunscreen, no hat. She will burn and peel, and that is okay. Brand new skin for her fresh start.

One of the houses comes into clearer view, but it isn't as close as it seems. When she gets closer, she sees a glistening blue rectangular swimming pool. It even looks clean. She wishes she knew how to swim. She can tread water for a few seconds, but she never goes under, afraid of some force pulling her down. She saw a movie once where a woman dove into a pool and as she tried to surface, realized she was trapped.

Ida approaches the ivory stucco facade and reaches for the door. There is no knob, just a hole. She puts her hand on the door and it opens. It is so bright inside. She looks up and sees the sun. There is no roof, only wooden beams and grey concrete. Building a pool before a roof. Weird.

Something moves in the corner. Something grey.

It's an armadillo, looking to her like a cross between a piglet and a knight in shining armor. Ida shrieks and the armadillo jumps a foot in the air, lands, and begins crawling backward, its claws scratching at the concrete. She runs outside and tugs the door closed.

"Holy Jeez!" she laughs. Maybe it was trapped in there, had gone inside to look around and the wind pulled the door shut. She pulls the door open again and walks away quickly, so it doesn't have a good chance to come after her. She doesn't know anything about armadillos, what they eat, if they bite people. She jogs back to the road.

The weather is changing. Dark grey clouds coalesce, sweeping across the pale blue like a tidal wave. The sky crackles with lightning and it begins to pour. She runs, laughing, toward her house. She is a moving target, but she is no longer hot.

THE NEXT MORNING, THURSDAY, she wakes to the sound of her brother Robert's voice.

"Ida, quick, come in here," he says, his voice so clear and real that she can see him as he looked that last day, the unlit cigarette between his two fingers, the brim of his fedora over his eyes, fingertips drumming on the thigh of suit pants that were too floppy for his bony, teenaged legs.

"I'm coming," she says, and props herself up on her arms.

"Jesus, Ida, hurry up!" He sounds so impatient with her that even after she is fully awake, she can't shake the feeling that she has disappointed him, once again.

He used to tell her to make sure she got out of Aster. "Don't fester here. Don't let yourself get ruined." And she would nod as if to say *of course, why would I*, but she almost had. She'd forgiven him for leaving her behind and not looking back, not writing, not telling her what it was like to leave Aster and Door Hill behind. She'd thought they were the same, but the day he left, he treated her like part of everything he was trying to escape.

Robert told her that their parents had once tried to give them away to an orphanage. The image of the orphanage would sit there between the two of them, unverifiable, dark, strange, and very easy for her to believe. She did believe it. There was never any real malice—just ambivalence—but their parents were rarely around; when they were, doors were closed. They displayed no curiosity about whether Ida and Robert were hungry, feverish, failing at school. There was no pretense of family dinners, and she and her brother had turned into all-day snackers, eating tuna from the can. And Robert was the one who had to say, that day she couldn't stand up straight, *We need to take Ida to the hospital. I think it's her appendix*, and it took them an hour to take him seriously enough to load her into the car and stop insisting that she probably just had to fart. They made a pretense of griping about how much it would cost, but in the end, the state of New York paid for it anyway.

They'd lived in a cluttered, sunless house at the bottom of Door Hill that her mother had inherited when her own parents died. It was the lowest point in town, where the rain runoff turned the yards eternally muddy. Red-eyed men walked out of the ravines, clutching bottles. Collarless dogs came out of nowhere, barked, disappeared back into the woods.

Where had Robert gone? Her guess was somewhere warm. He hated winter, his shivering, skinny body.

Ida takes a cool shower, using the pear shampoo all over her body, but the lather and scent don't take the feeling away. Any good feelings she had are gone. She feels empty, ugly, doomed, transported right back to Door Hill. Robert is free, but she is still stuck. It's because she has her mother's lashless brown eyes, her father's bad posture. She is like them, but Robert is Robert; he looks like himself and only himself. His dark hair isn't Overdorff hair. The farthest she had ever made it from Door Hill was three quarters of a mile, to the basement apartment at the center of town. Unless now counts. It probably doesn't. Will the taxi come tomorrow? Will Ken have a check for her? She had been so stupidly certain.

She steps outside and stands in the sun. Walking is the only antidote.

It isn't until the house is almost out of sight that she realizes she forgot her water bottle. Already she is thirsty, but she has gone too far to turn back. She left her watch, too, and can't tell how much time has gone by. She stops several times, crouching to rest.

She can't see her future anymore, can't see herself living in Linda's apartment, baking in that big kitchen with the window that overlooks the park, can't see herself getting out of here alive. She lets herself cry for a moment. Just a few tears.

Inside her house, she finishes the last bottle of water, then drinks glass after glass of the sour water from the tap. She paces while she eats potato chips and popcorn, not tasting them, until her jaw begins to ache. The house is grotesque. She hates it, hates the damp concrete smell, the cruel blackness of the bathroom, the hot echo of her own breath. Inside or outside, she is trapped. She stares out of the window, hoping to see the egret again.

And then, there it is, only now there are two of them. One takes a step toward the other, its long neck a dainty S.

One more night.

AFTER THE SUN SETS, she hears the high pitch of the mosquitoes and swats around her face. In the dark, she imagines the worst: yellow eyes watching her, Robert gone from her life forever because she didn't get to him quickly enough.

On the day before he left, he asked her if she wanted to come with him, to leave Door Hill behind forever. Where would they sleep, she wanted to know. Wasn't he worried about ending up homeless? *We already know how to take care of ourselves. We've been doing it forever.* She didn't take him seriously. Why should she have? For so long, he was all talk and no action, like her. He was going to be a bluesman, he was going to write a science fiction comic book series. Yeah, yeah, yeah. He was just as stuck on Door Hill as she was.

And she would miss Linda too much. And she heard a rumor that a boy was going to ask her to a party the next weekend, and she wanted to see if it was really going to happen. She didn't believe Robert would really leave, but he did, and the boy never asked her to the party.

SHE OVERSLEEPS. THE TAXI is due in six hours, if it comes at all. Ida gets dressed and walks outside. She remembers the gas station she saw when she was in the taxi, before the driver got lost. There is an adjoining food mart, newly built, but empty of people or goods. But there is a pay phone there, she is sure, black and rectangular, mounted by the air pumps.

She will find the gas station and call the taxi company. And then she'll call Linda. She has a stack of coins.

The lack of landmarks makes it hard to tell if she is going the right way, but she has her water and some crackers wrapped in toilet paper in her back pocket. The coins in her front pocket thump against her thigh. She longs for sunglasses.

The sweating begins. Ida stops and gulps the tap water she filled the empty bottle with. She can't mess around. Nothing is truer than the fact that she was born only to die someday, and the instruments of death—sun, heat, predators—surround her.

If she doesn't find it soon, she'll have to turn back. In the field to her left is a perfect tree for climbing, just tall enough, with thick limbs that start low to the ground. Ida takes bold steps through the tall grass to get to it. She pulls herself up on a waist-high branch and climbs around and up the tree until she is high enough that she can see the canals and the patchwork of razed lots. She is headed the right direction after all; there, not all that far away, is the gas station. Just a bit further down the road, there is an intersection, where she needs to go left. She climbs down the tree, proud of her grace and wishing someone could see her.

THE PHONE HAS A dial tone. She plunks in the quarter and punches in the numbers. Yes, the taxi is scheduled for three o'clock.

Ida dials Linda's number and a recorded operator asks for three dollars and ten cents for the next two minutes. She rests the receiver on her shoulder and counts the coins in her hand. A nickel short. But nothing has changed, no matter how unreal it feels now. Linda still needs a roommate and Ida is still going to be it. She starts her walk back.

Last week, when Ida had gotten up the guts to call Linda to tell her what had happened, that she was finally getting out of Aster, that she'd been too ashamed of her lame existence to keep in very good touch, and that she'd be flying out of LaGuardia, which was close to Linda's apartment in Queens, Linda talked her into coming early, to spend the day, spend the night. She pulled her into her life with flattering enthusiasm. *Fuck going back to Aster. Move in with me! I can get you work at my temp agency. This will be your room, once Melanie comes to get her stuff. Look at the view. That's Astoria Park and that's the East River beyond it. Look at the kitchen. You still into the baking?*

IDA HEARS SOMETHING BEHIND her. She turns just as it zooms past: a man on a bicycle. He flies by with only a few inches between them. She yelps. The man doesn't look back. He is kitted out like a magazine photo of a cyclist, with tight black shorts, a purple and green jersey, sleek little shoes, a white cycling cap. He didn't seem to notice her and he looks so out of place. More hologram than human being. He gets smaller and smaller until he turns and disappears.

Her house is coming into view. Maybe she can find a bus out of Florida tonight. With the check she'll be getting from Ken, she'll invest in serious pans and cookie sheets, mixing bowls, pastry tubes, some new clothes, the tall black Doc Marten's she has always wanted, her share of the rent, and enough left over to buy herself a little time if she doesn't find a temp job right away. She'll figure out a way to be a baker. Maybe open her own tiny shop someday, and the boots will be her trademark. She has a lot to learn, still: cakes have always intimidated her. When she does try, her anxiety makes her rush and forget things: they are dry, or she forgets to add the salt, or they fall when she lets the oven door slam. And no matter how carefully she frosts, they never look particularly pretty. She isn't great with her hands.

Ida hears the spinning wheels of the bicyclist behind her again. She can hear breathing, slow and loud. He wears mirrored sunglasses and has a tight set to his narrow jaw.

She turns and faces him as he approaches, hands on her hips.

This time, as he rides past—as closely as before—he turns his head to the side and spits. Not in her direction, but still. The yellowish gob sits on the pavement. She stops, waiting for him to turn back and pant an apology, but he keeps going.

"Hey!" she shouts at his back, but her voice is weak. She should have knocked him over when she had had the chance.

It is almost two when she gets to the house. She changes clothes, gathers her things, and packs her bag. The cushions and glasses and everything else she is leaving behind, piled in the middle of the living room.

THREE

ALONG THE WOODEN BOARDWALK of the recently completed Starlight River Park stand signs that name the genus, species, and history of the trees, and provide information about local animals. In the river just below it, the body of Mitchell Healy, a twelve-year-old boy, is guarded by a thirteen-foot female alligator. The body has been here twenty-one hours already and, except for the pale left hand with its bitten-down nails, is mostly submerged in the warm brackish water. His parents, unaware that he is even missing, are out by their pool, drinking cold Chardonnay in paper-thin glasses.

Mitchell's bicycle is gone from the house, and this afternoon, he is supposed to ride it half a mile down his gated community's palm-lined street on the way home from his friend's house. It was supposed to be a sleepover, but they had a fight about whether or not a car could really go from zero to a hundred in two seconds, and Mitchell (whose opinion was NO WAY) told his friend he was dumb for believing it. The friend shoved Mitchell a little harder than was appropriate, and Mitchell knew that he had to go home. He was angry, though, that the one friend he'd made here turned out to be a psycho, so he rode his bike to the park instead, pedaling along the unlit boardwalk. He wanted to stand in the dark and smoke the cigarette he had stolen. In the inky dark, he rode right into the barrier and flipped over the handlebars and into the water. What he saw, right before being rolled under and drowned by the four hundred pound alligator, was a dark and gleaming baby alligator. So cute and strange that it had to be a dream. He felt no pain or fear as he was pulled under; there was no way any of it could be real. The water tasted like ginger ale.

THE STARLIGHT RIVER BREAKS off into tributaries and newly-dug canals that thread through and beyond Starlight Estates, where the water turns murky, obscuring manatees, bass, snook.

Mitchell's possessions have already floated out of his pockets and made it out to the canals two miles east: the cigarette, never lit; a purple Bic lighter; a folded five-dollar bill.

The ten small and unremarkable houses that stretch from Ring Road northwest to Bell Lane—a distance of almost two square miles—are made of stucco and concrete, far apart. Not all are finished, but they have the same shoebox pattern: on the right, the living room and kitchen, and a screened porch in the back. On the left, three bedrooms. A bathroom in the interior hallway.

It rains almost every afternoon, sometimes for hours, sometimes just a few minutes. The sleek green lizards know the rain is coming; moments before the sky opens, they flash their red throats one more time, like a college boy's last glance around a bar before close.

HAIL HITS DONNIE. He is five. He sits behind the house, playing with lizard tails, which he and his seven-year-old brother, Carter, have collected and hidden under the drain pipe. They have five tails so far, either rotting and stinking or dried up like vanilla pods. When the boys tug, the tails come right off, and the lizards skitter away.

Donnie runs around the dirt yard to the front of the house and knocks at the locked door. "I have to go to the bathroom," he whines. He wears nothing but a pair of white briefs and a filthy pair of once-white socks. His face and shoulders are brown from the sun; his hair gleams white-gold.

There is no response. He knocks again, says it louder.

"You can't," Carter finally answers from inside. "Momma locked it and she got the key." Carter is also sun-tanned, but his hair is as dark as the wet dirt. He has bucked teeth. His soft stomach hangs over the top of his cut-off jean shorts and his arms stretch the blue cotton of his tight t-shirt to the point of semi-transparency.

She locked it without knowing Donnie was still outside. She'd been hitting their father with a shoe and he swung back with his fists, never landing a good shot. She was tougher and not as drunk. She let the shoe loose and it flew across the room, marking the wall with its black rubber sole. An uneasy peace followed.

Carter calls, "Go to the back window. You can get in if you climb up on the tire."

Donnie goes to the back of the house again, rolls the broken truck's old tire to the wall and climbs up it. He pulls himself through the open kitchen window and lands, hands first, in the sink, and pulls his body in, his legs sliding across the dirty dishes. When he lands on the kitchen floor, there is ketchup on his foot, but he doesn't notice.

Carter finds the key on the floor, a cool spot under his bare foot. As he opens the door, their small orange cat runs outside, disappearing across the field.

"Speedy!" yells Donnie.

Carter says, "He'll come back later. I'm hungry. I'll cook us spaghetti."

"Do you know how to make it?"

Carter doesn't answer. Instead, he goes into the kitchen, and takes a thick bundle of spaghetti out of the package. He puts the dry noodles on a dish, shoves the dish into the oven, and turns the oven knob to the right. They sit in front of it, waiting.

ACROSS A NEARBY FIELD is a trim man with thinning, sandy hair and a wispy, sandy moustache. He wears sunglasses that take the glaring sun down a few notches. Peter is glazed with sweat as he walks a shining black bicycle toward the trees. Moments before, he killed a small green snake by rolling over it with his tire. It is dying on the pavement a few hundred yards behind him, its inch-thick middle squashed. There is nothing he can do to help it. By the time he noticed, it was too late to stop or swerve.

Peter had lived in the tree house for almost three months when all of the new construction began. At first it was a few dozen large luxury residential eyesores in the area near the widest part of the river, by the new supermarket and golf course. The earth movers came closer and closer to his woods, until they felled trees along the edge of the forest to create a smooth line. They stopped there. A few crappy houses quickly went up, but since then, nothing more happened. The revenue stream must have been interrupted. Just as well.

The grass gets thicker and higher as he nears the entrance to the woods. Peter grabs the bike by the top bar and lifts it up and over his shoulder. He thinks that his father never would have been able to pull this off the way he has: building his own home in the wilderness, making it only with money he earned on his own. Surviving on nothing but the food he could find growing or swimming nearby.

His great-grandfather, Ogden Haggenden, probably could have. The rumor was that he began the Haggenden real estate empire with seventy-five dollars.

While Peter is proud of the way he's survived these past eight months, the way he has trained his body on his bicycle, he is far more proud of what he's accomplished here. After only a few days of living in these woods, catching catfish, gathering wild yucca, mulberries, and purslane, Peter realized that he also had to *do* something. Once he learned how to fill his belly, he found his creative impulse to be just as strong as his biological imperative. That impulse was a relief.

He has been working on a kind of music. He doesn't know exactly what the finished product will be, but he believes he will have captured what it feels like to be alive.

The warm rain hits him. He follows the path he has worn. Straight for fifty or so feet, ducking under branches of a group of chinkapin oaks, left for forty, a slight right for another twenty. There it is. It took three full days for Peter and six Mexican day-laborers to build the framing around the massive live oak. He remembers how they sweated under the canopy, how loud their breathing sounded, how they tripped over tree roots and were pricked in the calves by saw palmettos. At night, they slept in sleeping bags in the truck beds. The labor, trucks, and materials (the steel collar, Cypress planks, dozen panes of leaded glass, trusses, cables, a generator, a rain-catching system so that he could build a shower) cost just under twelve thousand dollars, money saved from two-and-a-half years' work as a landscaper. He has nearly thirty thousand dollars left. Not counting, of course, the family fortune, which he's ignored so far.

Peter built the tree house a few weeks after his father's funeral. The letters from the lawyers drove him to the middle of nowhere. Peter was the end of the Haggenden line. The major stockholders were waiting for his next move. People expected him to step into place. The last letter, sent overnight mail, said that the attorneys would come to his home in three days to discuss his estate. That letter had given him a decent head start.

Inside the bag around his waist are fresh batteries, and a half dozen blank cassette tapes. He has recorded wind-in-the-trees, rain hitting leaves, thunder, a dozen different bird calls. His plan is to put them together in a new way, and the music it makes will be like a dog whistle that can only be heard by people who know how to listen.

A HALF MILE AWAY, Nancy peels bananas and smashes them in a bowl with a fork. She thought her working days were behind her, but there isn't enough money left in her savings account. She sold her little house in Scranton and bought this cheap house so that she could retire in it. The humidity here gives Nancy's silver hair more shape and gloss and personality than it ever had in Scranton, but there is nobody here to compliment her on it. All those years setting and tinting the thinning hair of wealthy older women, and now that she is their age herself, though her own hair is thick and wavy, she will have to take a job at the supermarket to cover expenses. She wishes she hadn't spent the money to have the sheets of the soft Zoysia grass put down, to make the land here prettier than it could be on its own.

Two late half-shifts a week will give her enough breathing room. This will help keep them in decent food, keep the air conditioner running, and keep gas in the car. This will help keep Madeline's health insurance, which Madeline's father let lapse, so now the premiums are three times higher. Not to mention the cost of gas. Nancy takes her to the pediatric cardiologist every three weeks, and it is an hour and a half each way.

Madeline will have to stay home alone because a babysitter, even if she could find one, would likely charge as much as she'd earn. But Madeline goes to sleep at seven and doesn't wake until the sun rises. She will never even know.

As Nancy mixes in the flour, her pearl bracelet falls from her wrist and to the floor. The clasp, platinum with two small diamonds, somehow came loose.

Tiny Madeline is in the bedroom watching TV. She is Nancy's great-niece: seven-and-a-half years old, pink-skinned, her hair white and thin. Her lips are almost not there; her nose is pink, beak-like. Madeline will die of old age within the coming years. She has been living with Nancy for four months, which is three and a half months longer than it was supposed to be (her grand-nephew, who took a short-term trucking job, promised to send money each week, and to get Madeline once he found them an apartment, had sent only one piece of correspondence to her P.O. box so far: a single twenty dollar bill in an envelope without a return address). They are only now getting to know each other.

Nancy stands in the doorway, "You like the chocolate chips on top? Not mixed in?"

"Not mixed in," Madeline calls back, her voice helium.

Nancy says, "Do you want to turn the timer on for me?"

"Shhh!" says Madeline. "I'm watching something."

Nancy purses her lips. "No banana bread until you have your chicken salad. You were having a bad day last time when you got to have your treat first, but not today."

Madeline flicks the channel button on the remote control, looking for a darkly-lit television show. She finds a soap opera with a darkish bottom left corner. She gets down on her knees and stares at what she can see of her own face in the small patch of darkness, but the white sleeve of the show's actress begins to swing around in the dark patch of screen, and Madeline is unable to focus on her own face for more than a second.

IN A NEARLY IDENTICAL house a mile away, two men are still sleeping. The central air conditioning is turned very high. Ryan is on the bed in the bedroom, curled under a white duvet. Beneath the covers, his Irish skin is peach-pink and freckled. He is short and thickly muscled. His heartbeat can be seen right through his skin. He eats quinoa and live grain bread and mushrooms and organic meats. He meditates and knows everything there is to know about cleansing breaths.

Lloyd, six feet tall, dark-haired, dark-eyed, a hundred forty-seven pounds, is in his underwear on the living room couch. His long fingers graze a ceramic bowl on the floor that is full of smashed cigarette butts. He has been drifting in and out of sleep since two in the morning. He turns on his side and huffs into the back of the couch, waking and remembering that he is angry.

The plan, set in motion a month ago, was to drive to the Keys this morning and live it up for a few days. But last night the fight they'd been waiting to have finally got in the way and now they are not going anywhere.

His best line had cut Ryan hard and so, of course, he kept using it. *You want me to do this for you, but what are you willing to do for me?*

Lloyd maybe said that it could be fun to have a foster kid for a little while, but it was ages ago and he'd had a few drinks. *It would be fun for other people* is probably what he meant. But then yesterday, on the way home from work, Ryan told him that he had already filled out the fostering paperwork and signed them up for the first class, so that it would be done, just in case.

Lloyd wakes completely and sits up straight, the cowlick at the crown of his head pushing a shock of hair up and to the side. *And another thing*, he thinks, but he can't think of another thing, and anyway, nothing could possibly be as withering as the stuff he has already said. How he never wanted to move here, and how, in the time they have lived here, Lloyd has felt nothing as deeply (stressing the word *nothing* to make his point) as he feels the tug of every other city he has ever lived in and the lives he used to have in them. New Orleans, Boston, Sausalito, Charlestown, even Pittsburgh.

Ryan, his freckled face serious, said, "You're talking like I ruined your life."

"Yeah, well, something needs to change."

"Like?"

"I should leave."

He wanted Ryan to crumble, but Ryan did not.

He hears Ryan stirring. He listens to the drawers opening and shutting, then watches the doorway and sees Ryan emerge from the bedroom dressed in a t-shirt and running shorts. Ryan ducks into the kitchen.

He wishes that Ryan would lose his shit once in a while. Being the only loose cannon is getting old. He hears kitchen cabinet doors opening, water running.

Ryan calls in to him, "I guess we're not going today. We didn't get an early enough start. I'm driving to Erne City to get my run in while I can." Ryan never runs on the streets near here. It's too hot and there's no breeze.

Ryan walks into the living room, pointing to the full ashtray on the floor. "What's that?"

"I had the window open," says Lloyd. "Get a grip."

"You smoked all of that in one night," Ryan says, his hand on the door frame. He does not make eye contact with Lloyd, only stares at the floor, and then bends to tighten his shoelaces.

FOUR

IDA WORRIES THAT THE office will be closed up, and all of the furniture moved out. There will be no Ken and there will be no check. Predictably, the driver goes the wrong way at first, temporarily driving further away from town and cutting it close with the timing.

"Is there a bus station anywhere near here?" she says, chewing her thumbnail.

"Right over in Erne City," he answers. "A Greyhound stop near the fire station."

She rips the nail off too close to the skin and touches her tongue to the blood.

But the desks are there and the chairs are there and so is Ken. He smiles at her through the glass and motions for her to come in.

"I've got something for you," he says, reaching into the drawer of his desk. "Good things come to those who wait."

He hands her a sealed envelope. She sticks her finger under the flap and rips it open. The check is made out in her name, but it is from Ken Cantwell, President of Echo Development. $7,450.

She gasps and gives Ken a quick hug. He feels solid and reassuring.

"They made a mistake," he says. "See, they wrote their check out to us, so instead of signing it over to you, making it more complicated, I just wrote a check for the same amount to you." He holds out a white and blue box of Entenmann's cookies. "Have a cookie."

She takes one. "Are you sure that's the only mistake? This is more than you said it would be," she says, biting into oatmeal and brittle raisins.

"It's the fair market value."

The check is postdated for the next day.

"So that the other one gets a chance to clear," he explains, looking out across the plaza. "I believe in this place. I have to. I've risked everything I have to make Fort Starlight happen. You should come back in a year or two. You won't believe what this is going to turn into."

She leaves the office, her hands shaking. It is getting late and the bank will be closing soon. She runs down the plaza to get there before it does, and opens a free checking account, giving the address of the house, 80 Ring Road, as her own address. The branch manager tells her that the check will clear by Monday morning.

She devises a plan: she will come in early on Monday, the moment the bank opens, get a certified check for the entire amount, and arrange to catch the bus the same afternoon. She can just have the taxi wait while she does her bank business. In the meantime, she will live it up for a few days. She's still never stayed in a hotel.

Ida's head swims. She walks out of the bank and calls the taxi service, and takes it to Erne City, amazed at how quickly the landscape changes, once they are a few exits along the highway. When the taxi pulls off the highway, the air is salty. They cross a bridge and she opens her window all the way, breathing it in. The driver lets her out in front of a tall hotel on the water. The Grand Oasis. Fat, fragrant white blossoms fill vases all over the lobby. Ida craves this luxury: a real weekend, with seafood dinners and frozen cocktails, sleeping in air conditioning on a thick mattress and clean sheets. At ninety dollars a night, though (the off-season rate, the clerk tells her; at high season it is more than twice that), it is more money than she is comfortable spending. She steps away from the counter and walks out of the hotel.

On the main street, people are walking, laughing, eating ice cream. She comes to a motel with a vacancy sign. Dunes Inn, where the rate is forty-four dollars.

"Can I see a room?" she asks. The man at the desk shrugs and grabs a key. He stands outside, waiting as she looks at the room. The bedspread is red and brown, and torn on the corner so that the cotton batting peeks out. There are glass ring stains on the bedside table.

The man watches her walk out. "So?"

"That's OK, thanks," she says, and the man shakes his head and mutters under his breath.

She walks back to The Grand Oasis, pays for three nights and takes the elevator to her room. On the way up, she opens her wallet. $408 left.

She will send her landlord the money she owes him, once the check clears. She can afford to do the right thing now.

The room is on the eighth floor. She opens the blinds and looks down at the pool below, an enormous turquoise oval. Beyond it is the ocean, its water so clear that the sun penetrates to the ridges in the sand. The bed has six pillows and a celery-colored comforter. Underneath are bright white sheets. She takes off her shoes and climbs inside, inhaling the pale scent of the clean bedding. It will be wonderful to take a nap, if she can manage it. She concentrates on breathing, slows it down, soothed by the smooth, cool pillowcase under her cheek. She counts backward from twenty, backward from thirty, and then can't remember which number she is on or why she is counting at all. The door opens. The man in the cycling gear walks into the room, wheeling his bicycle. He leans it against the wall. He walks over to her and sits on top of her chest, his face turned away from her so that she can only see him from the side. The brim of his cycling cap is pulled far forward. His weight is too much and Ida can't get a breath. She tries to yell, tries to gather enough strength to push him off, but she can't move at all.

She figures it out: she is asleep. *Wake up*, she tells herself, and she does, sitting up and gasping for a breath. Nobody is there.

In the bathroom, Ida finds thick towels and tiny bars of soap. She lathers the soap on her cheeks and rinses it off, patting her face dry. She pulls her hair out of its braid, and looks in the mirror. It has been almost a week since she has seen her reflection. The sun has turned her skin pinkish gold. Her hair is crimped and glowing and she looks vaguely slim. She changes her t-shirt, grabs her key, closes the door, takes the elevator down to the lobby, and walks out of the hotel and out to the small main street.

Both ends of town are visible from where she stands. The air smells of seaweed and of piña colada sunscreen. There is life here. Couples hold hands and little children run ahead of their parents.

A group of boys with shaggy haircuts and drooping shorts skateboard along the sidewalk, their wheels clacking as they shift their weight from side to side and back to front. Clearly they are friends, but they don't pay attention to each other; they don't look at anything but their own sneakers.

As she watches them, she remembers that Ken didn't make her sign a contract. She doesn't remember signing anything at all. Still, the check was for almost twice as much as she'd thought it would be, and that surprise makes it not matter. She already deposited the money. Ida thinks of the Kitchen Aid mixer she'll be able to buy now. A shiny red one. Jesus, what can't she buy? She lets herself think farther into the future, about the *Sweet Ida* logo, about the plain white packaging with the thin ribbon holding everything together, about selling her goods at farmer's markets and restaurants, and how those will lead to recognition and more money and a storefront of her own.

She walks up and down the short strip full of bathing suit boutiques, sandwich shops, tiny stores that sell shell jewelry. She buys herself a blue two-piece bathing suit without trying it on.

She is very hungry. She walks until she sees what looks like the most expensive restaurant in town: *Laughter Cay*. It is early for dinner, just before six.

"Go ahead, get the lobster," the waiter says. He is tall and skinny, with dark hair, dark eyes, and a smirking mouth.

"You know that's what you want," he says. "It came in on the boat about an hour ago. I'm Lloyd and I'm going to be your waiter tonight, if you hadn't already guessed."

"I do want the lobster," she says, even though she has already decided not to get it since it costs nineteen dollars. She almost ordered the eight-dollar hamburger, something she could have anywhere. Lobster, though. She has never had it. She is going to be the first

Overdorff to eat lobster.

He sets a basket of warm rolls in front of her, a ceramic ramekin of butter curls. She quickly eats two of the rolls, the butter spread thick.

When Lloyd tops off her water glass, he asks her if she has come in for the day on one of the boats.

She laughs. "Sure. I sailed here on my sixty-foot yacht from Bora-Bora. For dinner. Do you think I'd make it back before sunset if I left right after dessert?"

"You're funny," he says.

Ida smiles, and as he walks off to tend to another table, she stares at the wrecked beauty of the butter curls. Her heart pounds. She wishes they knew each other, wishes she were having dinner with him, with anyone. She wishes she had somewhere to go after dinner other than her hotel room, where she will hear her own breathing over anything else.

When he sets the lobster down in front of her, she stares at the big red body, the fanned tail, the metal lobster cracker, the bowl of melted butter. She frowns, reaching for the cracker and setting it down again.

"I'm really not sure what I'm supposed to do next," she says.

"Here," says Lloyd, lifting the plate. "I'll have our kitchen take care of this for you."

He brings her plate out again a few minutes later, the tail open and the middle split with a knife.

He doesn't walk away as she spears a chunk of the meat and chews it, but all she can taste is butter. She wishes the lobster tasted more special than it does. He looks so invested in whether or not she is enjoying it that she flashes a fake smile.

When he comes to her table the next time, he places a glass of white wine in front of her.

"You can't have lobster without a glass of good wine," he says. "It's actually illegal in the state of Florida. You don't want me to call the cops, do you?"

She doesn't protest, but in her mind, she adds more money to her bill.

Delicate things are expensive. Ida was never one for wine, but she lifts the glass for a sip. It tastes sort of like butter, but with none of the grease. She takes another sip. And flowers. She loves it. She could drink a bottle of it. The warmth in her stomach radiates through her arms and legs and she nods at the sky.

She focuses more carefully on the lobster: it is firm and fresh. It doesn't have a taste as much as an essence. She orders a second glass of wine, pitying her mother and father, who have never tasted such a thing, have never seen anything like these bright white tablecloths, this thick silverware, the yachts that she can see bobbing outside by the docks. Maybe on TV, but that doesn't count.

She tries a forkful of the couscous, tasting the green in the fresh parsley on top.

When she is done, the waiter brings her a short glass.

"On the house," he says, setting it in front of her. He places both of his hands on her table and leans forward. "Oh Jesus, you're legal, right? I should have asked before I served you."

"I'm sixteen," she smiles, picking up the glass. "And I really LOVE this wine stuff."

He frowns.

"Gotcha," she says, aware that she is just a little drunk. "I had you for a second. Should I drink this? I'm not sure I should."

"It's already been poured," he winks. "Go ahead. Taste it. I'll be back."

He steps away. A new table has been seated next to her—a mother and daughter, she guesses. They don't touch the bread. The daughter cries, silently and intermittently. The mother reaches over and holds her daughter's wrist, moving her thumb gently across the pale inside.

Ida tilts the glass and dips her tongue in for a taste. It is tart, bright, bitter, slightly lemony. She takes tiny sips to make it last. When he gives her the check, folded inside of a leather cover, she is prepared for it to be a lot more. He hasn't charged her for anything more than her entrée, and she leaves him the difference in a big tip. She leaves the money in a neat pile next to the bill.

"You don't want to miss the last of the sun," he says. "Why don't you take your drink to the patio?"

Ida lets him take her by the hand and lead her out to a deck chair. It feels good to be pulled somewhere, to be told to enjoy herself. She watches as a pelican lands with a light thud on the wooden pier.

The sun is warm on her legs. She stretches, flexing her feet. White boats bob in the blue water. Men step off the boats and walk into the restaurant, nodding hello as they pass her. A man is seated at the other end of the patio. She watches as Lloyd brings out a brandy glass and a small plate holding something dark and sets it in front of him. She saw it on the menu: *warm, flourless chocolate cake.* Though she was too full to consider it earlier, she wishes she could have a bite now. She isn't sure she knows how to make one. This is something she needs to learn.

And she will learn it. There is no magic. Cakes are like anything else; it is just a recipe that she will have to make time to practice. She loves the experience of starting from nothing but sugar, flour, fat, and heat and ending up with something so mood-altering. She checked a few baking books out of the library in Aster, knowing full well that she would never bring them back. They are in her apartment still and she wishes she brought them with her. Besides doubling the cinnamon, or adding a pinch of some other spice, she never does much to change the recipes, but the people who run the community center were crazy about her blackberry crumbles, banana walnut muffins, pecan tarts, and caramel squares, as though she gave them some incredibly special touch.

The sky goes from orange to pink, the sun still glowing softly. Lloyd sits down in the deck chair next to Ida's. He takes off his bowtie and apron, and rolls up his white sleeves. His hands and arms are tanned, covered with fine, dark hair. Beautiful hands. He is tall and thin like her brother. On the tray on the floor in front of him is a bottle of beer and a pink drink, which he gives to her.

"Not that you probably need this," he says, leaning back. He lights a cigarette and reaches for his beer, his long fingers curling around the neck. "But I'm waiting for my boyfriend, Ryan, to get finished and I don't like to drink alone."

"Your boyfriend," she says. "Oh." She isn't thinking quickly enough to hide the disappointment in her voice. She can feel the water underneath the deck, the back and forth tugging of the tide.

"I've gotten you drunk."

"I ate like a horse tonight," she says, "so I'm not all that drunk. Almost."

Lloyd leans back. He takes a long drag from his cigarette and closes his eyes.

"When's your birthday?"

"The seventeenth of May."

"A Taurus," he says, exhaling. "Like me. We're lazy, but somehow reliable at the same time. This other server here, Mona, is always telling me my horoscope. She told me that today was supposed to be an exceptionally good day."

"It *was* an exceptionally good one," says Ida. "For me at least. And not just because of the free booze."

He sits watching her for a few moments.

"Listen," he finally says. "This might sound weird, but I'd really like to paint you. Do you live around here?"

A man walks over and stands behind Lloyd. He puts his palm on the back of Lloyd's head. He has reddish blonde hair and a squat, muscular body that reminds Ida of an Olympic gymnast.

"Is this who you're getting me into trouble over?"

"I'm Ida," she says.

"This is Ryan," says Lloyd. "He's bartending tonight."

"Thanks…for all the freebies."

Ryan nods at her, loosens his tie and unbuttons the collar of his white shirt. "How many is that today?" he says, pointing at Lloyd's cigarette.

"The first. Probably not the last."

"Your choice," says Ryan. He sits down on the deck chair on the other side of her.

"I switched to Marlboro Lights." Lloyd turns his head toward the water. "I was just asking Ida if I could paint her."

"Why would you want to paint me?" says Ida, picturing herself on a tall stool, a sheet draped over her bottom half.

He puts a hand on her shoulder.

"I like to do portraits sometimes. You don't have any calm in your face. There's just something about your…bearing, I guess. You look… like a fighter."

"A fighter?" she laughs. "Not exactly the stuff the masterpieces are made of."

"They should be. It's in your eyes, your mouth, your forehead. You look like you're ready to pounce."

"Huh," she says. Her forehead. "I don't know how I feel about that. But I don't live here. I live in New York."

"Ah. The big apple."

She nods and leaves it at that.

"You're on vacation?" asks Ryan.

"Sort of. I'm here because I had a piece of land. I just sold it. In this place called Fort Starlight. I'm putting the money into a baking business." She sounds to herself like a smart person who has invested some money. Like someone capable, good at planning her future, first a land owner and soon a businesswoman. She would believe all of it, if she were listening to someone else say it.

"I hate you. I wish to God we were leaving to go to New York, too." Lloyd lights another cigarette.

Ryan shakes his head and turns to Ida. "Wait, where in Fort Starlight? Over near the Karr's, where those fancy houses are?"

"Farther out than that. There's nothing out there. Just a few houses, mostly empty streets. The weird thing is that there's a house on the lot. The guy who bought the land told me I was crazy, but it was there. I even stayed in it for a few nights."

"We live out there," Ryan says. "Right near there. You were smart to invest in Starlight. We just moved in about six months ago. Our house is already worth a good bit more than we paid for it, but in a few years, it will be worth a whole lot more. You may wish you waited longer."

"Really?" she says. "There's nothing going on there."

"Less than nothing," says Lloyd. "What's going on there is in the negatives. We fell right into that whole Florida swampland trap.

Tropical breezes, a town is coming, all that bullshit. The air is stagnant, and it doesn't look any better than it did when we first moved in."

Ryan turns to Ida. "You watch. In a couple of years, the market is going to really take off. Think about it. How many places are there left like that in this country? A brand new town, with a beach just a few minutes' drive away. The really smart investments always seem unattractive at first. You have to have patience. And faith."

"You sound sort of like an infomercial," she giggles.

"He does," says Lloyd. "False advertising. If by 'a few minutes,' you mean almost twenty, well, maybe. It's so depressing to leave this view at the end of the work day and have to go home."

She nods but wonders, fleetingly, if Ryan is right. If she had waited a few more years, perhaps she would have made a lot more.

It was found money. No need to be greedy.

Ryan says, "There was just a house on the property? No explanation? I'm trying to picture where it is."

"There's a big blue plastic sheet thing on the back," she says.

"I know that place," says Lloyd. "We're pretty near there."

"I went for a few walks, but I never saw a single human being."

"That's no surprise." Ryan says. "There are only a few people besides us living over there. That one woman, the people with the pick-up truck…"

"I almost forgot," she interrupts. "There was this one guy. This complete asshole. On a bike. He blew right by me, and then he almost spit on me."

"A bicycle, not a motorcycle, right?" asks Lloyd.

"We know that guy," says Ryan. "His name is Peter. He sold us a bike in the beginning of the summer. A beautiful old Bianchi racing bike. I told him I liked it and he said he had more than one. He gave it to me for almost nothing. I don't know where he lives, though. I can't figure out which house it would be." Ryan turns to Ida. "We didn't see you, either. How long did you stay there?"

"Just a few days," she says. "The longest few days of my life."

"Doesn't surprise me," says Lloyd.

"It isn't Fort Starlight's fault," says Ryan. "It's because she was in an unfurnished house without air conditioning. In July. Of course it wasn't any fun."

"Turn and look at me for a second," Lloyd taps Ida on the shoulder.

Ida turns her head and looks into his dark brown eyes.

"If you can't pose for me, then you have to let me take your picture. I'm going to get the Polaroid."

She watches Lloyd walk inside.

Ryan shakes his head. "He loves that Polaroid, and I'll tell you why. He's too impatient to wait for film to get developed. He needs to have everything right away."

"Hmmm," she says, to be polite, though she knows whose side she is on.

Lloyd comes back, holding the camera in front of him. "Look at me," he says, and snaps her picture. He tugs the picture out, sets the camera down on the table and waves the undeveloped picture in the air.

"Amazing," says Lloyd. "See?" He hands it to her.

He is right: her nose is freckled; her hair is a tumbly, windy mass; her eyes glow like amber held up to the sun, alert, ready, a little wild. Her shoulders are tight. She does look like she is about to spring.

"A lioness after a meal. Only still a little hungry. Mind if I keep it?"

She wishes that Robert could see it. She has never looked this pretty in her life. The sun and the wind make her look like things have turned out even better than they have. He'd regret what he said to her on the day he left.

That tooth. It's about to fall right out of your head.

And he'd grimaced, disgusted, like it was her fault.

Well, it didn't fall out. And she'd gotten it fixed.

The three of them sit together, sipping. Night comes, and tiny white lights illuminate the patio. Ida's mind feels beautifully empty. She can hear the water slapping against the hulls of the boats. She wants to see what the water looks like at night, but when she looks, she can't see anything but the gentle moving darkness.

Lloyd is snoring softly. Ryan has his hand in his chin. His eyes are open, but he is lost in some thought, and isn't paying attention to her.

She stands up and tiptoes back through the restaurant and out the door. She is a little dizzy as she walks down the main street until the hotels and stores end and she finds a path.

Ida takes off her shoes and walks in the still-warm sand until she comes to the ocean. She sits at the bottom of a dune and watches the water. In the breeze, there is a super-fine spray of sand, and she crunches a few grains of it in her teeth. She imagines Robert as he might be now—with shorter hair and wiser eyes—sitting in a restaurant with a sweet girl who understands him.

"What are you looking at?" the girl will say.

"This," he will answer, handing her a magazine article: *30 Successful Women Under the Age of 30*. Ida is #6. She looks like she did in the Polaroid, with sunlight and wind in her hair, only she is wearing an apron that says *Sweet Ida* and is holding a tray of blondies.

"Who is she?"

"That's Ida. That's my sister." He will shake his head, smiling. "I knew she'd figure it out."

The girl will reach over and take his hand. "You miss her."

FIVE

IN THE STARLIGHT RIVER Park, the thirteen-foot female alligator suns herself. Her three babies are by her side. The body of Mitchell Healy has drifted away. It had only been superficially trapped, the collar of his t-shirt caught on a knot on the bottom of a log, when the current grew swifter. It floated far away from her, down the river, and into one of the muddy canals to the west. Along the way, his thin, white body swept over curious manatees that nudged his torso and peered from below.

The blackbirds are still here. At the end of the winter, they never returned north. The male broke his wing and it healed badly. He no longer can fly any real distance; the best he can do is a few dozen feet at a time, or hopping from tree branch to tree branch.

In the spring, they built a nest in a live oak. The female laid four eggs, turquoise speckled with rust. Soon, four chicks were born, fed, taught to fly. They are gone now. It is just the two of them again. They are always together. Though her wings are fine, she has stopped flying, in solidarity with her mate.

In the living room of the most expensively built house in all of Fort Starlight Estates, nestled between a green golf course and a natural rock swimming pool, five people sit on two white sofas. The sun comes through a skylight and hits the very center of an ebony coffee table. Mr. Healy, who is short, dark, slightly thick around the middle, sobs hoarsely into a handkerchief. His wife, painstakingly blonde and painstakingly thin, disappears into the kitchen and returns carrying a silver coffee pot. She sniffs delicately, bends forward, and fills the bone china cups.

The three policemen drink the coffee even though they neither want nor need it.

A pile of posters, which they have been taping all over the tri-county area for days, sits in the middle of the table.

Mitchell Healy, Please Come Home!!!!!!

Mitchell is almost thirteen, and was last seen riding a blue mountain bike on Werner's Lane in Fort Starlight in Western Star County, one mile from the Turnpike. He was wearing cut-off shorts and a white Bart Simpson t-shirt.

Mitchell has dirty blonde hair and blue-green eyes. He is 5'2 and approximately 100lbs.

If you see Mitchell or have any information, please call the police immediately.

Tonight, his picture will be shown on *America's Most Wanted*, right before the final commercial break.

"I blame this stupid, stupid place," says Mrs. Healy. She points out the window, at the shadow a royal palm casts on the lawn.

"Jesus Christ, there's no reason to pick out a casket yet." Mr. Healy says this under his breath, but still loud. They have lived here for ten months. He was hired as a consultant to oversee Fort Starlight's development.

"Who said anything about a casket, for God's sake?" Her hand shakes; she places the coffee pot on the table and sits down, looking closely at the policeman whose face she likes the most. He reminds her of Tom Selleck as Magnum PI: thick brown mustache, curly brown hair, bright eyes. Officer Sternbach. When she looks at him, she feels the slightest bit optimistic. Mitchell has run away. He hated it here. Hates it here.

Her husband wipes his nose and says, "Mitchell is a very

independent sort of kid."

"He could walk in the door," the oldest officer says with a wave of his hand. "There's always the chance of that. Kids do run away."

"You've seen that lots of times before?" says Mrs. Healy. "Doesn't that happen more often than not? Even with happy kids?"

The police radio crackles. Officer Sternbach and the other policemen stand up, shake hands, promise that they will be by later in the day, or will, at the very least, call. Before walking out the door, Officer Sternbach looks back at Mrs. Healy and nods, but she can't tell what the nod means.

Peter saw this place featured in a PBS series entitled *Uninhabited America*. He chose it because it doesn't get cold here, and because there are enough natural resources to sustain him. And also because his family used to own part of this land. Twenty-six years ago, when he was just eleven, his father brought him here in a helicopter; he wanted to decide if his 700-acre parcel was worth keeping.

You could have brought a friend today, his father yelled at him over the noise of the propeller.

Peter had no friends back then. Not in Miami or Connecticut or San Diego or Munich. He sat still, ignoring this jab, trying not to remember the week before when he'd overheard his father describe him as an *awkward kid*. He clenched his teeth and stared out the window as they exited the clouds and came closer to the dark green swamp, to the even darker clumps of trees and a green-black forest. The helicopter dropped lower. Peter could smell the wetness and he wanted to stay there and feel the dark, wet green all around him and be alone with it. But his father shook his head disapprovingly at this place, at Peter, at the pilot, and the helicopter rose again. In the clouds, Peter indulged in a fantasy of the helicopter pilot leaving his father in the woods, pictured his father hungry, sweating, bitten all over by insects, all of his money useless.

He finishes his ride, two and a half minutes ahead of his goal, and heads toward the swimming pool on Melaleuca. He strips his clothes off and slips in, collecting the dried palm fronds that have fallen into the water.

In the distance, he notices two boys walking across the fields. He sees them frequently. Their parents let them run wild, which seems like terrible judgment, but he was always alone when he was a kid. When he was twelve, just after he read *My Side of the Mountain*, he came home from boarding school for Easter break and spent three nights sleeping next to a boulder on the hill on his family's Connecticut estate. He brought water and a bag of apples. It wasn't bad. His parents never knew he was gone.

Peter had been even fatter than the little butterball across the field. He had secret stashes of candy bars, potato chips, orange pop. There were always the remains of something greasy or mushy sitting in his teeth and on his shirt.

He always believed the three nights sleeping next to the boulder broke his habit of overeating. During that time, the trees and the air and the dirt became important to him, like he was part of them. He was nature, and potato chips didn't fit the scenery.

He is familiar with the faces of the few people who live here, but now there is someone new. A girl. From where, he doesn't know. He has only seen her walking. Probably some developer's depressed daughter, missing the shopping mall and Cinnabon.

Peter pulls himself out and waits until he is dry enough to put his things on. He gets back on the bicycle and rides beyond Marine road, toward the forest. He thinks he sees a panther, small and lean, skulking around in the shadows of the trees. He hopes he will see it again soon. Maybe it will hiss at him in its heavy-breathing, big-cat way. He hopes so. He will try to catch it on tape.

Madeline is crying. Aunt Nancy will not take her to Gatorburg. Madeline saw the commercial on television and was entranced: *Watch him as he puts his whole head in the alligator's mouth, full of some of the sharpest teeth in the world! Unfortunately, it is too daring to show on television, so come on down to Jessie King's Gatorburg, on State Road 16, two miles north of the Valponia exit.* She even checked the map and saw that it was only two knuckles away from Fort Starlight.

But Aunt Nancy said no. *That's not worth the trip. It's nothing but a cheap carnival stunt*, she'd said. *And cruel to the poor animal, besides.*

Nancy is not feeling up for the way that other children will stare at Madeline. Especially the type of children whose parents would bring them to a place like Gatorburg.

Madeline is in the bathroom, the door locked from the inside. The sounds she is making are not authentic; they are dramatic sounds she has heard on television shows. She can hear Aunt Nancy on the other side of the door.

"I know you get bored here," Nancy says. "So do I."

Madeline doesn't answer.

"How about a drive to Erne City?" Nancy taps the door.

Nancy wants to bring her bracelet to the jeweler there. The owner told her she'd have to leave it overnight, but Nancy thinks that if she brings it in early enough, he'll agree to fix it on the spot. She and Madeline both like Erne City. They go there and are calmed and refreshed by the salted air, the ice cream, the crushed seashells in the streets.

Madeline says, "I want to wear my new flip flops."

"Open the door, honey."

Nancy walks in and places her hands on Madeline's tiny shoulders. She gathers the wisps of the girl's fine white hair in her fingers and fluffs it. Soon she will be bald.

"Don't," says Madeline, shrugging Nancy off. "You touch me too much."

"Do I?" says Nancy, not believing it. She pretends to feel stung. She isn't, really. Instead, she feels indulgently sorry for herself about things that have nothing to do with Madeline. At least, she thinks, she can attribute it to reasonable causes: to never having had anyone to make her a tuna sandwich or take care of her in any way; to having an irresponsible grand-nephew; to steadily running through the money she'd saved over the years; to her age, which is almost seventy. Nancy can't blame a mutation in her DNA.

Already, it is clear to Nancy that the other cashiers don't like her. Their backs are turned away from her and they make private jokes with each other. No wonder they resent her. She starts long after they arrive and leaves at the same time they do.

But she has made a friend. Corinne works in the bakery. She introduced herself on Nancy's first day, gave her a stale oatmeal cookie, and called it an 'oldie but goodie.' *Sort of like me,* Nancy smiled. Corinne invited her into the break room, where she poured Nancy a cup of coffee and dashed some Cremora in, stirring until the lumps disappeared.

Tell me, Corinne said, pushing the cup across the table and right into Nancy's hand, *how's life?* As though they already knew each other. And Corinne's gaze was so direct and comfortable that Nancy looked right back at her. Her eyes were warm and brown, and her gaze was motherly, despite the fact that she had to be twenty years younger than Nancy. Nancy started to cry. She didn't know she had crying to do. She bent her neck and sobbed, her shoulders shaking. Corinne reached over and took Nancy's hand. *You can tell me,* she said, squeezing lightly. *Go ahead. I'll listen and Jesus will listen, too. We'll both make you feel better.* And though Nancy found the Jesus part a bit off-putting—not that she didn't believe—she found that she did feel better.

Corinne's hair is the problem, Nancy thinks, as she shuffles Madeline out the door and into the Cadillac. Mousy brown and dull grey. Pin-straight and so fine that it looks damp. She should help her with it.

DONNIE AND CARTER SIT on the old couch. The couch, found on the side of a road in Tennessee, covered with some other cat's hair and piss, has always smelled bad. It used to be the main thing in the house that smelled bad. The whole place smells bad now. Half a loaf of mold-covered bread sits in front of the boys on the low table. In the middle of the floor is a stack of *Weekly World News*. For the past week, Carter has been reading to Donnie from them. He knows a few words as soon as he sees them, like *red, hot, one, dog, banana,* but not many others. Sometimes they get the whole gist of what they are reading, especially when there are pictures. Aliens, a woman with four eyes, a dog that ate cats every day for its afternoon meal. Their own cat, Speedy, has been gone a week, and Donnie worries that this dog has eaten him. He's just now stopped crying about it, a hard thing to do when Carter does not dispute this as a possibility.

Donnie says, "I want to take a bath." It will be nice to smell soap.

"No. You know you shouldn't go in there."

"OK, but I want to wash my legs."

"No!"

"Real quick!"

Carter leaps up to block Donnie's path. "Don't go in there!"

But Carter lets him go, because Donnie whines and pushes. "Keep the light off," he says.

In the bathroom, Donnie takes off his clothes and leaves them on the toilet. He doesn't turn on the light. He doesn't look at anything at all. He takes a big step over the body of his mother and then he is in the bathtub. There is a sliver of soap in the built-in soap dish. He turns the water on, rubs the soap on his face, his legs, his hair. He tries not to look at her, but he does. He can't help it. A quick peek out of the corner of his eye, and he thinks he sees her move, so he looks again, whispers, "Mama?" After a minute of this, he feels scared, turns the water off, and stands up on the edge of the tub and is out of the room in one leap. There is no towel. The soap has not been rinsed out of his hair.

"Want some popcorn?" Carter offers.

"Yellow, like at the movies?"

"You got to have a big machine to make it that exact way. We don't got one. You want some or not?"

"Yeah."

Carter looks through the kitchen cabinets. There is no popcorn, which he already knows. He'd only said it to pretend there might be some, like the game he remembered from when he went to school and the teacher had a box wrapped up in wrapping paper and a ribbon. She held it up in the air and said, *Let's imagine what's in this box*. One of the girls said, *Just open it, that way you can find out what's in it*. And the teacher said, *We're here to pretend*. Kids said *Transformers, a Barbie car, diamonds, a giant Hershey's kiss*. When Carter thought about what the girl said, he couldn't get the idea out of his own head, and he snuck back in the room and ripped it open during lunch. There wasn't anything in it, except a few pieces of crumpled up paper.

He used to say that he hated orange jelly, which once got him a smack in the face because it was on clearance and already spread on his sandwich, but now it tastes very good to him, so good that he never brings any to his brother or ever mentions that it's there. In a few days, he'd finished up this first jar, and there are three jars left up there.

He takes a box of Tasty Os and pours a big pile of it into his t-shirt, puts the bottom hem of the t-shirt in his teeth and grabs two handfuls for his brother before he goes back to the living room.

Donnie points to the TV.

"Carter, see if Willy Wonka is on."

"It's not on! It was only on once."

"You know how they get shrunk?"

"It's not on just cause you want it. Don't be stupid. You know the TV is broke."

But Donnie gets up and presses the button anyway.

Nothing happens.

"I want to go somewhere," says Donnie. He is as energized by this new idea as he had been about Willy Wonka. "Can we go look for frogs?"

"OK. Later. After we're done."

They eat silently; the only noise is crunching.

THEY ARE REALLY GOING. The forecast is clear, the car is packed, the driving music picked out. Lloyd is wearing a nicotine patch and does not feel like it is working.

Lloyd runs in for the beach towels, and Ryan checks the oil. Last week they attended a day-long foster parenting workshop. Ryan swore that Lloyd had promised to do this, but Lloyd thought he was fucking nuts, because there was no way he would have *ever* promised such a thing. Lloyd went, but after, told Ryan to never mention it again. Ryan said that was unreasonable. Of course he could mention it again. It was important to help others. That's what humans who have their own needs met are supposed to do.

For the past two days, though, they have been taking a break from the fighting. It was getting too scary and exhausting and pushing them both into saying the kinds of things they weren't sure they wanted to follow through with.

"Listen," Ryan says when Lloyd comes back.

"I'm listening." The way they have been speaking to each other feels robotic, but better than the default alternative.

"I'm glad we're going. We need this. We're going to have a lot of fun."

"We *will* have fun," says Lloyd. "As soon as we get in the car."

"I'm going to get in the car then," Ryan says, reaching for the door. He opens it.

"And I want to tell you," he says, his voice trembling, "that I love you because you're funny and I like my life much more with you in it. You're my best friend. Let's be nice to each other."

"OK," Lloyd says. "It's a deal." He gets in the passenger seat, turns to him halfway. "I love you because you're smart and have a great body."

Ryan puts his open hand on the back of Lloyd's neck.

They drive through the streets and toward town where they will get on the highway. "Sayonara," Lloyd says to Fort Starlight. "Don't throw a big party while we're gone and bust all the good china."

IDA SITS IN A booth by the window of a coffee shop in Erne City, right in the center of town, waiting for the pancakes she has ordered. She has a half hour to eat and then she will be on her way back to Fort Starlight, where she will go to the bank and get a certified check for the balance in her account, and then take a taxi back to Erne City's Greyhound station. She is looking forward to the long bus ride, to the landscape changing as she moves north. The trees will get taller, the grass finer. She is more confident with every passing minute, and sees the long bus ride not as a hardship or a money-saver, but as a chunk of time to reflect on how brand new she is. She will take pictures in every state.

Ida can't wait to see Linda. In high school they used to leave Aster behind for weekends, taking the local buses into the surrounding towns and making up new identities on the way: both of them were unwilling whores, on the run from Lobo, their abusive yet strangely alluring pimp. *Lobo*, they would murmur, raising their eyes to the sky, as if hypnotized, as if he were up there in the stars looking down on them. *Oh, Lobo.*

Or stylish German girls, with clipped accents and brusque mannerisms. They'd pick up store merchandise, dismissing it quickly; everything American was *nicht gut*.

Or the favorite: Linda was Ice Fern, the stoic, powerful daughter of a Mohawk chief, and Ida was Clarabelle, a mute genius who had escaped from an insane asylum. Clarabelle sometimes had episodes that had to do with past lives, mute frenzies, with lots of frantic blinking and arm-grabbing. Ice Fern was the only one who could calm her.

They sometimes went as far as the shopping mall in Liberty, where they would interact in character with salespeople for as long as they could manage before they had to find a place to collapse with heaving laughter so intense that Linda once threw up from it.

But on the bus ride home, Linda would start talking like Linda again, and this depressed Ida. She wanted to take it home with her, to fall asleep as Clarabelle, to wake as Clarabelle.

SIX

THE MORNING SUN COMES in through the window, and as it begins to warm the skin on her cheek, Ida is awakened by a knock on the door. She rubs her eyes and squints; there is no car visible through the window, and the knock was so soft. Maybe she dreamed it. She turns over, curls up and falls back asleep, dreaming about walking across a fishpond, frozen in winter, with goldfish trapped under the ice. Their fins and tails are still, but their gills are still moving. When she opens her eyes again, she sees children, sitting on the floor by the window. Two boys—a dark fat one and a light-haired skinny one—sit next to each other, dirty bare feet splayed out in front of them.

"Are you real?" she mutters.

"Yup," says the fat boy, wiggling the toes on one of his feet. "I'm real."

Ida jumps up and wraps the sheet tight around her bare body, wondering if they had seen her naked.

The boys aren't watching her with much interest; it is more like they were patiently waiting for her to wake up. The skinny one holds a long, crumpled strip of toilet paper under his nose. He wears nothing but a blue t-shirt.

"He got a bloody nose," the fat one says. He is older by a few years. They both look younger than ten.

"One second," Ida groans. She takes her clothes from the floor and brings them into the bathroom, where she rubs her eyes. She closes the door, shutting out the boys, the light of day. She holds her shorts out and lifts her leg, feeling for the leg hole with her foot. She misjudges, staggering, and grabs at the sink to keep from falling. She has to be dreaming still.

"Do you like pancakes?" She hears the voice through the crack of the bathroom door. One of them is down there on the floor. The shadow of little fingers moves across the strip of light.

"Jesus, can you leave me alone a minute?" she says, smacking the door for emphasis. "I don't even know what's going on. I'm not even awake yet." She pulls up the shorts and zips them, yanks her t-shirt over her head and pushes through the opening.

And then she remembers why she is there in the house again. She puts her fingers to her eyes and feels the lids, swollen and fat as earthworms from her crying the night before, something she hasn't done since she was a little kid.

She opens the door and the smaller boy scrambles back to his feet. He stares at her, his bottom lip drooping, showing his lower front baby teeth. Tiny. His fingernails are caked in blood.

"What are you doing here?"

He smiles and it unnerves her.

"Why aren't you wearing underwear?"

He shrugs. Dried blood covers the inside of his right forearm.

She goes to the living room and says, to the older one, "Did you punch him, or something?" And her voice sounds indignant to her, as though she is involved, as though these boys are real and matter to her.

The fat one looks back at her. "Nope. He was picking it and then his nose was just bleeding and bleeding. Maybe it stopped. Donnie, did it stop?"

The little one opens up the crumpled toilet paper to inspect it. He searches for a clean, white spot on the tissue, compresses it and pushes it up his nostril, then pulls it back out. No fresh blood.

"I think it stopped," he says.

She says to the fat one, "What are you two doing here?"

He stares back at her like she is supposed to know that already.

"We wanted to talk to you," says the little one.

"You don't just walk into someone's house," she says. "How did you know I was here?"

"I seen you across there yesterday when I went outside," the fat one says. "I got eagle eyes. I can see all the way to the end of the sky."

"We both got bit," says the little one. He sticks out his foot and shows pink welts. "Fire ants."

"Who are you kids?"

"We're Carter and Donnie. That one's Donnie," the fat one says, gesturing toward the skinny, half-naked boy standing next to him. Their clothes are filthy; the fat one, especially, smells like rotten fruit and dirty laundry.

She remembers the note from her teacher that came home with her in fifth or sixth grade, when the water had been off for several months.

Dear Mr. and Mrs. Overdorff,

This letter is to bring to your attention some hygiene issues related to your daughter. Weekly baths, at a minimum, are necessary for the comfort of your daughter. Good hygiene also creates comfort for her classmates and teacher.

She remembers her mother melting snow in a saucepan, remembers a rough and humiliating going over with the still-cold water, a rag, and orange dishwashing liquid. She remembers crying out of shame, her mother scrubbing at her harder as she cried. It was her fault. She was gross. The kids thought so and her teacher thought so, and even her mother, just as dirty, thought so. She stood there in the kitchen, naked, worried her brother or father would walk in and see her body, shameful, her breasts beginning to bud.

"We're hungry," Donnie says. "We walked here because we want something to eat."

"Don't you have food at home?"

"Nope," says Carter, and stares at his thumbnail, the tip of which is bruised blue-black.

"Not anymore," says Donnie, his voice high and squeaky. He hops from one bare foot to the other.

"Well," she snaps. "Time for your parents to go grocery shopping."

"They're not gonna go grocery shopping."

"Does your mother know you went out by yourselves?"

"Nope," says Carter, pushing thick brown hair away from his eyes.

"She's asleep," squeaks Donnie.

"What about your father?"

"He's asleep, too," Donnie squeaks again, and his face looks so pretty, with his pink lips, blue eyes, a tiny nose at the very center of his face. A little boy doll. His prettiness is annoying.

"You have to go. You have to go." She walks to the front door and opens it, points at the outside. "I didn't invite you in here."

"We can't go," Carter shrugs. "We're too hungry to walk the whole way back without having some food first."

"Okay," she says, raising her hands in surrender. "I'll give you a snack. First, though, you need to go into the bathroom and wash your hands. You guys look pretty…dirty."

"Yeah, we'll go clean up. We'll take a bath," says Donnie.

"Are you kidding? You're not taking a bath here."

"We can take it together," says Donnie. He walks over and takes Ida's hand in his. Ida shakes herself loose.

"No bath," she says.

"I don't want to take a bath with him cause he got worms."

"Shut up!" says Donnie.

"He does. Little white ones."

Donnie starts to cry. He shuts his eyes tight and snot drips out of his nostrils.

"Quit crying," says Carter. "I'm going first. I don't want worm water."

"Jesus," Ida shouts. "Calm down. Go ahead. Take a bath one at a time. I don't care. Just do it fast."

She walks into the bathroom, pulls the metal rod that plugged the tub, and runs the water.

"Then can we have pancakes?" says Donnie.

"Pancakes. Are you serious? A snack, and you'll get what I have.

And as soon as you eat, you have to leave. Got it?"

On the counter, she has a full bag of barbecue potato chips, a partly-eaten package of cream-filled cookies, a lemon. She also has packets of white sugar she took from the diner in Erne City so that she'd have them on the bus.

The bus she isn't on.

"Just so you know," Ida says, not looking at either of them. "It's bad manners to walk into someone's house. It's called trespassing. If you were older, you would definitely go to jail."

"We *knocked*," Carter says. "You didn't open it like you're supposed to do. But we could see you in here through the window. Didn't you know you're our neighbor?" He skulks off to the bathroom. After a moment, she hears him splashing in the water.

She calls, "If you keep doing that kind of thing, you'll end up in jail someday."

Donnie sits on the floor, staring at her. He says, "I don't want to go to jail."

She almost says, *Not you. Him.*

Donnie is Carter's opposite: thin and angelic, his beauty and goodness shining through the grime. His knees are drawn up to his chest, little bones pushing against the fabric of his t-shirt. She has to turn away. She goes to the kitchen window and looks out at the morning; it is already impossibly hot.

One of them coughs. She doesn't know which. She is angry at herself for being mean. Usually she is good with kids. She used to babysit in high school and all the kids would beg her to come back.

She softens her voice. "Where did you kids come from?"

Donnie walks toward the window and points left.

"Over there."

She sees nothing where he points. The ground doesn't dip or rise anywhere. She can't imagine where the boys have come from.

"I don't see any houses over there," she says.

Carter comes out, dressed again in his dirty clothes, his hair damp. It is Donnie's turn in the bath, and while he splashes around, Carter walks around the empty rooms of her house. He doesn't look at her or talk to her; she can hear him talking to himself, but instead of listening to what he is saying, she opens the chips and the cookies and puts portions of both on paper towels. She squeezes lemons and empties sugar into her two glasses. No matter how long she lets it run, the cold tap water is only lukewarm; the sugar sits, un-dissolved, at the bottom of the glasses. When she squeezes the lemons, several seeds fall in and float to the bottom. The sight of them annoys her, but she doesn't bother trying to get them out.

"I want that one," says Carter, pointing to one of the glasses.

"That one is for me," she says, just because. "You two can share the other one."

When Donnie comes back in, the three of them sit on the floor. The boys take alternating sips. They eat the chips quickly, and then the cookies. They want more, and she makes them another glass with the lemon she's already squeezed, the two last sugar packets she has. She eats potato chips and drinks her glass of lemonade. Her mouth is a mishmash of tartness and salty starch.

"Hurry up," she says.

She takes the last sip and crunches the un-dissolved sugar, watching their jaws moving.

"I'm done!" shouts Donnie. "Let's go play outside in the yard!" He wipes his hands on his t-shirt, leaving oily stripes down the front.

"Not a chance," says Ida. "No playing. You have to go home. Right now."

"We don't want to go home," says Carter. "We want to stay here and play outside. You don't have to play with us. We don't want to play with you anyway."

"Go to your own house. It's the same outside of your house and outside of mine. What difference does it make?"

"It's better here."

"Sorry. You've got to go home now. That was the agreement." She slips on her tennis shoes and opens the door.

"Go," she says.

"We don't want to go home," says Carter, his voice gruff.

"Have you seen a orange cat?" says Donnie. "Ours ran away."

"I'm not getting into any more talking about this," she says to Carter. "You're leaving. I need to be alone. Let's go. I'll even walk you."

"You don't have to walk us," Carter scowls. "We can walk ourselves."

Donnie stands in front of her, his blue eyes sad and wide. It hurts to look at him. "If you see a orange cat," he says, "ask him if his name is Speedy!"

They leave. Carter pulls the door shut behind him.

She stands for a while at the window, staring out as they walk away, their heads down, their arms swinging. Ida watches until she can't see them anymore. She cleans up the sugar crystals, the lemon pulp, and the crumbs, using only water and the back of her hand. When she finishes, when all the evidence of them is gone, she looks out the window at the black streets and yellow-green grass of the fields.

Empty and dead. It is nothing like Aster's landscape, where there is a thickness, a texture everywhere. When you look up, you see trees, tall and majestic. Even the ones at the bottom of Door Hill.

There was a neighbor there, Mrs. Glack, an old widow, whom she and her brother Robert used to visit when they were in middle school. Mrs. Glack must have felt sorry for them, because she made them a full meal every time, and never told them they should come less often. Sometimes the meals were as simple as boiled hot dogs on white bread, a bowl of sliced apples. At other times, while they sat in her living room, looking at the Hummel collection, and the black and white pictures of the man and three boys in lederhosen, she broiled pork chops and boiled and mashed potatoes. Sometimes, there was strudel for dessert, but if not, she served them toasted white bread topped with the tart, seedy jam she made from the raspberries that grew in her own backyard. Always, there was some old-world pageantry involved. Cups with saucers, pats of butter on delicate plates.

Once, while Mrs. Glack was cooking for them, Robert stole three dollars out of her wallet, the only time he'd ever stolen anything. The next morning, he put the three dollars, loose, into her mailbox.

Ida especially liked one particular Hummel—a kerchiefed,

rosy-cheeked girl pulling a white puppy by the tail—and stuck it into the back waistband of her pants. All through that meal, it poked into her spine. Mrs. Glack died a few months later, and when Ida found out about it, she threw the Hummel into the woods. She couldn't throw far, though, and for several months, saw the red, white, brown, and blue of the Hummel peeking out of the trees. She was grateful when the first snow finally came and covered it up.

In the dark bathroom, she splashes her face with water.

Ida's real future figured out where she went and came here to reassert itself. There is no new life. There is no new self. No victory.

Yesterday, when everything about her life felt perfect, she took a taxi back from Erne City and walked into the Sunshine Settler Savings Bank. A bus was departing from Erne City in two hours, and she planned to take the taxi back to meet it.

The teller's first words were, "I'm sorry." The manager was called over; a telephone call was made. The teller and the manager whispered to each other. She stood still, pinching the inside of her arm.

There was no money. The account had been emptied on Saturday morning at the branch in Miami. First thing that morning, right when the branch opened at 8am. It seemed she'd been given a bad check. Maybe it was a mistake. The teller advised her to go out the door and to the Echo office and clear it up with Ken. Maybe he'd meant to write it from a different account, since he had more than one. Or maybe he'd forgotten to deposit a check that would have covered it.

She ran down the plaza to look, but there was nothing there but the two desks. The drawers were pulled open on one of them, and she could see that there was nothing inside.

She went back to the customer service desk at the bank. They would investigate it, the teller said, but she shouldn't get too worried yet. Maybe Mr. Cantwell would make a big deposit that day. They would re-deposit this check; perhaps it would go through overnight.

"No," she said, "He's not coming back. The office is empty."

"I don't know what to say." The teller smiled sympathetically.

The manager didn't smile. "If a new deposit isn't made in the next few days, we have to start a formal investigation. We'll keep you updated."

There was no place for her to go but the house. The shelter of that house was all that she had, that almost-finished rectangle, its back corner bright blue plastic.

At Karr's, she bought some junk food, a bottle of seltzer and a package of light bulbs.

"Paper or plastic?" said the cashier.

Ida didn't answer. She wasn't listening. The cashier put her things in a plastic bag.

Money was too tight for another cab. She had to walk. Her bag weighed heavily on the right side of her body. A sedan stopped after she'd gone a couple of miles, and an elderly man called out, gently, from the driver side window, asking if she wanted a ride. She said yes and got in, directing the man all the way to the house, not even asking him if it was out of the way. The man talked the whole time: his daughter was driving down from Jacksonville that night; she was getting a divorce, and even though he mostly believed that every single divorce was a shame, this one was really a good thing because the guy was a lousy sonofabitch.

Tears streamed down her face.

"You okay, honey?" he asked.

She shook her head and held her hand up: please don't ask.

"I didn't know you was crying till I looked at you. You wasn't making any noise."

What she noticed as they got close was the way the razed lots sat across from wild fields, the way the smell of damp vegetation mixed with the chemical smell of the asphalt. And there was the house, a rectangular box with a sad cement step, the blue tarp brightening its side.

Ida got out of the car and closed the door quietly behind her.

She would have done anything to be back in her apartment in Aster, a short walk from the house on Door Hill, back in that life that had recently seemed so shitty.

She'd spent *all that money*. It was like she'd done this to herself on purpose. She sat down on the concrete floor of the house and thought about when she was a sophomore in high school and decided that she was going to change herself: she would work hard and see if she could be different, do well. All she had wanted to know was whether or not it was possible. She listened in class and took notes and studied and rewrote and pulled straight A's the whole semester. And though it was easy at first, it was too hard to sustain. It was easy to fall back into reading magazines instead, into closing her eyes and thinking about other things. Over the long Christmas break, she lost her momentum and came back as a fuck-up again. Even worse than before, and none of her teachers mentioned it or asked her what happened.

A few hours after the boys leave, she hears a car's engine idling in front of the house. When the knock comes, she doesn't get up to answer the door. It can only be something bad. Like the parents of those boys. They probably went home and said that they were at some lady's house. Some lady who bathed them and fed them and yelled at them.

Ida will not answer it. She doesn't look out of the window. She stretches out on the cool floor of the living room. The backs of her legs and arms heat the concrete up quickly, and she moves a few inches over, onto cooler territory. She hears more knocking, but she doesn't move from her place or even look up. She hears a shuffling of feet outside, scraping on the concrete stoop. Another knock. Harder. An official sort of knock.

Ida inhales, exhales, and closes her eyes.

There is a tap at the window. When she looks up, she sees someone peering at her through it: a tall man in a police uniform. Sunglasses, glossy dark curls, thick hands shielding against the glare.

"Shit," she whispers.

"Ma'am?" he says. "Could you open the door, please?" A southern accent.

She stands up. Outside, she sees two cars, one a police cruiser, one a red sedan, idling on the street. Both are crowded with people. She opens the door.

"What?" She is out of breath, her heart going crazy.

"We're looking for a missing little boy. It's over a week that he's been gone and we could use all the help we can get."

"How many boys?" she says.

"Just one."

He hands her a flyer with a picture on it of a boy with dark blond hair, sitting in front of a birthday cake. The lit candles give his face a golden glow. A black Labrador retriever sits by his side, its tongue out and its eyes on the cake.

"Mitchell Healy. He's twelve, almost thirteen. He was wearing cut-off jeans and a white t-shirt. He has a black bicycle with chrome handlebars."

"I definitely haven't seen him."

"Mind if I take a look around?"

"I'm not from here. I don't even know anyone here."

"If you wouldn't mind." He steps closer.

She opens the door wide enough for him to come in. She steps outside when he goes in, and sees the people out in the cars; she feels their eyes on her.

He comes back out.

"Didn't know anyone lived in this particular house. You got furniture coming?"

She shakes her head. Even that slight movement makes her perspire. She wants him to leave so that she can stretch out on the concrete some more.

"Doesn't seem all that comfortable."

"It sure isn't," she says, but then is ashamed. Someone's child is missing.

"We've got room for one more. We'll drive out by the woods and pair off."

For a moment, she considers squeezing into the car full of elbows and shoulders, riding off to search through hot swamp grass. Being a part of something other than these walls, this tarp.

Out in the street, the people in the cars still watch her, as though they are anxious to hear what she has to say.

She shakes her head. "I really don't know this place," she says.

"And I haven't seen that little boy."

When they drive off, she goes back inside and sits on the cool concrete, listening to herself breathing, to the house breathing. The house's breath sounds raspy, greedy, as though it isn't getting enough oxygen. And she is here in its belly, watching it try to stay alive, breath by breath. She should have gone to help. She waits like this, glowering, until it gets dark, and then she takes off her clothes, spreads out the cushions and stretches out to try to get some sleep.

She remembers that she bought light bulbs, and she fishes around for them in the dark. Ida climbs into the kitchen sink and stands up to screw one of them into the fixture in the ceiling. When she gets down and flips the switch, the light comes on, white and unreal. Naked, she only feels more vulnerable, and so she turns it off. There is nothing for her to see inside this house but her own body, the bare walls. All she has accomplished is that she can now be seen by everything that might be watching from outside.

Ida sleeps terribly that night, waking, over and over, to the noises around her. She hears a strange scratching, and runs to the kitchen to throw on the light. The sound turns out to be a skinny green lizard, making its way across her pile of plastic Karr's bags.

SEVEN

I DA HAS NO CHOICE but to walk to Karr's. She has no idea how long it will take; all she can think about is that every single bit of food is gone. Better to go now than waiting until the afternoon, when it will be even hotter. Her shadow looms next to her, freakishly tall and skinny. Sweat rolls down her cheeks and her sides. She is so hungry.

Ida has been walking for more than an hour and needs a rest. She sits on the pavement, tucking her head between her bent knees. She imagines never getting up again. Maybe dying will not hurt; maybe it will be an irresistible sleepiness, a comforting white light that she can slump toward.

A shadow passes over her head. She looks up and is startled to see an enormous brown bird, directly overhead. It looks as if it is floating, without even a shiver in its broad wings. It is bigger than any bird she's ever seen from this close, and more graceful. When Ida was eight and Robert was nine, he told her that he flew to the top of a tree at recess. There was a robin's nest at the top of it, and three little blue eggs. *What else did you see up there?* she'd asked. *An inchworm on a leaf,* he answered. *How did you do it?* she asked. *I just stood still, closed my eyes and believed that I could. Then I just went up in the air.*

She hates Robert right now. For so long, he was the one person in her family that she loved, and this bit of family love used to make her feel like she had something decent and normal inside of her.

The bird passes over her again and lands in the nearby grass. There, on the ground, it loses all grace. Its head and neck bend hideously forward; it walks as though it is on invisible crutches. She sees its raw, burned-looking face and neck, devoid of feathers, its hooked beak. Repulsive scavenger face. It stares at her and takes a few ugly steps in her direction. She screams and her strangled voice tears through the blank sky. The bird lifts from the ground with a single beat of its heavy wings and swoops away.

She stands up and smacks the dust from her behind.

The plaza finally comes into view. Her throat is dry. She needs water. Still, when she gets there, she takes the time to walk past the Echo office and peer through the glass. She sees the same two desks, one with the empty drawers pulled open.

At Karr's, Ida pauses in the entryway, just past the automatic door. She closes her eyes, savoring the way the air conditioning chills her damp skin, and bends over the steel water fountain, drinking and drinking and drinking, pausing for air and to wipe her chin with the palm of her hand. She stands a minute, catching her breath and reading the ads and notices on the bulletin board: *Live-in companion needed for elderly woman; Dan's Custom Car Detailing; Join the Karr's team. Experienced help needed in several departments.* A poster of the missing boy, the same one the police officer showed her.

She looks around at the mounds of bright grapes, bars of soap, packages of pink frosted cupcakes, whole roasted chickens at the deli counter. She stares longingly at the glossy magazines, at a thick paperback called *Ghost Lover*.

Surely, she can buy a roasted chicken, some cupcakes, a box of granola, a book, for Christ's sake. Ida puts all of these things into her basket. She has a vague idea of how much money she has left, but she knows that she needs to face up to the exact sum before she comes to the register. She gets out her money and counts it. A twenty, a ten, two fives, six singles. She bites down hard on her lip. There was more, she is sure of it. She remembers two more twenties, soft and crumpled. She turns her pockets inside out, sits down on the cold floor. She takes out the bills and sets them down, one at a time, on the floor, remembering shelling out for her diner breakfast and the cab back from Erne City.

Forty-six dollars. And a few handfuls of change back at the house. Maybe there are two more twenties there, too, in the pocket of her other pair of shorts, but probably not. She squeezes her eyes shut, reliving the excesses of the previous weekend: meals half-finished, frozen yellow drinks at the hotel's bar (and those she'd bought, like a drunken fool, for the couple on their honeymoon), the sixty-dollar bikini she hasn't even had the guts to put on even once after she paid for it, because once the high of that weekend wore off, she knew her breasts were too small, her waist too thick, her thighs too white and shapeless to look right in it.

Ida puts the box of granola back on its shelf, puts the book back. She puts the soap back and the $2.99-a-pound grapes, though not before yanking three of them from their stems and shoving them into her mouth.

She moves down the soup and canned goods aisle. It can't be about taste or diversion; she has to be strategic. The no-name ramen noodle soup brand is on sale for six for a dollar. She walks to the housewares section at the back of the store. If she buys a cheap aluminum saucepan and a $10 single-burner hotplate, she can make herself ramen for every meal, enough to live on. And though she knows that they'll be heavy on her walk back, the cheapest fruits are the juice oranges. She picks out a cheap flashlight and a pack of batteries. Spending just over twenty-five dollars, she can buy enough to last for almost two weeks.

And then what?

She looks at the dozens of Maine lobsters in the tank at the seafood counter, their claws held closed by thick pink rubber bands. Some of them clamor at the glass. How conscious are they of their shitty predicament? If the tank were to break and they floated out free, onto the tile floor, what would they do then? It's a long walk to the ocean.

At the register, she turns around and scans for the stock boy— what would he think of her now?—but she doesn't see him. She points to the phone cards on display behind the register and asks for the five dollar one. She isn't ready to call Linda.

One weekend back on Door Hill when their boredom and daring had reached equally high levels, she and Linda thought that it would be fun to dress up as old ladies and take these personas on a bus ride to the county mall. They wore old dresses that no longer fit Linda's mother, and pulled their bras up above their breasts, pushing them lower and flatter on their chests. They baby-powdered their hair and tied kerchiefs around their heads. On the bus, they peeked out over the disorienting reading glasses they'd bought from a display carousel at the drug store. None of the other riders noticed them.

Linda was Louise and Ida was Minnie.

During the ride, they talked, loudly, about their imaginary sciatica and hemorrhoids, the benefits of prune juice, how the Life-Call panic button was the most useful invention ever.

When they got to the mall, no one looked at them. They wanted to be madcap old ladies, but where was the attention? They were invisible, the opposite of what they wanted. They went along with it, walking slowly and arm in arm, taking turns pausing as though they needed to take rests.

After they took a couple of circuits around the shops, they sat down at a table in Joseph's cafeteria and, in her best old lady voice, Linda asked the waitress to bring them two Manhattans. The waitress did. All around them, they noticed other old women; some were in pairs, but many were alone. None of them were having cocktails, like Louise and Minnie were, but all of them looked as though they had already been sitting in Joseph's for a long time and were in no hurry to leave.

The waitress brought their drinks, bitter and awful. They sipped at them. The only thing they could hear, other than the low murmuring, were the melancholy sounds of coughing and of forks and spoons clinking against plates.

They sipped until their drinks were half finished, until they couldn't bear another taste, and then Ida felt a lump in her throat, her eyes welling up. Tears slid down her nose. They didn't look at each other. Linda left the money on the table.

It's going to be real someday, Linda said on the way home. *We'll remember that we did this and we'll know that it really was our future. And then we'll die, wondering why we wasted a day when we were supposed to be young.* She put her head on Ida's shoulder and closed her eyes.

The oranges weigh her down. It is hotter than it was on the way over. She sets the saucepan and the oranges down and knots her damp hair into itself to get it off her neck. When she makes it past the town center and into the beginning of the series of long and empty streets, she reaches in and gets a fat orange out of the bag. She peels it, throws the peel into the tall grass, and eats it two sections at a time, spitting the seeds onto the street. The tip of her tongue burns for another, and she reaches in to get one. She eats it the same way, and after, the bag is a little bit lighter.

The soft asphalt completely absorbs the sound of her footsteps. She wonders if the missing boy is still lost, thirsty, walking and walking, trying to get out of the nowhere, the endless wild grass that probably goes on for many miles, but only finding his way deeper in.

Ida takes a turn on a different street, hoping to find a shortcut, pretty sure that it will loop around more sharply, so that she can circumvent the longest stretch. She doesn't know the street, but commits to it, and walks until she sees another house shaped just like hers: white, with beige shutters and a pink azalea bush planted by the front door. The grass on the front lawn is different from any of the grass nearby; it is soft and green, with slim blades, just like the spring grass in Aster. It isn't the kind in her house's yard, which is thick and reedy and sharp enough to cut your feet. Ida sets down her bags and slips off her tennis shoes. The softness calls to her like a rare, pretty thing from her childhood.

The bedroom on the far left side of the house has the shade pulled down most of the way. Ida creeps close and peers inside at the sleeping back of a small child taking an afternoon nap. She can see the child's back rising and falling in the dimness of the room, scattered toys on the floor beyond the bed.

She tiptoes around the back of the house, seeing what she can through the windows. The bathroom has a neat stack of yellow towels on the shelf, and a wooden comb. On the edge of the bathtub stands a bottle of pink bubble bath. She can see right into the toilet bowl—it is sparkling white. She can even smell the air inside, fresh as a new bar of thick, white soap.

She passes the kitchen and looks at the sink and stove, the refrigerator that is no doubt full of good things. There is a pie on the counter. The crust is pierced with a deep criss-cross, and she can't tell for sure, but it looks as if the filling is either strawberry or cherry. Something red and tart. Her mouth waters.

She can see into the living room on the other side of the house. Something moves. A leg. Someone is sitting on a chair. Ida creeps to the next window and, through a filmy curtain, can see a woman sitting in a chair, a book in her lap. It isn't fair. Ida wants everything in that house, to sit in an actual chair and read a book in the cool air conditioning, to eat the pie with a fork right out of the pan.

On the way back across the soft lawn, she feels something under her foot. A small, hard pile. Ida bends down to pick it up and sees that it is a pearl bracelet. She tucks it into her pocket, picks up the grocery bags and doesn't turn back.

Once she makes it to her house, Ida takes the bracelet out of her pocket and fastens it onto her wrist. She wouldn't have seen it if she wasn't supposed to have it. She doesn't know for sure that the bracelet belongs to the woman sitting in the chair. Probably, but it isn't an absolute. And if it does, there are probably a dozen others in some neat wooden jewelry box.

She moves her wrist slowly from side to side, watching the pearls as they slide over her skin. On the clasp are three small diamonds. It is probably just costume jewelry: plastic pearls and rhinestones.

She remembers seeing someone on some TV show testing for genuine pearls with their teeth. If the pearls are fake, the faux-pearl coating is supposed to scrape right off.

She takes off the bracelet and brings it to her mouth, bares her teeth to test one of them, but the pearl is small and slippery and she can't get a good grip. She tries another, holding it firmly. Nothing. It might be real. She tests another pearl and feels something loose in her mouth. She moves her tongue around, trying to figure out what it is because the bracelet is still intact. She spits it into her hand.

It is her tooth. Her make-believe tooth, the one that took the place of her rotted upper canine. The one that she paid off over the course of a few months. The one that covered up the weak, dark spot of rot that she worried would find a way to come back. Her tongue goes to the soft, raw gum. She wraps the fake tooth in a paper napkin, puts it next to the kitchen sink. She moans; the sound comes from her very center.

It feels like something that she cannot survive.

EIGHT

DONNIE AND CARTER ARE in the forest before sunset. They have been drawn to it recently; the air is cooler and they sometimes find slimy frogs on the ground. Donnie stops, panicking; his brother is out of his sight.

"Carter!" Donnie calls. "Where'd you go!?" He stands, his fists clenched, listening for Carter's footsteps, and they finally come. Donnie can see him.

"I checked all around," Carter yells. "No lions. You can come on in."

"Are you sure?"

"Yeah. I take care of you, don't I? So come on."

Donnie does. Carter runs ahead of him.

"Go slower!" Donnie shouts, and Carter does, just a little bit. Donnie feels okay, as long as he can still see his brother, because Carter isn't afraid of anything. He looks at everything as he walks, turning around every few steps to make sure there is nothing behind him. Ever since Carter told him it was the jungle, he gets excited, hoping to see the monkeys and the parrots. But not the lions. Lions eat people. But Carter made sure that each of them has a butter knife in their back pocket to stab a lion in the eye, because that's the fastest and best way to kill it. Donnie slows down every once in a while, in order to picture how he'll actually do it. Carter said he'd have to attack the lion and push the knife all the way in and not stop until the lion is dead. Sometimes he thinks he could do it, and his arms and shoulders get tense, already feeling the end of the knife go in. Other time he pictures those teeth and that big mane of yellow hair and imagines getting his arm bitten off before he can even get to the knife.

Carter runs ahead and is out of sight again. Donnie is further into the forest than he has ever been. He can't see the outside anymore.

"Carter! Don't go away from me!"

"I didn't!"

Donnie runs forward and can see Carter's t-shirt between the trees.

"What are you doing?"

"I found something."

Carter stands there, holding onto the bottom rung of a wooden ladder, which is hanging from a massive tree.

"I need you to come over here," says Carter. "So that I can get up that thing and see where it goes. Come on over here and get on your hands and knees so I can boost up on you."

Donnie does. He has his hands and knees in mud, his feet on a saw palmetto palm. He grits his teeth because Carter outweighs him by thirty pounds, but one quick, big step on the middle of Donnie's little back is all he needs to get one hand on the second rung and one foot on the bottom. Donnie flattens out in the mud to recover, but he is okay. Carter extends a hand for Donnie. Carter lifts him until he can get his legs over the bottom rung.

"It's a little house!" says Carter, climbing up the last rung and running ahead.

He opens a screen door for Donnie and they go inside where the floor and the walls are wood and the windows are glass. They see a small, white canvas cot, a table, a red chair, books, paper, pens, a lamp, a small flashlight, a big one, a box of cassette tapes, a contact lens case, neatly-folded clothes on a wooden shelf.

Carter explores quickly: ducking, opening, peeking.

"There's no fridge." He frowns.

"So what are we going to do here?" Donnie sits on the cot.

"I wish we could live here." Carter sits in the red chair. He picks up the notebook from the table. It is open, and a pen sits in the fold.

"What does that book say?"

"Hold on," Donnie says, holding up his hand. He looks closely, moves his finger along the words. "I was lonely…true…b-but…it…was…be-cause…I…didn't…know…it…was…enough…to… I don't know this word." He sets it down again. "The rest of it is too hard."

"What's that?" says Donnie, pointing to a contact lens case.

"I seen this on a show once." Carter snatches it, unscrews the case and looks inside. He doesn't see anything, so he feels around with his finger. Something invisible sticks to it. "It's called contacts. You put it right on your eyeballs."

He tries to do just that, but when he puts his finger near his eye, he drops the contact lens on the floor. He crouches down to look for it, but he can't find it.

"Come on," he says. "Let's go. There's nothing to eat anyway."

"What are we gonna do?"

"Go back and sleep in the truck."

"I'm afraid to walk in the dark."

"It's not dark yet."

"Almost, it is."

"Dark only means night. Everything else is still the same."

They open the door and Carter waits for Donnie to go down the ladder first.

"Don't go ahead of me," Donnie says when he gets to the bottom. "Let me hold onto your shirt when we're walking." He looks up at Carter, his hands still gripping the bottom rung.

PETER FEELS LIGHTHEADED ON his ride back from Erne City. He knows he needs to ease up and buy something with some sort of sugar in it. His brain needs more carbohydrates than he has been giving it, and he can't always find them quickly enough. There are no mulberries this time of year, and the yucca doesn't grow quite as fast as he can eat it. He is not crazy about it, either. Last night he took the last of what he'd gathered, peeled the brown skin from the root, sliced it thinly, and fried it in fish fat. When he ate it, he was glad that it was gone.

It is nearly dark when he gets close to the Karr's plaza. Inside, the metal clips of his cycling shoes click against the cold tile floor and the cashiers all turn to look at him.

He is secretly glad to be near the motherly women who stand at the cash registers, waiting to take care of him, send him off with his food in a neat bag. Especially the one at the top register, with her cloud of gray hair.

Peter starts with the produce aisle, eyeing the green and purple plums. In these months, he's forgotten such things existed. He takes one of each and clicks down the aisle.

He stops to look at the bakery display. Except for loaves of bread, it is mostly empty. Behind the counter is a woman with lank hair and a green apron. Her chin rests on her hand.

"Are there any muffins?" he says.

She takes a while to respond, as though his question has woken her up from an eyes-open sleep.

"No," she shakes her head. "We haven't had muffins for a while. There's Hostess and all that down aisle eight."

He is disappointed. He doesn't really care about the muffins all that much, but he refuses to slum it with preservative-laden garbage.

"Hopefully we'll start up again soon," she calls to him. She gives him a sympathetic smile.

Three days before, Peter had come back from Erne City with handlebar tape and sweat-proof sunscreen and a police officer was waiting for him at the base of his tree. He told him he was there to investigate a missing boy. The policeman was friendly enough, but Peter was uncomfortable, aware of how suspicious a man living in a tree house had to seem to someone searching for a missing kid. He turned Peter's driver's license around, studying it.

"Are you a Haggenden, as in, the *real estate* Haggenden?"

Peter nodded. "That's my father."

"I thought I read he died not too long ago."

"Yes, he did." He scratched his arm.

The officer frowned. "Why are you living in a tree in the middle of nowhere? Not exactly your station in life, is it?"

"It's only my last name. It's not who I am," Peter said. He noticed the officer's moustache, brown, so thick that it gleamed.

"This is a pretty neat little place you've got. Mind if I see it up close?"

"Be my guest. You have to pull your legs up," he said.

But the policeman was already halfway up the ladder. Peter followed, his face hot. The officer tapped at the glass in the windows, stood on the porch, turned the shower on and off, asked how long the batteries lasted on his stereo system.

He patted the dark wood windowsill. "Nice job. You do this all yourself?"

"I had some help."

"How long did it take?"

"Three days. Long days."

He nodded. "It was in all the papers when your father died." The officer tapped at the glass pane. "When was it?"

"Almost a year ago."

"Heart attack, right?"

"It was a stroke." Sometimes, he thought of that moment when his father must have sank to his knees, knowing something was seriously wrong with the most integral parts of his body. His father had reached out to him in the months before, and sent him note cards on which he rambled about spending time in the Miami house, about a beautiful Jaguar he'd restored. He always thought that with the next card, he'd know how to respond, but he didn't, and then he couldn't.

The officer sat on Peter's cot, took the picture of the boy out of his pocket. "This sort of thing kills me," he said. "His mother…the last time I spoke to her, she asked me if I was really there. She said she thought she might only be dreaming the whole thing. What do you say to that?"

Peter said that the boy didn't look especially doomed to him. The picture didn't have that already-dead quality that so many of these pictures had.

Peter puts a box of muesli in his basket. He takes a carton of eggs, imagining how they will smell frying in a pan on his Coleman stove.

He'd like some salted butter. He finds the butter and a carton of milk.

He picks up a package of goat cheese and sets it back on the shelf. He touches a jar of pickles with the tip of his finger and the cold glass stops him. What could he use the jar for, once the pickles were gone? He really shouldn't buy so much. Just because it's here.

NANCY LISTENS FOR THE clicks of the man's funny shoes. When she hears them, she turns her head, looking down the aisles for him. Her shift has just begun, and she is feeling alert and energetic. Her station tonight is register #1, her favorite spot, close to the exit.

Though the other cashiers are still unfriendly—she would have liked to make a joke about those shoes, something about Fred Astaire tap-tap-tapping down the aisles—sometimes she enjoys the job a little bit. She likes reading the headlines near the register. She feels as if she knows some of the celebrities and thinks of advice to give them to fix their painful lives. *There is no reason on earth to starve yourself.* Or *Try being single for a while.* Or *No more plastic surgery for you.*

Something about the man tugs at her. Maybe the way he pursed his lips as he walked in, as though he were steeling himself. She thinks he looks lonely, too. And so thin. He needs a few weeks of good meals and to drink milkshakes in between them. He reminds her of Philip, her one love, the one who gave her the pearl bracelet. He gave the bracelet to her on her twenty-seventh birthday, just a few months after they'd met. She looks down at her arm and sees that she is not wearing it. She must have left it on the windowsill by the kitchen sink.

When they broke up, Nancy thought she'd meet someone else and get married. She thought she'd have children of her own. Once in a while she met a man or was set up by her sister or a well-meaning neighbor, but the men always told her, before she even got a chance to know how she felt about them, that they only saw her as a friend. So it went, until she gave up.

Madeline is what life has to offer Nancy. Madeline's mother left when she was just a few weeks old, panicked, maybe, by the idea of having given birth to such a sick and tiny baby. She couldn't suck; she didn't gain enough weight; her skin was strange. The diagnosis didn't come until after her mother was gone.

A girl pulls up to Nancy's register with a basket full of junk food: potato chips, cookies, gummy candies, soda. She smiles at Nancy as she puts it all on the conveyor belt. She is seventeen or so and her blonde ponytail swings as she moves.

"I'm on a road trip with my older sister," the girl says. "We need gummy bears." The girl reaches into her pocket and pulls out a wad of rumpled dollar bills.

Nancy smiles back and scans her items. She thinks of Madeline, who won't ever get to be a teenager going on a carefree car trip, who is in the house right now, asleep, so small, curled up under her comforter, unaware that she is alone. Madeline has brought her some degree of peace, and there are times when she sees what she would have been like as a mother. Yesterday, they made lasagna together, spreading and pouring the layers one at a time. Madeline ate a decent portion, and Nancy told her to have more, because she was a growing girl. But she isn't. Not really.

When she hears the man coming toward the front of the store, Nancy has almost forgotten about him. He sets the basket down on the ground, empty, near her register.

"Oh no! You have to get something!" she blurts out.

"I am," he says. He puts a hand on the candy display and picks out a roll of peppermint Lifesavers. He pays for them with a dollar bill. Disappointed, Nancy hands him his change and watches him walk toward the door. One of his shoes slides across the floor and he lands with a thump, whacking the back of his head on the tile. One cashier laughs, and the mean sound of it makes Nancy's face hot. She rushes over to help him, but before she gets there, he has already jumped up, brushed himself off, and walked out the automatic doors.

Later that night, when her shift ends, Nancy notices his package of Lifesavers on the floor by the flower display. He must have dropped them when he slipped. They rolled a long way.

On her way out to the parking lot, Nancy sees the flyer about a missing boy. Her heart races, thinking of Madeline in the house alone. She runs to the car. It takes her three tries to get the key in the ignition.

IDA IS IN THE dark bathroom, up to her chin in cool water. She has been here since three in the afternoon, and she has let the water out and refilled it four times. Her tongue rests in the raw place where the tooth had been. She wishes she had a bottle of wine, so that she could drink it all and maybe find the guts to slip under the water.

Ida walked in the heat today for hours, hoping it would tire her out. She didn't put on sunscreen, and now the skin on her face, especially her eyelids, is tight and sore. Ida hasn't seen anyone all day. She walked until a road ended in dirt, then grass, which moved with dozens of lizards trying to get out of her way. She turned around and walked back, looking at the water level of the canals, too shallow to drown in without a whole lot of effort. And being eaten by an alligator would be far too unpleasant.

She has been thinking about Mr. Brinks, her World Cultures teacher from high school. She remembers his vulnerable, white backside as he bent down to pick up his grey-white underwear.

On the last day of class her senior year, he told everyone that he was leaving Aster, New York, for a new teaching job in California. The news made her a little sad. The B he gave her, which she didn't deserve, was the main reason she would graduate. She stayed until everyone else had left and walked up to his desk. She told him that it had been her favorite class, which was true. He turned to her, one hand propped on the corner of his desk, and invited her over that weekend for a going-away barbecue.

When she arrived, no one else was there, and it was pretty clear that no one else was invited. He was plain and doughy, but he seemed whole and significant, with a beard and enough cologne to show that he expected to be noticed. She held herself straighter, moved her limbs languidly, stopped being so schlumpy, stopped thinking and feeling like an Overdorff. He offered her a seat on his couch, and a glass of white wine. Every few minutes, he was closer, until (finally!) he was kissing her neck and pinching her breasts, reaching down and pulling her dress off. She sat on the couch in tan underpants. She'd had them for years, from the time they were too big until now, when they were tight. He took her small breasts in his hands and squeezed them together. She thought, *Something is happening.* Her hair came out of its pins and a hank of it stuck, damp, in the cleavage he was creating. He grabbed the waistband of her underpants and rolled them down and off. She was glad. She thought, *Maybe there's hope for me.*

It was her first time and she was glad that it was happening and was glad when it was done. She walked home in the dark, her inner thighs strained and aching. Everyone in the house was asleep. A virgin no more. She grinned in the dark, her teeth bared. Linda would have been both horrified and thrilled. (*You fucked a teacher!* Linda would later say. *Right on!*)

She went dozens of times over the summer. Maybe he would take her to California with him. He could kick her out in a week and she wouldn't care because she'd be away from her parents and Aster and Door Hill. Just like Robert was. When she called Mr. Brinks and said she needed to talk to him, that it was really important and couldn't wait, he whispered *Oh my God, no* and told her to meet him behind the grocery store later that night. She waited for him there, wondering how she would present the idea. She just wanted the ride and nothing else. She watched him pull up in a rusty sedan. He parked, got out, and handed her a brown envelope. He ran his fingers through his lank, thinning hair.

That will more than take care of it, he said, using the same stiff voice he'd used in class after telling the boys in the back row to cut out the chit-chat.

She opened it when he drove off. Ten hundred-dollar bills.

She opens the bathtub drain and lets the water out. When it is gone, she closes the drain and turns the tap on again. All of that walking didn't exhaust her the way she hoped it would. There is no way she will sleep tonight, either. There is no point getting out of the bath.

"I DON'T KNOW WHY it's so dead," says Lloyd, tightening the strings of his black apron. He leans against the server station to count his tips.

"Why isn't Ryan working?" says Mona, another server. "You guys always work the same shifts."

"Not this week." Lloyd folds the bills and tucks them back into his apron pocket.

"Why not?"

He shrugs and pours himself a cup of coffee. "I think this old couple on twelve is going to stiff me. You always know you're going to get stiffed when your table sends a baked potato back. Do you mind if I take off once these geezers pay up?"

"Sure, honey. Is everything OK?" says Mona. "This whole shift you haven't smiled even once."

"I'm just tired," Lloyd lies and walks off toward his table with the cup of coffee. It spills over the brim and onto the saucer. He and Ryan have opposite shifts all week. Ryan arranged for it. He said he was doing it for the good of both of them, but Lloyd feels like he is being punished.

They had a great first night in Key West. A delicious dinner with a seventy-five dollar bottle of unbelievable wine. The hotel was perfect, the bed sheets smooth and cool. They went on a snorkeling trip on the second day, out to the reef on a glass-bottom boat. They got in the water and watched barracudas, a tiger shark, angelfish. Underwater, they laughed-bubbled at how funny the other looked wearing a snorkeling mask, their noses pressed like pig's snouts.

Back on land, before dinner, they sat on the beach and piled sand.

"It would be fun to build a sand castle," said Ryan. "With a kid. There's no reason to do it on your own."

Lloyd pulled *ArtForum* out of his bag and flipped through it.

That night, they went to the same restaurant, both hoping to recreate the experience of the night before. The food wasn't as good. The wine was just as good, but Lloyd drank too much, and as he glugged the wine, he thought about what Ryan said about sand castles and he got steadily more pissed off. After a half hour, he was seething.

"You're in a mood," said Ryan. "What's up?

Lloyd stood up and pushed his chair in. He walked out of the restaurant. It was dark on Duvall Street and he walked until he found the beach. He hid in the shadows, tried to sleep, all the while thinking of Ryan and hoping he was upset and then hoping he wasn't. At three in the morning, sober and feeling foolish, he finally went back to the hotel.

Ryan was asleep. He didn't wake up, even when Lloyd got into bed and bounced on the mattress a little more than necessary. Ryan wasn't faking. His breathing was even and deep.

Lloyd calls home to tell Ryan that he is coming home early. "What are you doing?" he says.

"I'm painting the bathroom ceiling. Finally."

Lloyd pictures Ryan, the breathing mask resting on top of his head while he talks on the phone.

"How's it going?"

"It's a ceiling. There's not much to report. What's up?"

"Nothing. What color are you painting it?"

"White."

Neither says anything else. They hold the phones and breathe.

NINE

WHAT WILL SIXTEEN DOLLARS buy her? This is all that Ida has left, and two of those dollars are in the form of nickels, dimes, and quarters. The food ran out the day before yesterday. It lasted twelve days instead of fourteen, because eating was the only way she could help the time to pass. A whole day without food was the only thing that finally motivated her to stand up, put on her shoes, and open the door into the sunlight. She stayed inside for three days in a row, barely moving, the tip of her tongue resting in her exposed gum. Once the food ran out, she saw the whole thing the way that Mr. Brinks must have seen it: he got it on with a dumb teenager. Probably only cost him, when she broke it down, fifty bucks a screw. So Ida had been a cheap hooker. Linda would laugh at that, and Linda's laughing would make her laugh, too, but Linda isn't here.

As she walks, she takes the bracelet off and holds it in her hand. She counts the pearls, working up the strand with her fingertips. Twenty-seven. The same number of teeth in her mouth.

The policeman has been back. When Ida saw him at the window, she took the bracelet off and put it in her front pocket. *What bracelet?* she practiced as she went to open the door. *I have no idea what you're talking about.* And the policeman would say, *Please ma'am, empty your pockets.*

She let him in and then remembered why he was there. The

missing boy is still missing.

"Do you remember seeing a dark blue Volkswagen bug? Someone said they saw one driving slowly through the streets, looking around. It would have been on the morning of the 22nd of July." He spread his fingers out and glanced down at them.

"No," she said. "I'm sure I would have remembered it if I saw it. I like Volkswagens. They're supposed to be good luck."

He nodded and rubbed his eyes with his forefinger and thumb.

"You know anyone else who lives around here?"

She shook her head, but remembered that she did actually know someone who lived nearby, or almost: those guys from the restaurant.

"The problem with a search like this is that there's too much to search through. We had a copter over in the woods a few times, but it's hard to get a good look from above. The trees cover up the ground too much."

"How long has he been lost?"

"It's been three weeks," he said. "I don't have any kids. I can't imagine." He shook his head.

"Me neither."

She watched him drive away, realizing for the first time that Robert had technically, or legally, anyway, been a missing child. At least for those few weeks before his eighteenth birthday.

Only no one had bothered to look for him.

Robert had once told her that he looked out of the bathroom window in the middle of the night and saw a black unicorn snacking on the grass. In the morning, he took her outside and showed her where, sure enough, the grass looked as if it had been chewed. He pointed to marks in the mud. *Those are from hooves,* he said and they certainly looked like hoof marks.

SHE IS GETTING CLOSER to Karr's. On her right is the scrubby pine that lists heavily in one direction, as if trying in vain to evade the sun. She has passed the tree enough times to recognize it as a sign that she'll be at Karr's inside of twenty minutes. Her stomach is making noises.

She mops her brow with the inside of her forearm and forces herself to think the thought she has been pushing away for the past week and a half: she has to go home. And worse than just going back to Aster, she has to go to Door Hill. And not only does she have to bear that humiliation, but she also has to call her mother and beg for money for a bus ticket. If she even has the money. If she will even give it to her. Her father is more likely to give it to her, but he doesn't even have his own bank card, and the last she heard, he lives in some trailer by the highway with his half-brother, with no phone and no electricity anyway.

The last time she saw her father, he came to see her at her job at the Community Center. She saw him pull up in the back parking lot on a Yamaha motorbike, which he'd found at a junkyard and gotten running. He wanted to take her for a ride, but she wasn't done with her work day and he didn't have a helmet, and he left, shaking his head as though she were a huge disappointment.

She will buy more ramen, more oranges. Nothing else. She has to settle for avoiding starvation and scurvy.

The plaza is in front of her. She runs across the wide roadway and passes the hotel, the Echo Development office. She has called the bank from the gas station pay phone twice now; unsurprisingly, Ken hasn't made any deposits.

A red and white sign in the window of Fashion Bug says *Salesgirl needed*. Next to it is the poster of the missing boy, candles lighting up his face.

Ida pushes the door open, her heart beating fast. Career clothes. Everywhere. Polyester and wool blend blazers and skirts, shiny blouses. All three of these are put together on several mannequins, with bold beaded necklaces or printed scarves knotted at the neck. Ida's first thought is, *Who around here would need any of these things?* No one. That's why the job will be such a breeze. Standing around in the air conditioning all day, dealing with the rare customer. Much, much better than calling her mother, begging and explaining.

"You looking for something special today?"

The woman is a few years older than Ida, and dressed like one of the mannequins. Tan hose on her legs and white pumps on her feet. Her hair is pulled back, revealing a broad face that is enthusiastic about possibly making a sale, no matter how small, just to have something to attend to.

"I like this blouse," says Ida, fingering the button of a slippery green-blue one.

"That color would be great on you," she says. She picks it up and holds it under Ida's neck. "Great with your skin tone."

"Yeah, I like it."

"Oh, and it is really nice with a pencil skirt. A brown one. The fall colors just came in. And if you buy two items today, you get a third one for half price."

Ida nods, wondering why fall colors matter here. The leaves aren't going to change, they aren't going anywhere. "Also, it says, you're hiring? There's a sign outside and I'm looking for a job."

The woman stares at Ida. "Oh," she says. She walks, dejected, to the front of the store, and grabs the sign. There will be no sale. Ida trails after her.

"I have lots of work experience," Ida says.

"Look, we're not hiring anymore. I was supposed to take the sign down a few weeks ago and I just forgot. But…even if we were, you don't really have the right look for selling professional clothes."

Ida looks down at her cut-off shorts and rumpled t-shirt.

"I was just gardening," she says. "I was planting some rose bushes in my yard. I just came by here spontaneously. I don't usually look like this."

The saleswoman shrugs. She turns to straighten a rack and Ida's tongue goes to the empty space in her mouth. As she walks out, she clenches her jaw so tightly that she feels it in her shoulders and chest.

She passes an empty storefront and stops in front of the glass. Without a mirror, she hasn't yet seen what she looks like, only has an idea of how bad it might be. She steels herself and opens her mouth.

There is the black space and also the tooth the dentist had shaved down so that he could attach the bridge to it. Without the fake tooth, the stump is the color of iced tea. She looks like a hillbilly, and not the cute kind. She turns away from the glass. She is rotting from the inside out. Her mother has lost six of her teeth. Her father's teeth are brown from the Skoal he is always chewing. Both of them look a decade older than they are. They didn't fight it. Being an Overdorff means no doctor when you were sick, no dentist ever. Your teeth aren't worth taking care of. Let ruin proceed. When Robert was twelve and there was no money and nothing to take for lunch, he'd opened a can of red beans in chili sauce and put them in a plastic baggie. The bag opened up and the beans had gotten all over his math textbook and stunk up his entire year.

The Karr's parking lot is fuller than she has ever seen it. In the entryway, she takes the calling card out of her back pocket. She'll call the house on Door Hill first, and get that over with. Then she'll call Linda and let her know she isn't coming. As she picks up the receiver, she notices the Karr's sign she has seen before but hasn't registered until now: *Experienced help needed in all departments.*

She hangs up the phone and quickly, as though the opportunity might disappear in the course of a minute, straightens her hair and walks over to the customer service counter. She takes a breath, her mouth open just wide enough to get the words out, and asks for an application. The man behind the desk stares at her through his glasses, and hands her a clipboard with an application and pencil on it. The man's nametag says, *J.B. Higgins, Your Karr's Store Manager—How May I Help You?*

"I need as many cashiers as I can get," he says. "And I needed them yesterday." His waist spills out, like dough, over his belt. "We're the only superstore around for forty miles, so we do a big business. Where do you live? Valponia? Or are you in Erne City?"

"Neither," she says. "I live here."

"In Fort Starlight? You live over there?" he says with disbelief, gesturing in the direction of the gated community with its fine houses.

"No. Further out. I just moved here. And that's why I look like a wreck," she says. She holds her hand up, her fingers splayed in front of her mouth. The words come out sounding tight, self-conscious and suspicious, but she has to keep going.

"Ordinarily I'm much more put together, but I decided to come by for an application at the spur of the moment. I have been gardening all day. I'm looking for a job. And I can start right away."

He holds his bent knuckle to his mouth. "You talk like a northern girl," he says.

"Yeah," she says. "Upstate New York."

"I'm from Boston." He picks up the ringing telephone.

"Yep," he says into the receiver. "Speaking." He pauses, frowns. "Ah, you need even more special treatment. I'm not sure I can help you out, but go ahead and ask me anyway."

Ida takes the application and begins to fill it out. She bagged and cashiered at the Food Town in Aster for seven months. She hated the bagging, having to worry about the heavy cans crushing the delicate things, having to think about balancing the weight out. She hated the cashiering even more: at least five times a shift, some customer would roll up with a heaping cart and then act shocked at the total, take a few minutes to stand there, blocking the rest of the customers, as she searched the receipt for overcharges or pulled out a coupon when it was already too late. Ida hated it, but she knows she can do it long enough for bus fare.

The man shakes his head, the phone cradled on his shoulder. "Look," he says, "it's up to you. If you want to switch days, it's your funeral, as they say. The other ladies aren't going to like it and I don't know if I can handle the infighting. You'll have to smooth things out for yourself. Okay? Alright. Don't thank me yet. I really need people who can make a commitment."

He looks at Ida, rolls his eyes.

"Yep. I know. I've taken care of kids myself. Yep. Okay. Goodbye."

He sets down the receiver and picks it up again.

"J.B. Higgins from Karr's here. I'd like to run last week's ad again," he says. "Cashiers and baggers. Will train. And the rest is a little bit different this time. Change the wording to *assistant manager* in the seafood department and *manager* in the bakery. Relevant experience required. And tell you what, run it again all month, just like it is, unless you hear different from me."

J.B. Higgins raises his eyebrows and hangs up. "I'm getting too old for this," he says. "Yesterday I bagged for two hours and rang for three."

"Did you say you needed someone in the bakery?" she asks.

"What I need is a bakery manager," he says. "I have a bakery clerk, but I need someone to run it. It's been closed for a while and we're losing money. I tried to run it one day last week, but it was too much for me, with everything else I have to do. I started off in the bakery. Twenty-seven years ago."

"I have some experience," she says. "With baking. Actually, I have a lot of experience."

He frowns. "Problem is that I can't train anyone. I need someone who knows what they're doing and can run things, too. The whole deal. I can't be worrying about it. I need to get someone in there and I need them to take off running right from the get-go."

"I *was* an assistant manager," she says, nodding and smiling and nodding. "At a bakery in New York. That's the job I just left, actually."

He squints. "What kind of product did you do there?"

"Oh, cookies, pies, cupcakes, tarts. The basics."

"What sort of volume we talking about?" He doesn't believe her, but she can tell that he wants to.

"I mean, it wasn't a big business, but I could have handled bigger." She rocks on her feet, trying to look relaxed.

She has one of her arms wrapped around her back, pinching the flesh on her waist. This is a gift, right here.

"Wasn't a big business, eh?" He grins. "OK, let's see what you know. Tell me how to make buttercream."

"Buttercream," she says. "Let's see…um, butter, an equal amount of Crisco, whipping cream, vanilla, and powdered sugar." Ida made it once from a recipe in *The Complete Baker*. By some stroke of luck, she committed it to memory. She is impressed with how sure she sounds. "I start off mixing the butter and the Crisco, and then the vanilla and cream and then the sugar, and…I stop when I get the right texture."

"Consistency?"

"That's what I meant."

"Hmm," says J.B. Higgins. "But tell me something. Why Crisco? Why not all butter?"

"The Crisco holds up longer. It loses its shape fast if it's all butter."

"Okay," he says. "The truth is that most everything is air-conditioned in these parts, so that isn't really a worry. Shortening is cheaper, though, and that's something to think about. We don't make cakes anyway." He puts his hands on the counter and stares at her for a moment.

"Tell you what," he finally says. "Write down your references for that place you worked."

"Sure thing," she says. She writes *Clarabelle's Bakery*. She puts down her own telephone number in Aster as the *Clarabelle's Bakery* phone number. She never had her telephone turned off. When she decided to come to Florida, packed her things, and dropped the keys on the floor of her apartment and stepped outside, she checked the knob to make sure she was indeed locked out and that there was no turning back. Maybe her phone was still on. Maybe the landlord hadn't done anything more than a half-hearted knock yet. It hadn't been that long.

"The owners usually take off for part of the summer," she says. "They go on vacation." She puts the clipboard on the counter.

He picks up her application and looks over it. "You don't have a phone number written down here for how I can get in touch with *you*."

"That's because I literally just moved here a few days ago. I didn't get it hooked up yet. If you want, I can call you tomorrow. Or I can come back. Just tell me when."

"I hope I can get a hold of them," he says. "It sure would make my life easier. You don't sound completely inept. Tell you what. Let me try right now. Before you go anywhere."

He dials her number and she can hear the ringing on the other end. Her heart pounds. She counts. Five, seven, eleven, fifteen, twenty. He hangs up.

"They must be in Maine," she says. "They have this vacation house."

"That doesn't do me any good," he says, and puts his hands on his hips.

"Why don't you just try me out?" she pleads. "I'll work for free for a day or two." She jingles the bracelet on her wrist. She hopes he will notice it and think better of her. Owning such a thing makes her look trustworthy.

He holds her application against his chest. Lank white hairs at the sides of his bald, pink head lift in the breeze of an air conditioner vent. "Up north, things are different. Here we have to operate a business with hospitality." He shakes his head. "You can be rude up there and get away with it. Here, if we don't give good service, we don't survive. Our baggers take the carts out to the customers' cars and load them up and they don't accept tips. That's the reason we do so well, why our customers think nothing of driving thirty, forty miles to shop here. I tell anyone that I hire from up north that they need to lose that northern attitude that the customer is a pain in their ass."

"I'd never be rude," she says. "Especially not here. This is a really great market."

He is going to give her a chance.

"Six days a week. It's a tough shift. Five a.m. to three in the afternoon. I've gone through two bakery managers in the past five months. People seem to have trouble getting here on time. They can take it for a little while, but then they decide they'd rather sleep. I don't need that to happen again…"

"Don't worry," she interrupts, "because one thing for sure is I'm a morning person."

He looks at her over his glasses. She is laying it on a bit too thick.

"I'll give you a try out," he sighs. "You can begin the day after tomorrow. Bring a photo ID. You'll get six an hour for the first few days to start off, and ten and a half an hour if I hire you. If you manage even the first day, I'll be glad I met you. Your relief will come in at two every day and that'll give you time to get away from the counter and do some prepping for the next day."

"I could start sooner, if you need me."

"You have some reading to do." He reaches beneath the counter for a spiral-bound book, the bakery's operating manual.

"Oh, right," she says. "I promise you'll be glad you gave me a try."

"We'll see," he says. It is called *The Karr's Bakery Way: How Sweet It Is.* She flips to the end of it; there are a hundred and sixteen pages and the font is small.

"Is there an employee discount?"

He shakes his head. "But there's a free meal at the prepared food counter so long as it's after two."

"Great," she says, and for a second, considers asking if she can get the free meal that day. Instead, she buys a king-size chocolate bar, four packets of ramen, a half dozen oranges, and a bottle of cold, celebratory ginger ale.

The bags are heavy, the sun intense. She walks away from town and into the emptiness, stopping to peel and eat oranges.

If she can last a week, she'll have enough for a bus ticket.

Ida hears a soft whirring and whistling behind her. She turns around and sees the cyclist riding toward her, his head down. The chrome on his handlebars glints in the sun. She remembers the two guys from Laughter Cay, saying that this man had sold them a used bicycle. If she gets a hold of an old, junky bicycle, then she can get back and forth to Karr's much faster than this, and hang her bags of groceries from the handlebars.

"Hey!" she shouts. "Can you stop for a second?"

The man doesn't acknowledge her. His mirrored sunglasses don't reveal whether or not he even saw her. His body is crouched flat over the frame so that he is parallel to the top bar of his bicycle. He leaves a hot breeze as he passes her. He keeps going, until he is a colorful blur in the distance.

"Jesus *Christ*," she says. "What a weirdo."

The colorful blur turns back in her direction. He stops several feet in front of her and pulls his feet, one by one, out of the pedal locks.

"What," he says. His chin drips sweat on the pavement.

"Someone told me you have a used bicycle business."

"I don't have a business. I have a few bikes. Sometimes I happen to have an extra."

"Fine. I figured it wouldn't hurt to ask anyway."

"You slowed me down."

"Yeah, well. Sorry," she says. "I am so terribly sorry that I caused you such inconvenience." She stares meanly at her own reflection in his sunglasses.

"I don't bother with girl bikes."

"Yeah. OK. Thanks anyway."

He puts one leg into the toe grip on the pedal, then the other, and he takes off. She gives him the finger, her arm raised high.

Her shirt is soaked at the underarms when she passes the scrub pine. The cold ginger ale! She'd forgotten about it. Ida sets her bag down and gets it out, unscrews the top and tilts it back.

Two figures are standing by the canal. As she gets closer, she sees that they are the two dirty boys, Carter and Donnie. The younger one, Donnie, jumps up and down, waving at her and yelling something, still wearing nothing but the t-shirt. For a second Donnie looks as though he is about to sprint toward her, but he doesn't. She pretends not to notice them. They give her the creeps. Children of the Corn. The older one crosses his arms and turns the other way. A blackbird lands on the grass next to Donnie. She sees its feathers bristle. The bird lifts one wing, as though it is about to fly off, but lowers it again. Ida keeps walking.

She hears the bicycle again. The man rides a few feet past her and stops his bicycle by dropping one foot to the ground.

"I do have one," he says without turning around. "It's in bad shape. It needs new rims and brake pads."

"How much do you want for it?"

"I'll take twenty for it. I can give it to you tomorrow at noon." He gets on his bike again.

"You sure? Great. Thank you." It comes out smart-assed; she isn't able to help herself.

"I didn't ride by to tell you. I'm riding a circuit," he says, pushing off. "I would have gone by anyway."

"Where will I meet you?" she shouts after him.

He doesn't turn around as he calls back. "The gas station. That one up around the bend."

"The empty one," she calls, but he doesn't answer. She stops walking. She doesn't have twenty dollars. She only has eleven and half of it is now in quarters and dimes. "Hey!" she shouts, as loud as she can, but he is too far away to hear her.

The house is coming into view. She is looking forward to getting there, to closing the door behind her and eating the cool oranges in the shade of the house. When she looks to the left, far off toward the line of thick trees, she sees three cars in front of it. She recognizes the red car from the search party. They are still looking for the boy.

WHEN SHE GETS TO the gas station the next day, it is just past noon, and he has the bike, as he told her he would. His hands are on his hips. The bicycle is white and quite tall, with thick black wheels. Old but not too old. When she sees it, she gets nervous thinking about how he will react when he realizes he has come out here for eleven dollars. Both that bicycle and his own bicycle are leaned up against the two gas pumps.

As she approaches him, she musters a close-mouthed smile. His face doesn't change.

"Hello," she says.

"I put the parts on this morning." He pushes his sunglasses back towards his face.

"Look, I'm really sorry. This is going to sound terrible, but I don't have twenty. I really thought I did." She looks down at the pearl bracelet on her wrist and thinks about offering it instead.

"You don't have the money," he says, and she shrinks into herself.

"I have eleven bucks…" She looks down at the bracelet again. "It's partly in coins, though."

"Don't worry," he says, nodding and pushing the bike toward her. His forearms and calves are darkly tanned and lined with veins.

"Really? That seems unfair. Even though I really need this bike."

"Of course it's unfair," he says. "But I found the bike in the trash and it's not worth the other nine bucks for me to wheel it back. It cleaned up pretty well." He points to it.

He holds his hand out for the money.

"God, thank you." Ida is a touch disappointed. She thought for a second he was going to give it to her for free. She digs the coins out of her pockets and hands them over in three fistfuls. *Ha. That's what you get for spitting at me.*

He has a pouch on the back of his seat, and he pours the coins in without spilling a single one.

She climbs onto the bike, gripping the handlebars with her hands. The handlebar tape is sticky. It feels too tall. She gets off again and wipes her hands on her shorts.

"It's a little high," she says. "The seat."

"You can fix that."

"I can't," she says. "I don't know how. I don't have any tools."

"Puhhh," he says, shaking his head, and snatches the bike away. He uses his hand to loosen the bolt, and in less than a minute, lowers the seat and tightens it again. He pushes the bike over to her.

She takes it. "I can give you the rest of the money in a week or so."

"We're square." He gets back on his own bike.

She watches him ride off. It takes him only seconds to disappear from her sight.

She pushes down on the bike pedal and moves forward, shakily. It has been a long time since she's been on a bike, but she finds the rhythm of it and builds up enough momentum to coast down the street and feel a breeze touch her neck.

A car passes her, a white convertible with the top down and a forearm hanging over the driver's side door. She watches the back of a man's head as it drives past her. The car slows and reverses.

"Hi there," says the man. It is a moment before she realizes that he is the bartender from Laughter Cay, the one who made her the drinks. "I'm Ryan. Do you remember me? What are you doing around here?"

"Just going for a…bike ride," she says. She stops and puts one leg on the ground. She smiles, making sure to not open her mouth all the way. She thinks of the deckchair she sat in at Laughter Cay and the picture Lloyd took of her, the gold of the setting sun lighting up her face and how belief in something can create the illusion of beauty.

"Hey," he says. "Why are you still here? I thought you left in a blaze of glory. Left this lameness behind."

Ida focuses on the handlebars. "It's really not the best story."

He stretches his hand over the mirror. "Lloyd and I are having this...little dinner party tonight. He would want me to invite you. If you're not busy."

"I appreciate it," she says. "But that's okay."

"He'll be mad at me if I don't at least try to convince you," he says, and his smile looks sincere. "Seriously. You'll make his day. Why don't you come by between six and six-thirty?"

"I'm not sure," she says. "I just…"

"Well, if you decide to. You know where we live, right?"

"I do," she says. "The house nearest to mine."

TEN

S HE PULLS THE DOOR shut behind her. She isn't there to make friends. There is no point in trying to impress either of them with any pretensions of good taste. It really doesn't matter that all she has to bring with her to a dinner party is the big chocolate bar that she was planning on having for dinner, which she even started to open before she thought better of it. The chocolate bar is in a plastic grocery store bag, hanging from the handlebar of her bike. Before she left her house, she peeled off the $1.19 price tag. Only the top layer had come off, and she had to scrape the gluey paper with her fingernail. It didn't come off completely; she can still see the stickiness of it.

Ida is only going because she needed to get out of the house. It is probably built on some lost souls' burial ground. Haunted with misery. The tarp has a death rattle lately; at night, it takes all of her energy to block it out so that she can sleep. Relief doesn't come in the daytime, either. There is nothing to see when she looks out the window, no way to distract herself from her tongue touching the tender, empty space. The cool baths give some escape, at least from the heat, but the darkness of the bathroom makes her imagine a sarcophagus. The other night, she climbed up on the bathroom sink to screw a light bulb in, but there was no fixture. Just a hole for one.

The Karr's bakery manual is in the house, sitting on one of her sleeping cushions. Its heft is unnerving. She opened the front cover and scanned the table of contents; there were chapters on Precision,

Multi-tasking, and Appetizing Presentation. There was a never-ending list of products and supplies and ordering instructions. Bakery Manager. She isn't fit to manage a sock drawer. There is no way that she can pull it off; this experiment will end the very first day, and afterward, she'll have to beg for a cashier job. By the time she got through the first quarter of the manual, the letters and the words began to look like symbols of nothing; she knew that something else would have to transpire before she could really concentrate. Dangerous weather. A fever. A change of scenery. Maybe a dinner party.

The late afternoon rain has just ended and it is a small freedom to be outside in the temporarily bearable air. And the bike sure beats walking. She pedals so quietly and slowly that she can hardly hear herself. She likes this bike. Perched up on the seat, she feels separated, as though she is not really part of this place.

She still has not managed to call Linda. Every time she thought about riding to the pay phone, she instead took off the bracelet and held it in her palm, the pearls piled upon each other. Linda would say that it wasn't going to work, that a few more weeks wasn't soon enough. She needed to find a roommate now. And why was she still in Florida, anyway? What had happened with all the money she was supposed to get? What happened, what happened, what happened? Genetics. Predisposition to fucking up.

Ida peers across the horizon at a line of low, bright clouds. She does not have to go. Where the street brings her near a canal, she stops the bike and re-ties her shoe and sees a fat, pale fish floating on its side at the surface of the murky water.

Ida follows the curve of the road to their house. In the side yard, shrouded with shrubs, the house's central air conditioner buzzes.

Their Fort Starlight is a pleasant place; their lives are good because they deserve good lives. They are good people, from good families. Life has treats in store for them. They have a house with air conditioning. They have good teeth. They have lovers who are in it for the duration.

In their front yard, there is a soft-leaved tree, low to the ground, its roots protected by bright red mulch. Shrubs on both sides of the front walk are shaved into neat rectangles. Great care has been taken.

The Ida that Ryan invited is not really her and she won't be able to hide that. She reaches out her hand to knock on the door and pulls it back again. As she moves, the bracelet slides around her wrist. She takes silent steps backward and gets back on her bicycle and glides back onto the street.

There will probably be cheese. Beautiful cheese. God, she loves cheese. Even Kraft singles would cheer her up right now.

Ryan will smile at her with his healthy teeth.

She never said she'd come. She rides back to the canal where she saw the fish floating. It is gone. Now she sees a blackbird—smaller than the other ones she has seen, small as the ones in Aster—standing on the water a few feet away, like her children's bible picture of Jesus calmly standing on the surface of a lake. She gets off the bike to get a closer look and sees that the bird is standing on something. She takes a step back, realizing what it is: the thick, dull back of a lifeless-looking alligator, the waxy ridges of its spine just peeking out of the water. It doesn't look real, like a statue that slipped down the canal walls and into the water.

The bird flutters its wings, shivers, and is still again.

The alligator registers nothing.

She read about this kind of relationship in her high school biology textbook: the shark and the remora, the bird that picks the food out of the crocodile's teeth, keeping them clean and in turn keeping itself well-fed. Symbiotic relationships. They did for each other so perfectly that each other's presence was taken for granted, even forgotten, the *other* just a shadow.

Snap! The bird is gone. The whole of its body disappears into and past the lurching muscles of the alligator's fleshy, pale throat. The alligator settles back into the canal, everything the same as it was, except for the missing bird and the rippling water. Ida backs up and jumps on her bike, her hands buzzing. Could it run after her?

She pedals fast, laughing.

The adrenaline has recharged her. She can go and have dinner with them. She can and she will. It will help time to pass.

She turns her bike around and rides towards Ryan and Lloyd's house, breathless. Relieved. She'll arrive at the door, panting, excited; she is bringing something interesting with her. As offerings, she will have a chocolate bar and this story about danger.

Also, they'll give her wine. She can ask questions that require long answers. *How did you two meet? Do you guys believe in God? What did your parents say when you came out?* They will talk and talk and maybe the love they have for each other will rise like a bright bubble floating in the middle of the room and distract her from herself and from the empty space in her mouth.

She gets off her bike, leaning it against the side of the garage, and smooths her hair. She knocks. The door swings open and there is Ryan, with Lloyd grinning at her over his shoulder.

The music fills her ears as she steps inside. Lloyd's hand goes to her arm and nudges her toward the living room. Two leather couches, one white and one grey, a peacock blue lamp, a coffee table made out of the cross-section of a big tree. How had they managed this, here? It looks like something out of a magazine. Even when she rallied enough strength and saved enough money to move out of the house on Door Hill, she never bothered to make her apartment in Aster look cute, never had a party, never invested in anything more than discount sheets and a tinny clock radio to listen to. Her shelves were plastic milk crates. It never occurred to her that she could ever live this way.

"Welcome," he says. He leads her to the couch. "This is Mona and that's Al. And the young one is Jamie. He belongs to Al."

She sits down, stiff and disappointed. A party. Of course. She didn't think about there being other people. She nods hello as she looks around the room at an older woman with long yellow hair and tanned brown shoulders, a middle-aged man with sunburned ears, a teenager with acne scars across his cheeks.

"This is Ida. Our New York City gal. You thirsty?" he says, turning to her. "Ryan's making gin and tonics for everyone."

"Except for me," the teenager mutters.

"You can have a sip of mine," says Al. "I guarantee you'll hate it." He turns to Ida. "How you doing?"

"Good," she says. The blonde woman, who is wearing a long pink dress, is perched on the couch right next to her. The white carpet is lined with vacuum cleaner stripes; it is pristine, except for a reddish-brown blotch that matches the color of the blotch on the toe of Ida's tennis shoe. Mud from by the canal. Hopefully nobody will notice. She takes some almonds from the bowl on the table and stuffs them in her mouth.

Mona reaches her arm across Ida's lap and grabs her wrist. "Look at this. Gorgeous. Bet it's an antique."

Mona tilts Ida's wrist to get a better look and Ida has to concentrate on not yanking her hand away. Mona is a toucher.

"It was my grandmother's," Ida murmurs.

Mona lets go of her wrist and reaches over her to a platter on the coffee table. She pops something small and flaky into her mouth.

"What's inside this, roasted peppers?" she talks while she chews. "Nice." She turns to Ida. "You're from New York? I'm from right outside Philadelphia. Nine times out of ten, people move to Florida to start over. Me included. I lost fifty-seven pounds and left my mean old ex-husband."

She locks eyes with Ida and smiles. A strip of red pepper skin is stuck to her front tooth. She tilts her chin up and shakes her hair, the wisps fluttering all over her shoulders and into her dark brown cleavage.

"I just started telling these guys about how I came back from Cassadaga last week. From this wonderful…well, it was called a *visualization* seminar."

She leans in closer, grabs hold of Ida's fingertips and closes her palms over them. "My friend, this will blow your mind."

Mona describes the seminar, smiling, squeezing any forearms she can reach from where she sits. Ida can smell her red rose perfume. How do people do this? Ida has thick walls up between herself and most other people. She would never in a million years grab a stranger's hand, lean in close, lock eyes, call them *my friend*. She used to feel embarrassed for people like this, but Mona is the comfortable one, wearing a real smile instead of Ida's stiff one, engineered to hide her tooth. Fruitcake or not, Mona, and people like her, know something that she doesn't.

She stares at Ida, giving her fingers one last squeeze before letting go. Al crosses his thick legs and smiles at Mona.

"What's it matter, the worst day of your childhood? What's it matter what your dearest dream is?"

Ryan hands Ida a drink. The glass is cold and the condensation drips down around her fingers and onto her wrist.

"The saddest day of my childhood was when I lost my Mickey Mantle baseball card," says Al. "Right out the window of my pop's Ford. We were on the highway and he wouldn't stop."

"Poor you," Mona winks at him. "You could have been a millionaire."

"Damn right."

"Mona, you didn't tell us," says Ryan, "What's your dearest dream?"

"Well," Mona says, reaching over Ida for another hors d'oeuvre. "When I was a kid, my mother only ever told me what I couldn't do. Couldn't ice skate. Couldn't learn a language. Couldn't ride a roller coaster. She made me scared to try anything that *she* was afraid of. Now that I've gotten through so much, I want to climb Mount Everest."

Al gives a pitying laugh.

"What's so funny?"

"You are," says Al. He reaches over and pats her brown shoulder.

"I'm not joking."

"And then what?" says Al. "You can die happy, knowing that you did it?"

"Yes." Mona takes a sip of her gin and tonic. "How about you, Ida?"

Ida stares down into her drink, at the two squeezed lime wedges at the bottom of her glass, trapped under the ice. She should have seen this question coming and made something up.

"I can't think of anything," she says, her cheeks burning. "May I use your bathroom?" She stands wrapping her arms around herself like she is hiding nakedness.

Lloyd points. She takes her drink with her.

The walls of the hallway are lined with mirrors and framed

photographs: Ryan and Lloyd wearing down jackets and backpacks, smiling as they stand in front of a waterfall; a sepia-toned and sad-looking Lloyd standing in front of the Eiffel Tower; a little girl holding the leash of a black puppy, a wilted dandelion in her hair.

The layout of the house is exactly like her own, the perfect rectangle, the kitchen and the bathroom in the same place. Instead of a tarp, though, they have a glass door that leads to a screened-in porch. She passes their bedroom, sees the high bed with the bright white sheets and wishes that she were sleeping there that night. Beyond that door is a second room. She pushes open the door and smells paint. There are canvases all over, on the walls and on the floor. The paintings are landscapes: snow-covered fields, mountains, fall trees, even one of the same flat land that is outside of this house. In each of them, there is a single figure, staring up or down or across at something.

She backs out, finishing her drink in one tilt. In the bathroom, she locks the door and sets her empty glass down on the sink. The medicine cabinet opens with a squeak. Shaving cream, razors, a blue toothbrush and a purple one. Sunscreen with SPF 45. A porcelain maneki neko cat, white with red ears, its left paw raised. A pharmacy bottle: prescribed to Ryan McCormack. *For Depression.*

The phrase is annoying. *Dearest* dream. As though she has so many that there is some sort of hierarchy in place. The only real dreams she can remember ever having were always about escape.

She grabs the prescription bottle, opens it, takes one out and holds it in her hand. There are plenty left. He will never notice. She turns the tap on and leans down for a drink to help her swallow it. She looks at the shelves: Q-tips, cinnamon mouthwash, a white ceramic figurine of a dog, small enough to hold in the palm of her hand.

On the way back, Ida stops for a breather in the kitchen. The kitchen in her house will look like this someday, with appliances, furniture, air conditioning, paint on the walls. The Polaroid that Lloyd took of her is stuck to the refrigerator with a magnet. Like they are good friends. She stares at it, the light of the setting sun in her hair, her mouth slightly open, and she can see the perfect little fake tooth, catching the last of the light.

So far, he hasn't brought up wanting to paint her again.

Ryan walks in.

"Hi," she says, disappointed it isn't Lloyd, who hates Fort Starlight. She feels kinship with him because of that. Shared hatred is the basis of every friendship she has ever had.

"Hi yourself," he says. His eyes are so blue and so bright.

Ryan lifts the lid of a pot on the stove. Steam rises up to his face. "You're not hot are you? I can't tell. I have to really crank the a/c when the oven's on."

"No," she says, "it's cool in here." She looks around. "Your house is really nice."

'Thanks," he says, and offers a toothy smile.

"How long have you guys lived here?"

"Just five months. We were like tornadoes, getting this place ready. We bought it for nothing but there was a lot to do because it wasn't completed. We hung drywall, put down the baseboards. We still have some work out on the screened-in porch. We want to put marble down instead of the concrete that's out there now."

"It looks great. The whole thing."

"Thanks. I appreciate that. If you could see the before and after... Remind me to take you to the back yard later. We've picked out the spot for the hot tub." He turns the burner up higher, peeks into the oven. A gorgeous smell wafts out. He puts on oven gloves and takes out a pan of roasted chicken, sizzling and spattering. He sets it on the stovetop.

"Do you need some help?"

"Thanks, that would be great," he says, opening the refrigerator and handing her a bag of lettuce. "Would you mind putting the salad together? You could chop up an apple or two, maybe crumble this goat cheese. If you don't mind. That way, I can make a quick wine sauce. The bowls are in that cabinet."

Ida takes the food from his arms and sets it on the counter in front of her. She washes two green apples in the sink and sets them down on the cutting board. She'd forgotten about apples. In Aster, there were orchards everywhere. When the apples were ripe, the town came alive for a little while.

Ryan hands her a paring knife.

"How long have you two been together?" she asks.

"Three and a half years," he says.

"You guys seem like a really great couple."

Ryan looks at her. "Three and a half years, though we knew each other before we ever hooked up." He scratches at his neck with bent fingers. "I was in human resources management back then. Moving here was my way out. I'd rather mix a drink any day."

With two forks, he lifts the chicken from the pan and sets it down on a platter. "We paid thirty-thousand dollars for this place. It was supposed to be a demo house. I guess they thought they'd get potential buyers to tour, see what their house might look like after it was built. Instead of doing that, the next developer just decided to sell them cheap to get the area started. It's not easy to convince that first buyer. Americans aren't really into pioneering anymore."

"Except for you guys," she says.

"I guess." He turns on two burners.

"Did you buy it from a place called Echo? Ken Cantwell was the guy's name."

"No. I think there are a few different developers, though."

"You guys got lucky."

"I think so," he says. "The brave are rewarded." He pours a glass of Chardonnay into the chicken pan and sprinkles in a palm-full of cornstarch.

"When you moved in, was my house already here? The one on Ring and Marine?"

"It must have been. There were four or five houses when we moved in. I remember counting them when we were driving around." He wipes his hands on a dishtowel. "Wait, I've been meaning to ask you this all night. Aren't you supposed to be in New York City? Why are you still here?"

He scrapes at the bottom of the roasting pan with a big fork.

Ida sucks in air. She feels her chest tighten, a lump sitting at the front of her throat. "Just...bad luck. I got screwed by Echo. He gave me a bad check and then disappeared. I don't want to think about it."

"God. That stinks. I'm sorry."

She unwraps the goat cheese and crumbles it into the salad bowl. It sticks to her fingers. She won't cry. It will get out of control if she lets herself start. Her tooth will show and she won't be able to bear the shame.

Ryan turns to look at her. "That's really terrible, Ida." He points to the empty glass she left on the counter. "Give that to me. Let me pour you another."

She dumps the ice out in the sink and hands the glass to him.

"This is why they invented alcohol," he says.

They sit down in the dining room at a long table. A glass vase holds three yellow roses. Above their heads is a tiny chandelier. Lloyd turns on a switch and dims the light. Ida looks through the windows at the fields of dark green, the lavender sky.

"You went all out. All this for us, huh?" says Al.

"Yeah. Pathetic, isn't it?" Lloyd says. "You'll know we've finally made some real friends when you don't get any more invitations."

They drink cold white wine out of long-stemmed glasses, except for Al, who sips a Bud from a can. The chicken has been sliced and arranged on a platter, and after it is passed around, a gravy boat full of Ryan's wine sauce to pour over it. The roasted potatoes are crispy with chicken fat. Thin asparagus spears, pan-fried with butter and basil.

Ida licks her fingertips; she has decided to focus on the food, and she is feeling better after a few more drinks.

"This meal," she says, "is way, way better than that one I had that night at Laughter Cay."

Lloyd smiles. Mona laughs with her head thrown back.

"Quit it, you," says Al.

"Laughter Cay is Al's place," Lloyd grins. "He's the boss."

Al turns to Ida. "I'm not the chef, so no offense taken, honey."

"Well, you hired the chef," says Mona. "My Amish grandmother had more of an imagination in the kitchen."

"The yachties who eat at Laughter Cay aren't complicated. They want their lobster and their whiskey. Their baked potato, green salad with ranch dressing and three cherry tomatoes. They got money. Give the people what they want and they'll keep coming back to pay for it."

"Dad, the food is pretty boring. You should put some other stuff on the menu already. People will eat other things. Maybe, like, French food or something."

"My kid, the gourmet. Are you sure you're my son? Some days I wonder," says Al. "Some days I think he belongs to some other guy with unlimited funds to pay for speeding tickets and twenty different t-shirts that all look exactly the same."

Jamie scowls. "I told you they caught me in that speed trap, right when the speed limit drops. You act like I do it all the time."

"Two hundred bucks so far this year."

Jamie looks as if he is going to protest, but then appears to add the numbers in his head and thinks better of it.

Al reaches over and pats Jamie on the shoulder. "Just a sip," says Al. "That's enough."

"Dreams. We didn't finish, before," says Mona. "The world turns and weather changes and we get older and our lives get away from us. It's Lloyd's turn. What's your dearest dream and how do you think you might get there?"

"Help," says Lloyd. He lifts his glass. "Somebody save me."

Mona reaches across the table and takes Lloyd's hand. "Listen to me. Close your eyes and breathe and try to picture your ideal life. Don't doubt it before you let yourself say it. Ignore any negative thoughts and just say what you see."

Lloyd closes his eyes. He squeezes them until there is strain visible in his forehead and eyelids. His eyes open again.

"I don't see anything other than this very moment," he says. "And I looked very hard. So everything must be going according to plan without my having to meditate on it."

Al laughs.

Ryan stands up and pushes his chair in.

"You," says Mona. "Show your sweetie how it's done. You're way more open-minded."

Ryan walks around the table, collecting plates. "Just a minute," he says. "I need to put dessert together."

"Oh never mind. I know already." She turns to Lloyd. "He told me."

Dessert is strawberry ice cream in tall glasses, with hot fudge sauce on top. They have it with hot coffee. The sky outside is dark blue and the light of the small chandelier gives the room a golden glow. Ida is very glad that she came. This takes her by surprise, but there she is, her elbows on the table, her chin resting in one hand, a sleepy smile on her face.

Mona looks over at Ida and smiles. "Do you have second sight?"

"Like ESP?" Ida laughs. "No."

"You might," she says. "It usually takes time to develop. Don't laugh just yet."

"I'd help with the dishes," says Al, "but I'm so bad at it that my ex-wife used to yell at me to quit helping."

"You're excused, Al," says Ryan. "We have a dishwasher anyway. I'm going to drive Mona home because we poured her a few too many."

"Yes, you did," Mona says, stretching, shaking her pale hair. "Shame, shame."

Ida is disappointed to see everyone stand up to say goodbye and move toward the door. It means that she has to leave, too. She sits at the table alone, finishing her coffee. She listens to the door close, to the car engines starting up. When she is done, she gathers the ice cream glasses and brings them into the kitchen. "Let me help you clean up."

"Don't clean," Lloyd says. "Just keep me company while I wash these. They're apparently too fragile for the dishwasher and I'm in trouble enough with Ryan as it is."

She sets them down and leans against the counter.

"Ryan just told me what happened with your bounced check. What are you going to do?"

"Oh," she sighs. "I don't know. I spent all of the money I had."

"Oh, boy," he says. "Wow. That sucks."

"I got a job at Karr's, though. I'll guess I'll just try to stick it out there until I have enough money saved for a bus ticket and then I'm going back to my mom's place. Which I really don't want to do," her voice cracks. "You have no idea how much I don't want to do that. But I don't really have a choice."

"I'd sell a kidney before I had to live in my childhood house," he says, rinsing the suds out of a wine glass and setting it upside down on the counter. "Not to mention with my family. I'm really not kidding. You have a choice. It's not like you're paying rent in the house here. You have a job now. Stick around a couple of months and then you can go to the city like you want."

Tears slide down both of her cheeks, and she wipes them with the backs of her hands.

"You think?"

"If you tell yourself that it isn't an option, then it won't be one."

She frowns and starts to explain how she'll never be able to handle the job at Karr's; she bluffed her way into it and she will never be able to keep it. She stops. Maybe it isn't impossible. Ida has a manual to tell her how to do everything.

"The whole thing is sort of funny, I guess. I'm being paid back for some crappy thing I did," she laughs, and as she does, she notices him looking at her mouth.

"Oh God. My tooth." Ida gasps. "I forgot. To top it all off, my bridge fell out. Another thing to make me feel like shit."

"Do you need a dentist?" he says. Without looking at her, he rinses the meat knife in the running water, drying it with a dishtowel. "We know a great one in Valponia."

Ida wipes her eyes. "Oh, you know…the money."

"If it just fell out, if it didn't break, it may be an easy fix. I have a bridge. You didn't lose it, did you?"

"I still have it," she says, and brushes bread crumbs from the counter and into her hand. They stick to her damp fingers and palms.

"Did it break or anything?"

She shakes her head.

"It probably won't cost very much to just re-glue it. I could lend you the money. I can give you a ride, too. It'll just have to be on a day I'm off."

"Oh," she says, picking up a towel and one of the overturned glasses. She dabs at the wet spots. They are so thin and delicate. "If you mean it, I'll take you up on all of that. Thank you. That would be just so beyond great."

"Cool," he says. "So that's that."

"Ryan said you guys have been together three and a half years. I've never had a real relationship," she says. "Nothing longer than a few weeks. I think I'm too fucked up of a person, honestly."

"You can be fucked up and have a relationship," says Lloyd, pushing his hair out of his eyes. "Have you seen people? Being fucked up is not an obstacle."

Ida takes the leftovers that Lloyd wrapped up for her in aluminum foil. She puts them in the plastic bag that still hangs from her handlebars. She forgot all about the chocolate bar. She forgot all about the alligator.

She rides back in the dark. It is hard to see with nothing but the moon to guide her, though she knows there is one turn that is followed by a long stretch. She can feel the house pulling her toward it. There are thousands of pinprick stars above her. At times, her bike wheel moves away from the road and hits the spiky grass instead, and she has to get off and squint in the dark to right herself. When she looks back, she can see the tiny lights of Ryan and Lloyd's house.

The asphalt is perfectly smooth under the bicycle wheels, soft as a cushion. The night is so dark that Ida feels like she is moving through velvet. She closes her eyes. Flying. The chirping of a thousand crickets fills her ears.

She hears a rustling and crunching; she's ridden onto the grass again. She gets off the bike; it is hard to know which way the asphalt is. She has so quickly become disoriented. There are canals all over. If she picks the wrong direction, she may very well end up in one of them.

When she stares straight ahead, she can see a light, white and long, and moving from side to side. Someone is looking for something in the dark. She watches it closely. The searchlight illuminates the tall, wild trees of the woods, which means that she has veered off to the left.

Ida walks the bike until her feet find the street. She can see her house, the dim outline against the navy sky. Next time she will remember to leave a light on.

Inside, she washes her face and stretches out on the floor, the Karr's manual open to the page she dog-eared. She flips through the *Quality Control* section. *Consistent excellence. We start with the finest ingredients, which are unbleached flour, creamery butter, and pure cane sugar.* Ida skips ahead to the *Anytime Pastries* section.

Every few minutes, she notices the searchlight in her peripheral vision, moving across the sky in a slow arc. That boy is surely dead. Too much time has passed.

A sick feeling rises in her stomach and spreads throughout her body. She remembers when they were kids and they would wrestle. Even though Robert was older, she had always been stronger. She sometimes overpowered him, watching him struggle to push her off. He was so skinny.

The tarp breathes in and out, quick and ragged. Maybe Robert never found some great future after all.

That was why she never heard anything from him.

"Stop it," she says aloud. "He's fine." She says it twice more, trying to sound certain, angry, even, at the house's suggestion that he might not be.

ELEVEN

HELL. FROM THE MOMENT Ida hops off her bike in the dark and walks into the Karr's bakery at 5:02 a.m., it is like an impossible Japanese game show with a depraved host watching her anguish on closed-circuit television.

The good news is that all of the breads and rolls are made elsewhere. She already knew that the cakes came from outside, but she didn't manage to finish reading the whole manual in time, and felt the presence of the dreaded bread section at the end of the book, ready to smack her upside the head. Loaves of rye, French baguettes, multigrain.

It turned out, though, that the last twenty pages were nothing but an index and a glossary of terms, and then a bunch of pages listing the phone numbers of every Karr's bakery in the whole Southeast. A truck delivered the bread every day before anyone else arrived, and left it all in deep paper bags outside of the employee entrance. All she has to do is drag them inside and put them in the right baskets on the racks, though this is still a challenging task, considering everything else she has to do.

Working in the bakery isn't even a distant relative of baking at home. While the strudel or the tart or the toffee brownies were in her own oven in Aster, she could listen to the clock radio or read or stare outside of her window across the green hills and the outlines of the white mausoleums in the cemetery and think of anything—of what

Morocco might be like, of whether she should go to the trouble of getting a passport just so that she had one, of whether it was worth it to try to stop biting her nails, of where Robert might be right at that second—as she smelled the crust beginning to brown, the sugar caramelizing.

The hours before the store opens are the worst. From five until eight, she is expected to make everything—chocolate chip and oatmeal cookies; banana nut, bran, and blueberry muffins; plain and currant scones; glazed, chocolate, and blueberry donuts that are supposed to be made in the messy deep fryer; brownies and blondies; cheese and raspberry Danishes; eclairs; cupcakes; three kinds of pies—and put it all into the display cases. There are four ovens and three mixers and she has to get the whole thing started the right way, right away.

She does not. Not at all.

The only good thing is that there are no witnesses to her early morning distress, because the ovens and the bakery walk-in are tucked in the back, and of no use to any other Karr's employees. Some of the ingredients are pre-measured, but not stored where the manual told her they were supposed to be, not stacked up on specific shelves with the label-side out. The walk-in is disorganized and full of unmarked white containers. No one sees her dipping her finger into the containers to try to guess whether they are batter or buttermilk. No one sees the way that the end of her ponytail drips sweat even in the chill of the walk-in, how more than a few drops of that sweat splashes onto the puff pastry dough. Or how she runs, stops short, runs, drops an egg on the floor. She spills donut batter, shoves pans into the ovens so that they splatter inside, burns her fingertips, slips on the donut batter she spilled. She doesn't bother with the donuts because she is too afraid of the hot oil. There are too many things to hold in her head at once; one alarm means that something is done and that something else has to start, but she can't remember what is done and what is supposed to start. No one sees that she forgets to set one of the timers and doesn't figure it out until the banana muffins are black on the tops.

No one sees her at 7:55 a.m., when she realizes that she forgot all about the cookies she is supposed to have already made and she sneaks over to Aisle Fifteen for two boxes each of Entenmann's chocolate chip and oatmeal cookies and presents them as Karr's' own.

When J.B. walks by the bakery at 8:30 a.m., her sweat has started drying and she manages a weak smile.

Her hands shake for the rest of the shift.

"Hot enough out for you?" says a friendly woman customer.

Ida nods dumbly and ties the woman's muffins up in a white box.

No one sees her crying as she rides her bike home when the shift ends, sweating and thinking about how she has to return to the horrible house, and then try to get herself to sleep, and then wake up and do it all again. In just a few hours. It is all too soon.

There it is. The truth. If she can't handle baking in a supermarket, what does she think will happen if she tries to go out on her own? As though anybody can make a living baking one stupid pie or crumble at a time.

The clouds come, moving across the sun, and the rain begins in an instant, running down her arms and hands. She steps off the bike and pulls it into the house with her, leaning it against the powdery wall. She sets the bag down. In it is dinner from the prepared foods counter—potato salad and meatloaf—but Ida can't eat; she hasn't eaten since the night before. She hasn't eaten enough lately at all. Her shorts are starting to hang on her, and she feels too sorry for herself to be thrilled with this.

She sits on the cushion with her head tucked into her folded arms. Her Karr's uniform shirt, white with a smiling orange sun emblem, is soaked through.

She thinks of her mother. Josie. Josie Overdorff never went beyond a quarter mile radius of the house. Why should she? Nearby, there was a Laundromat, and a store that sold coffee, milk for her coffee, cigarettes, Fritos, scratch-offs, and overripe bananas. There is a Western Union at that store, she is pretty sure.

Ida walked down from town to Door Hill every few months to check the pile of mail on the floor, flipping through the coupon books, bills, and collection agency letters. She hoped there would be something from Robert, but there never was. Sometimes her mother was there. Ida heard her upstairs, coughing, talking back to the television. And Josie could hear Ida downstairs. The back door didn't fit right, and shook the whole house when it opened or closed. And Ida knew her mother knew her sound. She chose to stay upstairs, watching *One Life to Live*.

Except once, when she rushed down the stairs and said *Ida, guess who just won three hundred dollars on Pick Six!* Their eyes met and Ida stared at her, hard, until her mother looked away.

It's about time I got a big win. I had enough of winning five bucks at a time.

Oh, said Ida. *You had enough.* But the tone was lost on her mother. The world owed her a living. It owed her food stamps and disability for a back injury that she would never tire of exaggerating when it suited her. It owed taxpayer-paid visits to the doctor who gave her unheeded advice to quit smoking and stop eating junk before her lungs and heart gave out.

I tried to work, her mother insisted. *Remember, after your father left.* It was a year after high school had ended. Josie had managed to get a job at the apple packing plant, which was walking distance from Door Hill. After thirty days, she would have been eligible for health insurance. After ninety days, she would have been eligible for a pension. She'd lasted most of a day.

Her job was to grab the undersized and spoiled apples from the conveyor belt as they rolled past her, and put them in corresponding carts so they could be packed up for the school lunch distributors or made into sauce. But the fear of managing alone, without her husband's unreliable income, was not enough to give her any determination. That afternoon, Ida was cleaning the kitchen, spraying the cabinets with Fantastic, thinking that maybe she'd do the floor next, that maybe things could change, when her mother opened the door slumped into the kitchen weeping, hysterical. There was no chair for her at the apple plant. She had to stand the whole seven and a half hours, putting strain on her lower back. *Ida, I can hardly walk!* The other women were nasty to her, telling her what to do and whispering nasty things. *Treating me like I'm stupid!*

Her mother blew her nose into a wad of paper towel. *I can't take it.*

Ida wasn't unmoved. Her mother, even with her bad teeth and wrecked body, cried like a poor little girl whom nobody had ever loved. And probably they hadn't.

But one thing she said made Ida harden herself, take on more hours at the Food Town and plan her own escape: *I could have had a real career by now. I wanted to be a nurse. Only I chose to stay home and be you and Robert's mother.*

THE ALARM GOES OFF at 3:30 in the morning. She puts the Karr's shirt on, brushes her teeth, pulls her hair back into a rubber band, and wheels the bicycle outside. She ties the flashlight to the handlebars with a shoe string, and it lights a thin path as she pedals. The dark morning is gentle with her, the air soft and cool on her face.

She will make it there a whole hour earlier than she did yesterday. She will make the muffins and brownies and pies and she will sort the bread. Forget about the donuts and the Danishes and whatever else. She isn't going to try too hard, or torture herself, and if she needs to hide in the walk-in for a few minutes, or go in there for a good scream, she will do so. If the customers complain, if J. B. calls her into his office, she'll admit that she is in over her head.

She rings the service bell and the lone janitor lets her in.

On the way to the bakery, Ida grabs the Entenmann's cookies from the shelf and, before she does anything else, sets them out on the cookie trays in the display case. The ones from yesterday sold out.

She is alone. She goes back over to the aisle where she got the cookies and grabs an armful of boxes of Dixie Grandma's Morning Muffins. There are blueberry and banana, two dozen of each. She puts the muffins in the case, and drops the boxes into the trash can by the register, flattening them with her foot. She ties her apron and walks through the swinging door into the baking kitchen.

❀

"No BRAN MUFFINS TODAY?" The old man is Ida's first customer.

"Someone just came in and bought them all," she says.

"In the first five minutes you're open?"

Ida smiles. "A real early bird."

"Damn it. I guess I'll take blueberry," he says.

J.B. walks by twice, looking in her direction. She avoids eye contact.

Customer follows customer. Most elderly, some not. There are young families, teenagers. Where are all these people coming from? By eleven, the muffins are gone. Her raspberry and cheese Danishes sell out.

Ida sees a tall woman, late twenties or so, standing at the case, scanning it, her hands on her hips. She shifts her weight from one foot to another, rhythmically, like she is dancing to some song in her head. Her dark hair is pulled back into a sleek ponytail.

"Can I help you?" Ida says.

"Brownies."

"How many?"

"A dozen. Well, thirteen. Give me one now, OK? I bring them to my clients, but you guys haven't had them for a few weeks. You haven't had anything for a few weeks."

Ida hands her one brownie on wax paper. These are her own recipe, but she remembers now that she didn't add the vanilla. Where is the vanilla, anyway?

"This is going to be my lunch." The woman bites into the corner and chews, seeming none the wiser about the vanilla. "I've been running ragged all morning."

"What do you do?" Ida says, nonchalantly, trying to hide her jealousy of the woman's purposefulness and simple sophistication.

"Makeup." The woman jingles her car keys as she chews. "For two different news channels. I go up and down the coast. Morning news and then evening news. God, I miss brownies. How come you guys didn't have anything the past few weeks?"

"Oh," says Ida, standing up straighter. "They needed a real baker. It took them a little while to find me."

"I'll take a baguette, too," the woman says, pointing to the one she wants. "I just saw that poster about the little boy."

Ida nods.

"Channel fourteen, WGNL, had his mother on yesterday. I was there. She said, *We just want our sweet boy back.*" The woman sniffs and wipes at her mascara. "Did you see it?"

Ida shakes her head. "I don't have a TV," she says, and regrets how smug it sounds.

As she watches the woman walk toward the registers, Ida remembers Mark D. from the Aster Community Center. He died unexpectedly, just a few weeks after she started. Mark D. was just a little older than her, a year ahead of Robert in school. She remembers the memorial, his mother standing at the podium, talking about the difference he made in people's lives, how fortunate she had been to be his mother. So many people got up to talk. His pictures flashed across the screen: toddler, blue eyed and nearly bald; a school boy, two front teeth missing, curly black hair; a teenager at the prom, his curls short but still glossy, a hint of stubble on his chin. Everyone loved him. A line of people went to the podium to talk about how he had changed their lives. Ida felt the urge to make something up, because now she loved him, too.

Mark D. would pull over on the highway and fix anyone's flat. Mark D. fed the stray dogs and rescued a baby bird. Mark D. had a baby on the way. His young widow wept. She couldn't speak, holding the microphone with one hand and clutching her belly with the other. Everyone lit a candle to show the light he brought into their lives.

If it had been she who had the aneurysm, nobody would have stood at a podium and said that she brought them any light or joy or that their world would not be the same without her. No one would talk about her quiet dignity, her willingness to help, the impact she had made on the lives of those around her. No one would say how grateful she was to be chosen to be her mother.

❁

AT NOON, THE STORE begins emptying out. It happened at this time yesterday, too. If this were her real job, she thinks, she'd be making a list of what she needed to do before she left. Pies, for one thing.

But it isn't, and J.B. will be by any second to tell her thanks but no thanks.

She picks up the bakery phone and calls 411.

"New Orleans, Louisiana," she says, thinking of how Robert had been trying to teach himself blues harmonica.

"Robert Q. Overdorff." The Q is for Quincy, and Robert had given it to himself. He doesn't have a middle name and neither does she.

No listing. And no listing in Albuquerque, New Mexico or San Francisco, California. Not the surrounding areas, either.

An old lady taps the counter. Ida hangs up the phone.

"No crullers?"

"I'm sorry. We don't have donuts today."

"You sold out? How can that be? I called this morning and the manager told me you'd have donuts again."

"I'm sorry. We don't have any. Can I get you something else?"

"No you cannot. I came here specifically for the donuts. I drove fourteen miles for the donuts."

Out of the corner of her eye, Ida sees red gold hair. Lily! The woman is still talking about donuts, but Ida moves away from the counter and fumbles with the latch and lets herself out onto the floor. The red-gold hair is walking toward the exit, empty-handed, and Ida sprints after her. She is going to grab her by the arm and hold her while someone else calls the police.

Ida rushes out the door and runs after her, noticing just before she grabs at her shoulder that it is not Lily's shoulder at all, that the shoulder belongs to a full-grown woman, carrying a tiny baby out front in a sling and walking toward a station wagon.

Ida's hands shake. She waits, trying to catch her breath before going back inside.

J.B. is standing at the customer service desk, apologizing to the blue-haired lady.

"A dozen donuts, free, next time you come in."

"That doesn't help me right now," the woman says, but it helps enough, because she takes the voucher J.B. offers her.

Back at the bakery, the phone rings.

You didn't make donuts. It's J.B.

"No," she says.

They're a pain in the ass. Once Corinne clocks in, I'll come back there and show you how they're done.

"O.K." she says, and hangs up the phone. She takes a deep breath and grabs a pencil.

Pies, she writes on a napkin.

Lemon bars.

Chocolate éclairs.

When Ida looks up, she sees the red-haired stock boy, standing in the produce section, right where the berry display meets the bakery.

"Looks like my dream came true," he says, his voice almost a whisper. He picks up a grapefruit and tosses it in the air, catches it.

The bakery phone rings again. It's the girl from the deli. Ida looks over and sees her waving her hand as she talks.

You gotta ignore that weirdo. If you make eye contact even once, he'll never leave you alone.

Too late.

TWELVE

IT IS STILL HELLISH and stressful, despite two and a half weeks. Ida comes in at four-thirty every morning and it is almost enough time, though she has to skip something every day. Nobody seems to miss the blondies, so those are on her permanent ignore list. So are cream puffs and éclairs. And she is still filling the cookie trays with Entenmann's.

Ida likes the view she has of the produce department, the pyramids of navel oranges and pale green apples, the rows of purple eggplants, the bright raspberries in green plastic baskets.

One morning, J.B. puts his hands on the counter and leans in. "You're on the new pay scale, kid," he says. "As of last week."

It's what she figured. Yesterday's paycheck was bigger.

"You ready for cakes yet?"

"Oh God, no," she shakes her head. "Not even close." She thinks of the lopsided layers, the stubborn habit crumbs have of getting caught in the frosting. She doesn't have to do them. J.B. isn't going to fire her.

"Well, they're coming. Better prepare."

She shrugs and smiles at him, displaying her newly fixed-up tooth.

Lloyd drove her to Valponia the afternoon before. When she opened her mouth, the dentist was not horrified. He didn't even grimace.

"It's this awful yellow-brown," she said, close to tears. "It's probably rotten all the way through."

"Just staining. The seal wasn't good with the cement your last… dentist…used. Open. I'm…polishing…it…right…now."

He made her rinse and re-applied the clean bridge with fresh cement.

"How about my molars. Do they look okay?" she asked, both hands tucked under her thighs.

"They're okay. It looks like you've lost some enamel. Do you grind your teeth?"

"Maybe."

"Try to stop," he said. "You should have some x-rays to make sure, but at first glance, they look fine."

He turned her chair around so that she could look into the mirror. She braced herself and opened her mouth to have a look. She looked fine. The pristine office, the walls painted a cool blue, changed her, pressed a reset button. She was officially human, no worse than anyone else. Things were better. She had four hundred and nineteen dollars in the bank. Linda said not to worry; Melanie was still paying rent, anyway. She'd move out when Ida got there.

CORINNE CLOCKS IN. IDA ducks into the bakery kitchen and gets started, hoping to be left alone. No such luck. None of Ida's obvious body language does any good.

"Well, gooooood afternoon," Corinne says.

Corinne is frumpy, has a lisp, her second husband just left her for someone younger, yet she never shuts up about how blessed everyone is, herself included. How *blethed* everyone is.

Corinne stands in the bakery kitchen while Ida creams butter with sugar. "What are you making?"

"Icing," says Ida, squirting in a few drops of red and blue food coloring. She adjusts it, adding more blue until it is a soft shade of lavender.

"That's a pretty color," Corinne says, pointing to the bowl. "Where did you learn to do that?"

"I learned it in Paris," she says. "In cooking school."

"Paris?" says Corinne, craning forward for a better look. "Well you certainly were *blethed*, getting to live in a place like that!"

Ida stays later than usual, experimenting with the colors, trying to make them intense instead of pastel. She makes an electric lilac, a bright spring green, turquoise, blood red. This is fun. She adds more sugar to one batch, experimenting with an icing bag and the different tips to make stars, flowers, leaves. Her inclination is to do it much too fast. *Slow down*, she tells herself. *Loosen up*. She takes a deep breath and lets it out slowly so that she can be calm and steady enough to let it flow and then pull the bag back and up at the very last second. She practices the flowers on wax paper, turning the paper as she adds petals, and after an hour, when they start to look like roses, she decorates three naked cupcakes, a red flower on top of her electric lilac, a turquoise flower on her spring green.

As she cleans up, she notices that her one arm seems a bit lighter. The pearl bracelet has fallen off. And there it is on the floor, at the toe of her shoe. She picks it up and inspects it. She closes the clasp and gently tugs at it. With a small amount of pressure, the clasp opens right up. She puts it in her back pocket.

She bags up the eight donuts that are left: one glossy blueberry glazed, two chocolate, and five plain.

"Honey," says Corinne. "Mind leaving me one of those? I'm trying to reduce, but a donut would really hit the spot."

"Sure," says Ida. She takes the glazed donut out of the bag and puts it on a piece of waxed paper.

"Thank you, darling. You got Jesus in your heart, and he *blethed* you so you'd be generous with that donut."

She stops at the payphone on the way out. She doesn't want anyone to hear.

Hello, Martin Jewelry.

"Hi…I'm wondering…do you buy jewelry?"

Sure. What have you got?

"A bracelet. It's pearl and diamonds, I think."

You think?

"They look real. The diamonds. And the clasp is gold. Do you know how much something like that could be worth?"

To me? It depends. If the diamonds are big, if the pearls are in good shape. If it's real gold. Could be as much as a few hundred. I won't know until I see it.

"Thanks," she says. She hangs up, slightly disappointed. She has been a little too excited over the idea, thinking it might be worth a few thousand dollars or something. The thought came to her in the night, that she has enough money, that she won't have to slum in that house or bust her ass at Karr's anymore. A few hundred dollars is nothing to sneeze at. It's a whole week she won't have to work. She needs to think about it.

As she rides home, Ida squints against the brightness. Just sun and emptiness. The bad personality of this place can't be erased no matter how many houses are built on it. Yesterday, when Ida stopped by Sunshine Settler to deposit her paycheck, the bank manager said that, although he probably shouldn't tell her, Ken Cantwell wrote a few other checks late the same Friday he wrote hers, without the funds to cover them. A letter from the Starlight County attorney was sent to his place of business. He had ten days to pay before a criminal complaint was filed and the ten days passed. Now it was a county sheriff investigation. Ken Cantwell was probably on some Brazilian beach, sipping a Daiquiri and eating from a box of supermarket cookies.

When she gets to the house, she doesn't see them at first. She hops off the bike and notices something peach-colored. It is the smaller kid's knee, sticking out against the line of the side wall of her house. She cranes her neck. Donnie is sitting against the wall, his bare behind square in the dirt. He is wearing the same filthy t-shirt.

Carter is nearby, bending to inspect the outdoor faucet, which she has never noticed before. He stands up straight when he sees her.

She climbs off the bike. "Let me go for a ride," says Carter. He gestures at the bike, his other hand on his hip.

"It's too big for you," she says, moving past him.

"No it's not."

"Yes. It is. I guarantee it."

Carter folds his chubby arms on his chest. "Lemmee show you how I can ride it."

"I'm not going to, Carter."

"If you let me do it, I'll get you a fish. Yesterday I caught one in the water by scooping it up with a pot. I could do it again. There's two different kinds in the water: Ones with whiskers and ones with no whiskers. You got a pot?"

"No thanks." She pushes the bike toward her door. "I'm busy, okay?"

Donnie jumps up and runs toward her, stopping inches away. "We came 'cause he wants to show you something!"

"Fine," she says. "Show me what you want to show me."

"He gots a new watch!" says Donnie.

Carter fixes his gaze steadily on her, and holds out his arm. A black plastic watch with digital numbers. He presses a button.

"It glows!" says Donnie.

"Lucky you," she says.

"You can't see it if the sun is bright," says Carter. "You have to look at it in the dark." He walks toward her, covering his wrist with his hand. When he gets closer, he lets his fingers splay a bit, and holds his wrist close up to her face. She looks, sees the green glow, and sees his dirty hands and the black under his fingernails. Smells the rotten smell. Something stirs in the center of her body. She is supposed to do something about their smell, their grime, all of this.

"Cool," she says, pushing the feeling away. "That's nice. Did your parents give it to you?"

"Nope," says Donnie. "He gots a friend. By that canal."

"You should really put some shorts on," she points at Donnie. "Seriously. The next time I see you, be wearing something on your bottom," she says, and leaves them standing there.

"When?" calls Donnie. "When are we gonna see you?"

There is a note taped to her door:

I,

Thanks for paying me back so fast. Nobody does that. Now we're really friends.

Love,

Lloyd.

Ida grins, opens the door, wheels the bike inside and leans it against a wall. She slipped the envelope under their door the morning before. A fifty dollar bill to pay him back for the dentist.

She washes her hands at the kitchen sink and sees them again out of the back window. They are walking away. The cheeks of Donnie's little rear end are streaked in mud. She opens her door and calls out to them.

"Hey, you. Wait right there for just a second."

Inside, she takes a t-shirt from her duffel bag. It is grey and long, a man's shirt. Right before she left Aster, she found it in the Launderette in town, in a damp heap in an otherwise empty dryer.

She hands it Donnie. "Put this on. But take that dirty one off first." She turns away from him, hears his tiny grunts as he lifts the dirty shirt over his neck and shoulders. The new shirt goes down to his knees. Thank God.

"Keep it," she says.

He turns around, admiring himself.

"What are you going to give me?" says Carter.

"Huh?"

"You gotta be fair. If he gets a present, I need one, too."

"Look, it's not a present. It's something he needs. Like a glass of water or something."

He glares at her.

"Stop staring at me."

"You. Aren't. Fair." Carter clenches his teeth.

"Oh, Jesus Christ, just go away!" She turns around and marches back inside, banging the door shut behind her. She wets her face in the bathroom, cupping the water in her hands and slapping it on her neck and throat. Back in the living room, she takes a deep breath and sits on the floor and opens the newest mystery book she bought herself from

Karr's; she is currently on the fifth grisly, unexplained murder. In the daylight, she can't resist reading it, cheesy as it is, but once the dark sets in, once all she is aware of is the blue plastic breathing in and out of the house, she regrets it.

Carter stands on the other side of the big window, his hands on his hips, glaring at her. Ida acts like she isn't paying attention to him, but when she can no longer fight the urge, and looks up again, she sees that he has come closer. She isn't going to let this little kid bully her into going into the other room. She can ignore him like a champion. But the next time she looks up, Carter's nose is pressed against the glass. He seems to think that the two of them are engaged in a staring contest, that each time he wins a battle, he is allowed to advance.

She shakes her head, sighing, and gets up to open the door.

"I don't have anything to give you. That t-shirt was the only thing I had. I don't have anything else so there is no point for you to wait for anything."

He glares at her.

"If you want, I can play with you. For fifteen minutes. I'll be playing with Donnie, too, but it's a present for you. It would be for you."

"I'll take it," he nods.

"Wait, wait. Never mind, I do have something. How about instead, you'll get a donut." She goes inside to get them. Two, though. They had to each get one. Carter, of course, needs a donut far less than Donnie does.

"Here you go," she says. Yes! They take the donuts—she's kept the chocolate ones inside for herself—and stand eating them.

"This is good," says Donnie. He smiles at her, this dirty little boy doll with dainty nostrils, thick-lashed eyes, tiny white teeth. "Where'd you get it?"

"I got it at work."

"You work at a donut place?" Carter licks his dirty fingers. "You're lucky."

They catch the crumbs in their hands and in their shirts and eat those, too.

"So you guys should go home now. I'm sure your folks don't want you out this long. Bothering people."

"You said you'd play with me," says Carter.

"I said that, but then I decided to give you the donuts, instead."

Carter sticks out his bottom lip and stomps at the dirt.

"Okay. For a few minutes, but that's it," she says. It isn't worth it. "What do you want to play?"

"Don't you got some games here?"

"I already told you I don't have anything. No games." She wishes she did. A jump rope, a deck of cards, a garden hose so that she could hold out a stream of water and they could leap over and under it and she could be done with them.

"What are we gonna do?" says Carter.

"We can go on a walk!" yells Donnie.

"That's a good idea," says Carter, his tone paternal.

"Yeah, we can take you for a walk!" Donnie's voice is loud and sharp enough that Ida wants to stick her fingers in her ears. "We can go to see Carter's friend. The one by the canal!"

"Sure," says Ida. "But I can only be gone for a little bit. I've got a lot of other things I need to do."

She follows them across a field, across a street, and across another field. She has never been over here on foot. There aren't any houses or even the beginnings of any houses on any of the surrounding streets. The boys walk, looking straight ahead, as though what they are doing requires concentration and solemnity.

"This way," says Carter, and she and Donnie follow him.

They walk close to a canal. Ida hangs back.

"Be careful," she calls.

"We do this all the time," says Carter, looking at her like she's crazy.

"Don't get so close!" she shouts. "Don't you kids know about alligators?"

"So?"

"An alligator could snap you up in two seconds," she says.

Donnie turns and looks at her. He runs to her and grabs her hand with his own sticky fingers.

"If you won't let us go close to the water, then we can't see my friend," says Carter, taking big steps forward. "So we're gonna go someplace else I know."

"Where?" she says, pulling her hand away from Donnie and wiping it on her shirt. "I told you guys I don't have much time."

Donnie calls to Carter. "I don't think that's the way. 'Member there was that big black stick on the ground?"

"Keep looking," says Carter.

Donnie turns to her. "It was a big stick," he says.

"This is a longer walk than I had in mind. I'm not sure I want to do this," she says, but they don't register it, so she follows them. They are close to a thick stand of trees.

"Maybe over this way?" she offers, pointing ahead.

Carter looks up at her. "Maybe," he nods.

Dark clouds begin to move across the sky. The same dark clouds that she sees every single day in the late afternoon or early evening. The clouds that bring rain for ten or twenty dramatic minutes.

"I have to go," she says. "You should go home, too. It's about to start raining."

"We're almost there already," Carter assures her.

They are close to the trees. Probably not the best place to be in a storm. Still, she follows them, walking until they are underneath them. The trees are thick enough that they can't see much of the sky. She can hear it, though, the low rumbling in the distance.

"We should turn around. Forget about visiting your friend right now. It's not safe out here."

Carter rolls his eyes. "We're out in a storm all the time."

Donnie squeals. "Look at that, look at that! We found it again!"

He points across the branches to a red towel, draped over something. They all move toward it.

"Huh," she says. "It's a *house*. Wow." It is square and significant in the middle branches of two wide trees. Finished planks of wood, pane-glass windows, a porch, even.

"Yeah, we know this little house!" Donnie cries.

"A tree house," she says. "An actual tree house. That's so weird."

Carter nods. "And it's fancy, too."

"Hush, I think I can hear somebody up there," she says. There are sounds coming from it, a coughing and also tinkling of some sort, a trilling. She takes a few steps closer to it, stepping over branches. The boys follow her.

Donnie begins to giggle crazily. The sound creeps up the back of Ida's neck. She shushes him, and for a few seconds he tries to stop, but then he only gets louder.

Something slams. She looks up.

"Hey," a man yells. "Who's out there?"

It's the bicycle guy, standing up above them on a platform, wearing his sunglasses and cycling clothes. All green this time. He isn't wearing the hat, but his blondish hair is flattened, damp-looking, like he's just taken it off. Ryan said his name is Peter.

She has seen him twice since getting the bike from him. She thought she saw him wave to her as he passed her on his bike, but she remembered his nasty, shithead smile from the day he gave her the bike and she felt no inclination to be polite. A few days later, he passed her again and said, *Hey,* in a clipped way that sounded both snotty and friendly, but Ida pretended he wasn't there. It had been fun.

Peter has something in his hand. The moment he catches Ida's eye, he holds it behind his back.

"No children allowed," he says, grinning.

They stare back up at him.

"Vamoose," he says.

The boys stand firm.

"Are you joking?" says Ida.

"Not even a little bit."

Carter waves his fat, grimy fist in the air. "It's a free country!"

"I have impeccable aim," says Peter.

Ida laughs. Carter and Donnie laugh, too.

Carter puts his hand to the top of his head. A thick peel of orange sits at Carter's feet; Peter has just thrown it. Another piece of orange peel through the air. Aimed at Donnie. It hits his shoulder.

"Dummy," Carter shouts. "That's my brother!"

"And guess what? It don't even hurt!" Donnie screams. He starts to run and Carter follows him, back out of the woods.

Ida looks up at Peter. "What the hell?"

He is grinning, and the grin is eerily gracious, full of teeth. He holds up an orange peel, pulls his arm back.

"You're seriously going to throw that at me?"

He does. Her hand shoots up, and she catches the peel.

"I'm like a ninja," she says, heading toward the clearing. "And you're an asshole." Out from the trees, back in the open, the air is thick; the water of the canal has gotten darker.

"I'm gonna go back and throw a banana up at him," Carter is saying, shaking his fist.

"You got a banana?" says Donnie.

"No," says Carter. "I hate that jerk."

"Yes, he's a jerk," says Ida. "You've got that right."

"You should throw some poo-poo on him!" screams Donnie. He stomps his feet and holds his fingers in front of his mouth. His high-pitched giggling hurts her brain.

"Stop it," she says. "Please."

He looks at her and stops mid-giggle. The rain begins, soft at first. The wind comes in a big breath. It blows one side of Carter's dark hair straight up toward the sky.

"*That* was the friend you were talking about?" says Ida. "Your friend is a bonehead."

"That's not his friend," says Donnie. The t-shirt she gave him to wear is dotted with dark splotches of rain.

"I'll walk you home."

They stare at her. Carter wipes rain from his eyes.

Donnie points vaguely to the left, where the clouds are darker.

"You live in that house with the beige shutters, right? And the pink bush and the soft grass?"

Carter frowns at her. He nods.

"I'll walk with you, but let's go fast," she says.

The boys look at each other before taking off in a run. Ida tries to follow them, but she is too tired to keep up with them. They will be fine. It is odd, though, that these two mongrels live in that perfect little house with the soft grass and the sweet pie on the counter.

The thunder shakes the air; parts of sky light up with streaks of lightning. She watches Donnie's bare, skinny legs, as he jumps, frog-like, through the grass, away from her.

IDA HAS BEEN AVOIDING this, but the sight of Donnie's tiny t-shirt, dirty and rumpled on the concrete floor of her living room, is too much.

She fills the sink with water and pours in four capfuls of pear shampoo. She changes the water in the bathroom sink and adds more shampoo. When the shirt is as clean as she can get it, she wrings it out and hangs it on a branch of a ficus tree; it will dry by the time she gets home.

The next afternoon, Ida finds the boys' house again. She leaves her bicycle in the driveway. The t-shirt is clean and dry, folded and tucked under her arm.

When Ida rings the doorbell, she hears a child's voice— Donnie's?—calling out. "Can I answer it? Can I answer it?" There is a murmuring back. The answer must be no, because a woman answers the door, opening it only a little. The woman blinks; a pair of bifocals make her water-green eyes enormous. She has a bath towel wrapped around her head.

"Yes?" she says to Ida. "What is it that you want?"

Cool air from inside of the house touches Ida's face. She can see into the kitchen, the sturdy wooden table with matching chairs.

"I'm Ida. I live nearby." She holds out the folded t-shirt, but the woman doesn't reach for it. "This belongs to your little boy. He was playing in my yard…his shirt was really…it got really dirty. I guess he spilled something on himself. So I gave him a clean one of mine. And washed this."

"I'm sorry," the woman says, stepping backward. "I don't have any idea what you are talking about."

"You don't have a little boy?" says Ida. "Two little boys? Maybe your grandsons?"

There are no other houses nearby. "No, I do not." The woman frowns. She begins to close the door. Ida can only see one green eye now, then the dark hole that is the woman's nostril. She hears movement from inside, a tiny voice. *Who is it? Who is it?*

Ida stands there listening to the lock click. Out of the corner of her eye, she notices a small something. The curtain in the room on the far left moves. Of course not. This woman wouldn't let little kids run around alone, without underpants.

Then Ida sees a tiny face, miniature, strange, ghostly. A tiny wave and the curtain closes.

THIRTEEN

IT IS THE SECOND week of September, and the temperature has been in the upper 90s for ten days running. The thirteen-foot alligator has dug a den in the mud so that she can keep herself and her babies cool. The afternoon rains are heavy but unrefreshing, and followed immediately by newly-hatched mosquitoes, crazed with blood-thirst. They feast on otters and squirrels and deer, on the breasts and necks of egrets, herons, wood storks, pelicans, buzzards, and terns.

A single private developer has made a deal with the state of Florida. They have bought the state-owned land and are in the process of buying up all of the land owned by other, smaller developers. The town of Fort Starlight will not be. This is not yet public information.

In the plaza, the Pampered Pet is closed, and so is the Fashion Bug. These stores have been cleaned out completely; the signs have been removed and there is no trace of what they were or what they tried to be.

Inside Karr's, Ida stands at the bakery counter. A man, tan-skinned, mouth over-filled with sparkling dentures, points to a blueberry scone, which is enormous and crusted on top with sparkling sugar.

"They're two for three dollars," she says. Alone, they are a dollar seventy-five each. She can't understand why she can never convince anyone to buy more than one at a time, as though a scone is too precious to stock up on. She likes it when, by the end of her shift, the case is mostly empty of morning pastries.

"My doctor says I need to stay away from sweets." The man winks; his irises are blue, the eyeballs yellowish white, the color of an antique tablecloth.

"Well, I'm sure he'd approve of these. They're not too sweet." She is not lying. She makes them with very little sugar, making the vague sweetness of the berries do most of the work. With a bit of extra salt, they are almost savory, the sparkling sugar on top an interesting contrast. *Pull back on the sweetness and the natural flavors will stand out more.* It was something she read in the cooking magazine she grabbed from the display at the cash registers.

Without letting the man see her do it, she puts two in the bag, but prints out a ticket only charging him for a single scone. She won't be here much longer, and besides, he is the type of customer that she likes. The type who has nothing to do but come nearly every day and linger for an hour in the cool, enormous store. The type who walks around these bright aisles happily, smiling at the bounty on the shelves, and with enough time to ponder the efforts put into the presentation. He is old, but he walks with vigor and grace. He is alone, and unoccupied, and takes pleasure in planning his meals. He whistles while he shops. He gets the point of Karr's, and makes Ida proud to be part of this place.

"If my doctor got a load of you," he points a forefinger at Ida, "he'd tell me to stay away. Much too sweet. Likely to give me a heart attack."

"Sweet things don't cause heart attacks, I don't think," she says.

He takes the bag from her, places it in his cart. Winks again.

"Yes." He stands still, stares at her wistfully. "Much too sweet. If you were a few years older, I'd take you out on the town."

She wants to say, *What town would that be?* Instead, she says, "If I were a few years older, I'd probably say yes." She doesn't care that this is a lie, only that this is what he'd likely want to hear her say and it causes her no trouble to say it. She smiles and turns her back to him to straighten the loaves of bread. She can still hear him there. *Go away now.* When she finally turns around, he is gone, but she can hear his whistle in a nearby aisle.

She takes her bag from the shelf under the pastry case. Inside is her latest bank statement, which she got after that morning's deposit. She likes the sight of the numbers as they build up. She has managed to get by with spending less than thirty dollars a week on herself.

Corinne needed to take three shifts off one week to help a friend out. Ida earned time and a half by covering her shifts.

Three more weeks of work before she can take a bus out of Fort Starlight. Ida takes a pen and a scrap of paper. Even though she knows this all by heart, she draws up a calendar for this month and the next month, circling pay dates in red, double-circling the day she thinks she may actually manage to leave, circling also the day she hopes to start some sort of work in New York. She does this calendar-making every day on the white, porous napkins that sit on the bakery counter. The red ink seeps into the napkin and spreads. She plans to leave on a day that Ryan and Lloyd have to drive to Erne City for work so that they can see her off from the Greyhound stop in the middle of town. She will be a bit sad to say goodbye to them. Most of her days off are spent with them, eating at their place, watching movies. She often feels like a third wheel, but she never says no to an invitation, even when she senses that they might want her to.

The old man is back. She notices that he is a natty dresser. No slouchy trousers and Rockports for him. He wears seersucker pants that fit perfectly, an oxford shirt, leather sandals that are somehow debonair. He is handsome enough that she imagines he was devastating before he got old. His body is…nice. Slim, toned, solid. He is not the type, she realizes, who cares about a free scone. He is on the prowl.

"You're a beauty. In a slightly unconventional way. It's pleasing. You look like a handful of wildflowers. I thought I should come back and let you know that."

She blinks at him, grins stupidly. *Wildflowers?* She wonders if this could be true. She has been looking pretty good lately, better, in her opinion, than ever before. But flowery? Not really.

"I have a swimming pool, you know. It's on the beach, built up above the dune. And my house is wonderful, too. The view would take your breath away."

"That's great." She tries to sound as though she means it.

"Built by a famous architect. You've heard of Martin Holt, I'm sure."

"Oh. Martin Holt," she says. "Yeah."

He bites the side of his bottom lip. "How would you like to see for yourself? For a late lunch? Today. I've got the Cabriolet out front."

"Oh, I don't know." She laughs. "Maybe some other day would be better."

"Dinner tonight. That would be better." He leans in. "I'll drive you myself. A bottle of wine. We'll have a good time." He leans far forward, slides his hand across the counter, wraps his fingers around her wrist. His skin feels hot and dry; the tips of his fingernails feel sharp, like he could use them to slice into the thin skin of her inner wrists.

There is something dangerous in his smile.

"A hot time. You pretend to be a good girl, but I think you're really more of a bad girl."

She tries to pull away but he holds on tightly.

"I run four miles a day," he says.

"I can't," she says. "It's against store policy."

He does not let go.

"Lay off, Grandpa," she snaps, and raises her other hand at him. She will hit him if she has to.

He takes his fingers off. "Oh, cut it out," he says, and turns and walks away, as gracefully as before. His sandals make a soft flapping noise on the floor.

She knows that she should feel disturbed, and does, a little bit. But she still can't help imagining what would have happened if she had gone with him. He would have driven her to his house, showed her the bedroom, and lunged for her immediately, and maybe she would have succumbed, out of curiosity and, she knew, desperation. Not at first. Maybe she would make him chase her around, first, show off that cardiovascular fitness. She is looking forward to the end of the day, when she can tell Ryan and Lloyd about it.

Dale, the stock boy, has been gone a week already. He quit.

After weeks of his suggestive one-liners and eye-contact, she couldn't handle it anymore, was through with fantasizing about it, and handed him a note one morning, telling him to meet her. He had nearly driven her crazy. She needed something to happen.

There had been Mr. Brinks and then only one other, a guy she saw sitting outside of the diner in Aster one afternoon, strumming a guitar. Older, scruffy, skinny. He smelled like coins. When she walked by, he said, *Come on over here and talk with me a while.* He had been on his way to Poughkeepsie but he got hungry and had to get off the road and get himself a grilled cheese sandwich. *Sit down with me,* he said. And she did. *Here, hold onto this guitar; let me show you a few chords.* The chords Robert had once taught her came back to her. Her fingertips stung. And then, *Let's go to your place and share this joint I got,* and *take that shirt off.* She did everything he said. And it was all fine, but it hadn't been her idea. None of it, and in retrospect, that made it no fun. No anticipation. She didn't have time to feel any desire. When he left, she took her sheets to the Laundromat to wash out the coin smell.

She wasn't a kid anymore. It was time to screw someone because it was her idea.

Her note said: *I will be in the bakery walk-in in a half hour.* It was a quiet time of the day. Perfect. No customers yet, and everyone too busy to be interested in what anyone else was doing.

She walked in and waited, leaning against the tall shelf. It was dim in there. What would he look like without his clothes? Did he have muscles or was he stick thin? You couldn't always tell with men. Their clothes hid the truth. What would he think of her? She slid her hand into the waist of her pants and rubbed her hip. She pulled it out and touched her bare stomach.

When he finally walked in, she was already beyond shivering.

He didn't have a slick one-line. It was like he'd never had them at all. His mouth was slightly open. There were freckles all over the bridge of his nose. "Here I am," she said. "And here you are." He looked at the floor; his hands shook, even when she led them under her shirt, and put them on her bare ribcage. She whispered, "Finally." She reached forward and tugged at his shirt.

He mumbled, "Hey, I'll be right back." He pulled away from her, unlocked the walk-in door and never came back. Not to the walk-in and not to Karr's.

Apparently, the experience inspired him to give the eleventh grade another try.

MRS. HEALY SITS UP straight on her white sofa, making the first of what will be many telephone calls. The policemen have just left. They found something.

She puts her hand to her neck.

It was his shoe. His left shoe. In the water, stuck in the mud.

The time has passed too fast and too slow at the same time, but all of it headed toward the point of no return, which she knew in her heart from the very beginning. They will still look, yes, but they aren't looking for *him*. They are looking for his body, for more of his belongings. His spirit is no longer on the ground. She feels it up in the air above her and knows that he is alone up there. There may or may not be a God, but her son's spirit is up there alone and he is afraid and doesn't know what to do next, where to go. When she inhales, she is inhaling part of him, and she feels him come to her, a baby, toddling across the floor and into her outstretched arms where she holds him too tightly.

The bicycle was found in the river, stuck in the mud on the bottom, across from a placard that described the attributes of the White Ash tree, native to this area. The police ran the fingerprints on his bicycle and she had to wait for the results as though she might learn something she didn't already know.

Her husband's prints and Mitchell's prints were on the bicycle. Nobody else's. Mitchell had had it for a few months. It was a good one, bought from a mountain biking store in Miami, of all places. More than a thousand dollars, even though there is nothing anywhere near a mountain to ride it on. Had she really never touched his bicycle? It seemed strange that she hadn't, but it was true; she'd only looked at it. The truth is that she hadn't seen much of him that summer, hadn't looked at him very closely. It had been one of those times when a mother steps away from her child and into her own head for a little while. She wishes very much that she had touched the bicycle, had taken an interest in it.

She told this to Officer Sternbach and he listened to her.

She told him that Mitchell was a part of her body. He once lived inside of her and when she gave birth to him, there was a pain different from her body opening and stretching and ripping. There was the pain of not wanting to let him go. To keep him where he was safe. She said that when she was in labor, she never felt the urge to push. That she thought the lack of this urge meant that he didn't want to exist outside of her. That he wasn't ready. *As strange as this may sound*, she said, *I think that if I had only listened to my body…and not pushed when they told me to…I know it sounds bizarre, but a few more minutes, and it could have shifted everything in time, just enough that he'd still be here.* He didn't say that she was wrong or that it sounded bizarre. But he took her hand and held it.

A PILLSBURY CHOCOLATE LAYER cake is baking in Nancy's oven. Madeline's birthday is today and tonight they are having a party. Corinne is coming. She has been watching Madeline while Nancy works her few shifts at Karr's. Corinne and Nancy are very different, but she is grateful for her, and not simply because Corinne is generous enough to baby-sit in exchange for Nancy simply tinting and cutting her hair, for promises of fixing it up again in the future, but also because for the first time in years, she feels that a few of her burdens have been lifted from her shoulders.

Someone is helping her and it couldn't have happened at a better time. Nancy's register drawer kept coming up short, no doubt because she was too frazzled about leaving Madeline to pay close enough attention. J.B. let her slide once, but the second time, he took the eighteen dollars out of her paycheck. And then nine-fifty. No matter how hard she tried, it never once came out exactly right.

Corinne volunteered to baby-sit, insisted, really, the day after

Madeline ran off. Or when Nancy thought she'd run off. It had been so hard until that day. Madeline had been acting up quite a bit: making calls to a television psychic, trying to paint her fingernails, spilling the bottle of pink polish on the white bathmat and neglecting to mention it. On that terrible morning, Madeline was sulkier than usual, sassing her at every opportunity.

When Nancy had finally had enough and asked her what was wrong, Madeline exploded, yelling that Nancy was a promise breaker, that she'd promised to take her to Disney that day. It just was not true. Nancy frowned, trying to figure out why on earth Madeline was insisting on this untruth when the front door slammed. It took Nancy a few minutes to realize that Madeline was the one who had slammed the door, and that she was no longer in the house. She stood still for a few minutes, trying to calm herself.

She should have run out immediately. When she finally did, she didn't see Madeline anywhere.

"Oh, Hell," she shouted. Her voice didn't carry; it stuck in the hot air right in front of her. "Madeline!" She circled around the house quickly, two times, sweating and gasping. Madeline was not in the yard; Madeline was nowhere. She looked at the canals in the distance and trembled. There was nothing else in the horizon that would draw anyone.

Madeline couldn't swim. Not even a little bit. Nancy thought of the boy she'd heard about in the news, the one who went missing. She ran inside and picked up the telephone to dial 911. She hung up before it rang on the other end. Bad things happened quickly. What she needed to do was get the car out and drive as fast as she could, right over the grass and to the canals. She pictured Madeline's legs, thin and white, the sun burning her face. She pictured the quicksand, the alligators, the mud-colored water, biting fish that could tear apart her little ankles. Her little hummingbird heart, beating too fast.

There Madeline was, in the back seat of the car, curled up small.

That night, Nancy couldn't sleep, wondering what had made Madeline so angry. The only thing she could think of was that Madeline must have woken up while Nancy was working at Karr's and found herself alone. Terrified. That was what happened. She was sure of it. Madeline was too stubborn to admit to it.

Madeline has her ear over her bowl of Rice Krispies, listening.

"What are they saying?" asks Nancy. "Are they singing happy birthday to you?"

"I have something to show you," Madeline says. She jumps out of the chair and goes into her bedroom.

Nancy stands up and peeks at the cake. She has canned white frosting in the cupboard and she has some happy looking rainbow sprinkles to go on top.

Madeline runs back to the kitchen, wearing her lilac dress with puffed sleeves and white patent Mary Janes.

"You're ready for the party very early," says Nancy, reaching into the refrigerator for the potatoes in the bottom drawer. "Be careful not to get your dress dirty." She is going to make potato salad with cubed ham and radishes. She looks at the bottle of white wine, chilling on a shelf. This is for her and Corinne, who, when Nancy asked her if she drank, said, *Jesus did, so I do, too*. But when Nancy thought about it, and she'd gone to Catholic school, she could remember Jesus turning water to wine, but not drinking it.

"Well?" says Madeline, stomping one tiny foot.

"Hmmm?"

"Don't you want to know what I went to get?"

"Oh," says Nancy. "I forgot."

"Guess what it is."

"Let's see…a ribbon?"

Madeline shakes her head.

"A bracelet?"

Madeline stares back, shakes her head. She brings her hand forward. It is a white paper napkin, folded over.

Nancy unfolds it and sees a small lipstick kiss print in bright pink. "What's this?"

"It's my kiss," says Madeline. "Corinne helped me do it."

"Oh," says Nancy. "When?"

"Last night. She put the lipstick on me very carefully and showed me how to make a kiss. She said I have sweet little lips."

"You do," says Nancy, looking at the napkin. "You do. Very pretty little lips."

"She said that it's a kiss on paper and I could hand it to you and you could carry it around and have my kiss. It's better than a real kiss because it lasts longer. You can have it."

"Thank you," says Nancy. "You like Corinne, don't you?"

Madeline nods. "Do you have a lipstick?"

"I'll see," says Nancy. She walks into her bedroom and rummages through drawers and at the very back of one is an orangey lipstick from years ago. She opens it and, leaning in front of her mirror, paints her own lips. It is an improvement; she looks a little bit better with it on. She decides that she will wear lipstick every day.

Nancy secretly thinks that Corinne got the bad end of the deal. It turned out that there wasn't much to be done about Corinne's hair.

Through the mirror, Nancy sees Madeline come into the room and sit on the bed. She holds out a napkin.

"Corinne gave me empty napkins so you could give me one too and they would match each other. That way I could have your kiss, too."

"You want my kiss?"

Madeline nods, so Nancy puckers and then presses the napkin to her own lips. Madeline reaches out for the napkin and studies it. "You have sweet lips, too," she says. "They're really big but still sweet." Madeline reaches up and pats Nancy's cheek and Nancy is so surprised and delighted by Madeline's touch that she stays as still as she can.

THERE IS NO LOCK on the front door of the house at Ring and Marine. This is the second time Lloyd will have gone inside. The first time was a few days before, and just to take a peek. It was much worse than Lloyd had imagined. Not livable. Lloyd wouldn't be able to spend one night here. The drying peel of an orange, neatly stacked on the edge of the sink, smelled bittersweet. A line of ants walked across it.

Ryan shuts off the motor of the truck they borrowed from Al, gets out and slams the door.

"Let's check the pipes first," says Lloyd. "Make sure there's gas." Today he's wearing two nicotine patches instead of one, and still, his nails are bitten down to the quick and he has chewed a bloody spot on his lower lip, which is scabbed over. Cold turkey. It has been twelve days so far with this attempt, and the only reason he has not given in is that he is so proud to have made it twelve days.

"We should have checked that before," says Ryan. "Before we dragged it all the way here."

"More than likely it's on," he says.

Things are better. It happened without effort, over coffee and green tea in their kitchen one afternoon two weeks ago. Ryan had turned to him and calmly said, "If you don't want to be a foster parent, I can deal with that. I want to be with you, so we won't do it."

Lloyd stood still for a while. He nodded and stayed quiet. Lloyd had just finished one of Mona's books about how you couldn't make the other person change; you had to change your expectations. It made sense, only he hadn't felt charitable enough to change those expectations.

Ryan had done this, without needing a self-help book. That night, over wine (Ryan's idea: toasting to this decision that freed him/them from further turmoil!), Lloyd told him that his own childhood—his parents' divorce, his father dying, his mother's cruel and stupid boyfriends—had been bad enough that he didn't want to be a part of someone else's bad childhood. He almost confessed that he loved the feeling of being taken care of by Ryan and thought it would be hard to share him.

And because he was grateful for Ryan not pushing the foster child thing, he said that he would shut up about hating Fort Starlight and just be patient. They had a nice home; they had more than enough money for the first time ever. Ryan was putting together a business plan for the Montessori school he wanted to start someday. They could afford to travel whenever they could get the time off. Things were good. They had each other. Lloyd said he knew that if he really wanted to do this art thing, he could do it. Nothing was stopping him. He didn't need to live in some overpriced city to show his work in that overpriced city's galleries.

And the day after that, the timing ridiculously perfect, Lloyd got a letter from an old friend who lived in Houston, who used to gush over all of Lloyd's paintings and talked about opening a gallery. It had been that friend's dearest dream, and she was finally doing it. She wanted him to be in her first group show; he needed to get ten pieces together and send them immediately. Rush, rush, rush. Did he still have the one that was the orange campfire, and the old man standing right behind it, hardly visible? He did.

On the wall of the kitchen in Ida's house, there is a pipe and a valve. Lloyd crouches down and turns the valve, holds his hand in front of it, sniffs.

"It's on," he says.

"You know, I don't think they ever found that little boy," says Ryan. "Did you ever hear anything?"

"No," says Lloyd. "Not a thing. Here we go," he says. He stands up and wipes his hands on his shorts.

"So strange," says Ryan. "The whole thing."

Back outside, Lloyd pulls down the truck bed and hops in.

"We have to *lift* it out. I don't want to scrape his truck up with this thing." A white stove. Their boss, Al, was getting rid of it, redoing his house with all stainless steel appliances. He just wanted it gone. They brought her the mini-fridge they found in a garage sale somewhere in Alabama on their way down here, but have never used. Also, the futon that had been sitting, unused, in the second bedroom, and a tiny radio. Doing this was Lloyd's idea, but Ryan is the one who really ran with it, made a list, made the phone call to Al.

"What made you change your mind about her?" says Lloyd. "I remember when you first met her you said she was annoying."

"The dinner party. She was so vulnerable. And hungry. She liked my cooking. And she was sad. I'm easy, I guess."

After they return the truck, they are going swimming at a beach that no one else seems to know about. It's an inlet, separated from the other beaches by a thin channel and a few hundred yards. Sometimes they swim out, one at a time, to a blue and white striped buoy. It takes a while to get there. They watch each other from the shore, look for signs of distress. The current is stronger than they ever remember. It draws them both out to the buoy, which they hang onto for a while before swimming back to shore again. When they return, the skin on their palms is mottled, sometimes even cut up a little, from the barnacles.

The stove is heavy and makes a tinny sound as the wire racks rattle on the inside. As they carry it, Ryan cuts his finger on a piece of sharp metal on the back. They set it down and Ryan puts his finger to his mouth, tastes salty blood. The cut isn't deep, but after they pick it up and bring it all the way inside, he washes his finger at the sink, lathering it with Ida's dishwashing liquid. He rinses his finger and wraps it tightly in a paper towel, holding it in place with his thumb.

They push the stove back until it meets the wall. They try the burners, one at a time, and all of them burst into their controlled flames.

It is nice to work side by side at something.

"Al is nuts," says Lloyd. "A new stove. I bet he's never cooked in his entire life."

They put the small refrigerator on the floor next to the stove.

They set the bed up in the bigger, sunnier bedroom. Never mind that her cushions are in the living room. People should sleep in bedrooms. Lloyd drapes Ida's sheet across the futon mattress and tucks the edges underneath. He plops a pillow on top.

"Do you have the flowers?" he asks.

"I already put them out."

Lloyd sees the four Gerbera daisies, pink and yellow, in the glass on the windowsill.

"It's like in *A Little Princess*," says Ryan. "Have you ever seen that movie? Shirley Temple?"

"No," says Lloyd, but then he remembers that he has, twenty or so years ago on a day when he was home from school, sick. "There was a Rajah, right?"

"Punjabi, I think. Is that something different? He filled her room with silk quilts and pillows and bowls of fruit. He did all of this while she slept. And when she woke up, she thought she was dreaming."

"That's creepy. Think about it."

"I only wish that there were stuff in the fridge. Do you think we should go back, get some milk and eggs or something?"

"Babe," says Lloyd, "that might be going a bit far."

"Milk and eggs is going too far?"

"Well, yes. She can get her own milk and eggs."

"Then eighty-six the milk and eggs," says Ryan.

"Stop it with that already," Lloyd groans. It is restaurant talk for when something has run out. Ryan has two master's degrees and sounds ridiculous when he talks this way, which is why he does it.

Ryan points at the blue tarp. "That's where the screened-in porch was supposed to go," he says. "Weird that it didn't get finished. That they just left it open. It can't be good for the house to leave it like this."

They back out of the house slowly, assessing the finished product.

"This is great," says Lloyd. "She's going to flip out. Too bad we didn't think of doing this a few weeks ago."

"It could be better," says Ryan. He walks out, waits for Lloyd to do the same, pulls the door closed.

"Everything could always be better. And anyway, she's leaving soon."

PETER HAS THE TAPES all stacked up. There are a hundred and twenty-six of them, far more than he'd planned. He sits at his small table, rewriting the labels for the tapes. *Toy piccolo. Cricket. Wave during Neap Tide. Cast of a Fishing Rod.* All of them quiet sounds, but infinite, somehow. Simple. Natural. Real. Powerful. More powerful than any sound that was being made for the purpose of being recorded. When they come together, the whole will be far more than the sum of its parts.

These are some of the words he writes down. He is writing another letter (his third) to the famous audio engineer in Los Angeles (about as famous as one could be), the same man who has worked on recordings of the pygmy tribes of the Ituri rain forest. This would be a very different project; it will be much more abstract than anything the man has worked on before. But important. Possibly the most important recording, he dares himself to write, of the century. The implications of it will likely not be understood for a very long time. Not until the human race has evolved further. Not until people are evolved enough to truly be able to hear the silences between natural sounds, and until they can understand those silences as sounds in their own right. It will be music for the future.

He has been up all night. Despite the early hour, as he writes, he drinks a glass of celebratory dessert wine, slowly nibbles three squares of dark, almost black chocolate. The Gewürztraminer is cold, as it should be. He admits to himself that this is exactly how he hoped it would happen.

The first letter was answered right away and with just five words: *Sounds interesting. Tell me more.* The second letter said, *I'm probably free for a week in late summer, if you are done/ready by then. I will have time and access to a great studio. Let me know.* Peter did.

When he gets the next response, Peter will leave right away. He is not sure if he will disassemble the house. Leaving it maybe isn't ethical, but he likes the idea of someone finding it and marveling at it, wondering about the thought that went into it. He will ride his personal things to the dumpster behind the supermarket. It will require four or five trips. Of course, he has to take one last ride to the beach, which is something he has enjoyed doing. He liked riding there, sprinting most of the way, letting himself get overheated and thirsty, dropping his bike and his clothes in the sand, and running for the water.

He will go at low tide, when the tidal pools are full and still, and so many things are trapped inside of them. Hopefully, as has twice been the case, there will be a lobster sitting at the bottom. If so, he will reach down and get it, spear it on a stick, roast it right there on the beach.

After that, he'll leave his two remaining bicycles where someone who will appreciate it might find them. He will take a rental car to the airport. After he's gone to Los Angeles and done the composing and the editing, maybe he'll go to Honduras, or maybe to Costa Rica. He will not come back to live here; when he is finished with a place, he leaves it for good. He thinks of the girl he sees here, how she is different than she first looked. She is no developer's daughter, anyway. Her walk is interesting, long strides, her arms swinging with every step, like she is marching off to battle. She is smarter than he thought she was, too, though she did get herself roped into hanging out with those kids.

Peter addresses the envelope. No more wine. He can't wait any longer. He stands up, seals the envelope. If he rides into Erne City now, he can get to the FedEx drop at the drugstore before the afternoon pickup.

DONNIE AND CARTER HAVE also been in Ida's house when she was out. And more than a few times. They like it there.

They watch from down the road, waiting for the two men to leave. Carter's nose has peeled; the white skin that was underneath it has also burned. It hurts. He holds his hand over it so that the sun can't make it any worse.

When the men drive away, Carter and Donnie walk down the road and onto the grass. There are fire-ant hills in the front and back yards. They have become experts at avoiding fire-ant hills, and this morning, Carter gets the idea to pour her shampoo on top of them to see what will happen. The ants panic, try to run out, their legs moving in slow, sticky motion, and they die soon after. The boys play superhero, but they don't take turns. They are both Antkillerman. They kill four whole hills, and then Carter goes inside to fill the bottle up with water to make it less obvious that they used so much. It is mostly water now, only a little bit green.

In the kitchen, there is a plastic bag halfway filled with oranges, and a white paper bag with cookies in it. There are only two, both chocolate chip, and Carter decides they should eat them both rather than to just share one of them, like they sometimes do. Carter is usually the hungry one, but today Donnie is hungry, too. After the cookie, Donnie starts to eat an orange, biting right through the skin. He spits out the peel.

"Look at the little fridgerator," says Carter. "Open it up and see if there's some Coke inside it." He very much wants to believe that there will be a six-pack of red Coca-Cola cans inside of it, waiting for them.

Donnie checks the fridge. He holds it open so that Carter can see that it is empty. There are two more oranges on Ida's counter, and he has to have another. Carter does, too. They eat them quickly (Donnie peels his this time) and they both gasp when they are finished.

Back out in the yard, Donnie tells Carter to turn on the faucet and drink the water from it. Yesterday, they didn't come here, and when they were thirsty, they tried to drink from the canal, instead, holding the water in their cupped hands. Donnie was so thirsty that he couldn't get enough of the sour brown water down. All night long, next to Carter in the bed of the truck, he coughed, and the dark, acid taste of the swampy water kept coming up and filling his throat. It made him feel like he had burns in his insides.

They walk. They pass the canal where, until recently, the remains of Mitchell Healy's body, except for a single arm, were mostly hidden under reeds along the bank. Weeks ago, it had been almost up on the bank for most of a day. They sat with it for a while, and talked to it, and politely asked if they could have his watch. Carter told Donnie that kids didn't die, only older people, and that this kid was just tired and sick or maybe a mannequin. The kid seemed to say yes about the watch, even though his face was down in the mud. After a heavy rain, the body slid back down. They were disappointed not to find it. Carter told Donnie that the other arm grew back and then the boy got up and walked away.

The boys aren't trying to go anywhere, they are simply moving, and they keep going until they see the swimming pool. They walk to it without taking their eyes from it. They both sit on the edge, put their bare legs in, and then their bodies drop into the water with a splash.

Donnie has copied Carter when he shouldn't have. It is the deep end; the water is a whole foot and a half higher than he is tall. He fights at first, tries to kick himself higher, but the kicks only pull him down. He can't breathe and his eyes are open. He sees his feet. He stops fighting. He goes limp.

He feels himself being pulled. At first, just across, and then upwards. He blinks. There is sun in his eyes. Water pours from his nose and mouth. He starts to sputter and cry.

"You need a swimming lesson," says Carter. "I could teach you. The first thing is, just don't never swim where you can't stand up all the way. Not 'til you're twelve years old."

"You're not twelve," says Donnie. He stops crying.

"I'm different from you. I'm like a older person."

FOURTEEN

THE CAKE IS CHILLED enough. Ida is ready to cut the rectangular layer in half, the long way. It's tricky work. She sets it on the bakery counter and measures the layer with a ruler, adding ten toothpicks to help her keep track of the halfway point. Using the sharpest knife she's ever held, she aims and hits her target. She holds her breath until she gets all the way across. Pretty good.

She slides the top of the layer onto a piece of cardboard that she cut to fit the cake, and takes the two thin layers to the walk-in to chill again. In half an hour, she will add the raspberry-lemon filling, and put one layer on top of the other. Next will be the buttercream crumb coat, and then it will go back into the walk-in. After that, she still has to do the final layer of buttercream, making sure it is as smooth as a bedsheet. Before she leaves for the day, she will decorate it with the silver and pearl candies, the golden sugar wedding bell, and then, with pastry tips and chocolate icing, trace the cake's border and write *Happy 50ᵗʰ Anniversary Roberta and Melvin* in a practiced script. Already she feels proud. Her forearms are sore from the stiff way she has to hold the frosting spatula and pastry bag. This is her third attempt at fulfilling the order.

J.B. Higgins told her she was doing a decent job. He had no idea that she'd totally quit making the éclairs and cream puffs. She never really liked either of them, and the filling was a huge pain in the ass.

She yanked the little signs for them out of the pastry case and tossed them into the trash.

This is serious business. With all the other baking she did in Aster, she was pretty much done as soon as whatever she made was out of the oven. It smelled good and looked like it was supposed to look, more or less. Maybe, with cupcakes, for instance, or cinnamon buns, you needed to do a little bit of work afterwards, but not much. A swirl of icing, a dollop of frosting were all that they required. She didn't have to be a beautician.

The work that is cake-making doesn't even begin until the cake is out of the oven and has already cooled. They are supposed to look so gorgeous that you almost hate to cut a piece, and while the taste and moisture matter, they are secondary. It's all about that first look. Ida will have to saw some of the top layer off where the cake peaked in the oven. After that, it might still be a little uneven, but she has just figured out how to build it up with frosting, and, after it gets firm enough, even more frosting, until it looks level.

So much artifice. No cake is ever perfect. Every single cake has a back, where mistakes hide out.

Chilling the cakes between steps is the secret. It cuts down on crumbs and lets the first coat of icing harden enough so that the next coat is smooth.

"Well," J.B. says, when he comes by at the end of the day. "That looks like the real deal." He stands for a while with his hand on his chin. "Maybe we should take some pictures."

He gets his camera from the customer service desk. They set the cake carefully down on overlapping doilies.

"Why do you want to take a picture?" she says.

"I'll put one in next week's circular," he says, stepping back, adjusting the lens. "Get the word out."

The day after the circular goes out, Ida gets a call from the assisted living center in Vernon, just north of Valponia, telling her how much the director loved the cake at her aunt's anniversary party the day before. *So rich. Next month, we'll be placing an order for our big Halloween party. There are usually a hundred and fifty people.*

"No problem," says Ida, as she makes note of the things she will need to order: marzipan for pumpkins and cats, orange candy confetti. The marzipan will take some learning, but it can't be any harder than Play-Dough. She can do a sheet cake with a small second tier, and use black food coloring to make it as dark as night. It will look great with a raspberry filling. Like blood.

When Ida puts down the phone, she realizes that she will be in New York City long before Halloween. She'll get to see the leaves turn yellow and orange and blow off the branches and into the streets, the way they are supposed to. Poor J.B. She thinks of the way he brings her a cup of coffee in the morning, like he is her coach, and says, *Have a little fuel, champ. The hard part's over.*

And her house, the comfortable bed, the refrigerator and stove. How Ryan and Lloyd came in and sweated and lifted just for her. It is almost a shame that they had gone to such trouble, but it really did make a difference. At night, she is comforted by the buzzing of the refrigerator now, and she can turn on her little radio and listen to talk shows when she can't sleep. It takes her mind off the blue tarp and its steady, unnerving breathing.

WHEN CORINNE ARRIVES FOR her shift, she puts her hand on Ida's shoulder.

"You were so good to me about my taking time off," she says. "Why don't you go home early? You deserve it. I'll clock you out myself."

Ida looks at the clock. It isn't even one, but she is done for the day.

"You're going to clock me out?" she says. "Is that what Jesus would do?"

"He's the one who told me I should do it."

Ida likes the way the two of them run things together. She takes care of the early part of the day, and Corinne takes care of the later part. When Ida comes into Karr's in the mornings, she finds the bakery pristinely clean, the work surfaces ready for her.

She bags up the nine donuts that are left over from the morning.

She will put them in her refrigerator, even though she knows that most of them will disappear again. The boys are going into her house while she is at work, leaving their muddy footprints, a dirty bathtub ring, taking her food.

Before Ida leaves for home, she goes to the back aisle and picks out two children's shorts and t-shirt sets, clipped together on white hangers. She stops at the bin of canvas sneakers and picks out two pairs that look like they might fit. At the register, she hesitates. It is twenty dollars, after all, and twenty dollars was unbelievably precious just a short time ago.

She stops at the pay phone on the way out.

We're not home, says Linda's outgoing message, *so spit it out.*

"It's me," says Ida. "I just wanted to make sure you know I'm definitely still coming. Really soon. I can send you my rent deposit if you want."

On the wall over the phone, Ida sees a flyer:

Lost. $100 Reward offered for a truly special bracelet.

Under that, a basic drawing of a small string of beads with a rectangular clasp. A phone number. Ida sets the phone receiver back down and leaves the store. And though a small part of her is picturing this very bracelet, in the same patch of grass where she found it, the rest of her mind overrules it and pushes the image away, because thinking about it is a reminder that she still is the kind of person to take something that isn't hers. Who was going to sell the thing she stole.

She will bring it back. Maybe even knock on the door and tell her that she found it.

SHE HEARS HIM RIDE up behind her.

He is next to her, his forearms covered in shiny dust, streaked with the salt of dried sweat. He smiles at her, the same smile he smiled that day as he hurled orange peels from the tree house.

"What do *you* want?"

"Hey," he says.

"Go to hell," she smiles back.

"I'm Peter," he says. "And there's no need for verbal violence."

"There's no need for throwing stuff at little kids. Something is wrong with you."

He shrugs.

"Seriously," she says. "Someone must have dropped you on your head."

"I've had it with their trespassing," he says. "They've been up in my tree house too many times. Taking things, breaking things. They leave their grubby fingerprints on everything."

"Huh," she says, disappointed that this is something she can relate to. "Then why'd you throw them at me?"

"Guilt by association," he snaps. "Look, I was teasing you. You look like you'd make a good goalie and I wanted to find out if I was right."

"What does a good goalie look like?"

"It was an orange peel. Not a hand grenade. Anyway, I'm going to the ocean if you want to come along." His tone is annoyingly confident, as though the only thing she can possibly say is yes.

"Why would I go with you?"

"It's a nice day," he says. "Come on."

"OK," she says. "How far is it?" She wants to see the ocean, to see something different.

"Thirty minutes, maybe. The afternoon is the best time of day for swimming."

"I almost forgot there was an ocean near here," she says. "You know? It doesn't look like there could be one so close."

He is tight-lipped and stiff again, facing every direction but hers. Like he will only participate in the parts of the conversation that he initiates.

She doesn't really care. The beach! He will show her how to get there.

"I need to get out of my work clothes, though." She starts pedaling toward home and watches him ride ahead of her at full speed, his head down and his eyes on the pavement. Halfway down the street, he makes a U-turn and comes back, still at full speed. When she gets to her house, she has the idea of making him wait and then telling him that she changed her mind. Or maybe just not coming out of her house at all. She wonders how long he'll wait before he gives up and rides off alone.

The problem is that she wants to go.

She leans the bike against the house and goes inside. An envelope was slipped under her door. The note inside reads *Cause Celebre! Lloyd's paintings are going to be in an art show and since we can't be there, we're having our own party, right here in Fort Starlight.*

She sets the card down and puts on cut-off shorts and a t-shirt. She pushes two dollar bills, thin and soft, in her front pocket. It is money for a bottle or two of water and the only cash she has. Everything else is in the bank.

She sits down on the floor and watches him through the window as he rides back and forth. While he rides with speed and purpose, there is nothing about the way he takes the turns that shows impatience.

She steps out of the house just as he is coming her way. He slows. Ida sees the corner of his mouth turn up and he gestures with a tilt of his head.

"Follow me," he calls, and rides ahead.

It is only a few minutes before all she can see of him are the beige stripes of the backs of his calves.

She wants to go to the ocean and look out at it, smell the seaweed and brine. Ida can feel her future. For real this time; it is just the tiniest bit ahead of her.

After the second turn, she almost loses sight of Peter's legs, his blue hat. She has to pedal like mad just to spot him again.

She pants, wipes the sweat from her hairline. They are beyond all of the roads that she knows, far more quickly than she knew it was possible to leave them behind. He is making her sprint, something she would never force herself to repeat on her own. Her thighs are on fire. She grits her teeth and pumps her legs until she is straining for breath. She almost catches up with him; for a minute, she is close enough that she can see the back of his neck, sweat-slick in the sun. Not once, though, does he look back to see if she is there.

The struggle quickly becomes evident: she has to keep him in sight while remaining calm enough to not fall off the bike; she has to not have a heart attack from pedaling so furiously.

Because she does not entirely know her way back.

She is on an access road, with no cars or people, no sign that anyone has been there in the recent past. Sweat drips into her eyes. There is no way that Ida can keep up this pace; she stops pedaling until she slows down enough to squeeze the brakes.

"Peter!" She yells as loudly as she can. Her voice shrieks across the sky.

Ida's blood pulses in her wet temples. She sets the bike on its side and collapses on the pavement, her shoulders heaving. She leans over, retching, but nothing comes out. She stretches out on the grass and tries to slow her breathing. She counts to ten, to twenty, thirty, breathes. A breeze touches her brow and the sun doesn't seem as punishing. She feels a little better. After a moment, she gets back up and on the bike again—cursing under her breath—so that she will have a chance of finding him.

"Fucker," she mutters. She will not turn around and try to get back. She will find the beach at her own pace.

Why didn't he stick around to see her bad fortune play itself out? Wasn't that the whole point? Maybe he is watching her from somewhere, willing her to go the wrong way, or hoping she will flatten her tire on a piece of broken glass. She never should have gone with him. He probably figured she'd give up and just sit there, waiting for a rescue that wouldn't come.

Not her. It is better to move than not. She keeps going, watching for glass on the road, riding in the direction that feels right. The air gets cooler and dries her sweat. The nausea is gone and she finds herself able to ride a little faster. The wind is at her back, pushing her on. The road forks and she sees bicycle tire tracks on the dust in the pavement.

She thinks she smells seawater.

The road ends and a new, narrower one begins. The greenery is thick here, and sweet-smelling. Tall trees drip with purple flowers. A road sign indicates that Erne City is two miles ahead. There are far more cars on the roads than she has seen anywhere near Fort Starlight: pick-up trucks, convertibles, vans, driven by busy and purposeful people. Two trucks pull trailers for jet-skis. A car honks at her; a man waves. "Keep on riding, baby!" the man yells.

She does.

She sees a green road sign that says *Erne City Island Bridge Ahead* and then the bridge spanning a wide inlet. On her last trip to Erne City, she went over this same bridge; how had she had not noticed that she had been on an island? She pumps her legs up the slight incline, and sees the inlet spread out ahead of her, a thick, navy blue body of water, and the long, slender island, as though a piece of the mainland has been snipped off with scissors. In the inlet are a half dozen wave-runners and jet skis, their riders chasing the wakes of the motorboats to catch a moment of air.

In the middle of the bridge is a stone tower, and inside of it, a man staring down the path of the inlet. A long barge approaches the bridge. The light on the top of the tower changes from green to flashing red, and a white barrier comes down, bringing the cars to a stop. The drawbridge rises. She gets off the bike and leans against the railing. The trucks, station wagons, long sedans, and motorcycles line up, waiting. All eyes are on the barge as it slowly passes below. The men on the barge's deck wave up to the people watching.

Finally, the bridge sinks slowly into place. The people in the cars honk and clap their hands, and the man in the tower, controlling everything, salutes them.

Ida rides to the land on the other side, where the saltwater smell fills her nose. She follows the curve of the road and looks across the water at the mainland. Here, sand edges both sides of the asphalt, and the cars that pass her do so carefully, moving to the center of the road. She rides through the town, passing the dentist's office, peach-colored condominiums, the diner where she ate breakfast, an ice cream shop, the hotel where she spent those three nights, Laughter Cay. She sees wooden houses on stilts, great big pink conch shells on the porches, frayed nautical ropes wrapped around the banisters.

The houses thin out. Ida sees a clearing to the left, and a path that leads to the beach. She gets off the bike and follows it on foot, struggling with the handlebars wobbling through the sand.

And there it is in front of her: the grey-blue water, tumbling softly. The only other people on the beach are so far down the shore that she can't even guess at gender.

Seagulls squawk overhead. A great big one screeches as it dives into the water with fury and determination. The bird doesn't come up for a long while, and when it does, it has a silver fish in its bill. Other seagulls beg and bully.

Ida drops the bicycle in the sand, takes the dollar bills out of her shorts and stuffs them into the toes of her sneakers. She walks, barefoot, toward the water, feeling cooked from the inside. The sand burns.

She walks through the warm water. With every step she takes, a cloud of sand rises before settling around her toes. Crushed scallop and clamshells crunch under her feet. She thinks of pearls. Of the bracelet. She still has not brought it back. Shit. She needs to write herself a note so that she doesn't forget.

Ida is so sticky and hot that she can't resist going further than calf-deep. She isn't going to swim, though. She isn't going to go deep enough that anything will have the chance to get her. Once she is up to her knees, she considers turning back, worried about the killer whales, the sharks. She'd once seen a show on television about killer whales. One of them came right up onto the beach, almost completely out of the water, and snatched away two baby seals while their mothers groaned from the shore.

She can see her feet, still. The water is so clear and the waves so gentle that she scans the shore in front of her and sees nothing but sand.

She goes on for a few more feet, and sees that the water is getting lower again. She is walking through tidal pools. She looks left and right; there are sand bars everywhere: flat, smooth strips, matte against the shining surface. It is low tide. The real waves are far, far out. Ida walks through a half dozen warm pools before she finds a deeper one, one where the water reaches all the way up to her mid-chest.

The water has been trapped for hours, and is warmed by the sun.

She doesn't feel refreshed yet.

Tiny, translucent crabs skitter across the bottom and she lifts up her feet, treading water, watching them, as well as a small school of tiny white fish. A slender, slate-colored sea snake curls around itself, straightens out again, nowhere to go. Whenever she moves in its direction, it backs away from her.

Ida is still hot. She climbs up out of the tidal pool and walks on a few steps, hoping to find a bigger, deeper pool, one that won't be so warm. But just a few more steps beyond that last pool is the drop off to the open ocean. She stands on the edge and looks down. She can't see anything in this deep, dark water. She dips her toe and the water is beautifully cool. She lowers herself into it. Just for a second.

It charges her limbs and reminds her that there are other places, other seasons. In Aster, the leaves are already red and orange and falling.

She straightens her legs, but can't feel the bottom.

She can climb back out. She will. In a minute. First, she needs this cool water all around her. God, it feels good. Weightless and clean. She wishes she'd taken off her clothes.

Steeling herself with a deep inhalation, Ida pushes herself underneath the surface. She forces herself further down with her arms, at first only to where the water covers her head, then further. And further. Her toes don't touch anything and her hair streams out above her. When she opens her eyes underwater, they burn. All is darkness. She thinks about baptisms in the water, how you have to be pushed under and then everything is new the second you pop back up. Then she thinks of the woman in the movie, trapped under the surface of the water, and raises her arms and kicks her legs.

The light of the sun is so bright when she surfaces. She sucks in the air and tastes salt on her lips. A small, soft wave rushes across her shoulders. She is facing a different continent. Africa.

As she treads water, her legs gently scissor kicking, something large and smooth brushes her foot. It touches her heel and feels solid and endless. She pulls her foot away and reaches, frantically, for the sand bar behind her. She scrambles up the sand bar, pulling with her hands, and lifts herself clumsily out of the water.

Once she is safely standing, Ida looks down. A gentle rippling under the surface gets bigger, faster. She stares at it, waiting for whatever it is to surface, but it never does. The ripples disappear.

She wipes the sand off her feet as well as she can, gets her shoes on. She feels the dollar bills, soft under her toes as she wheels her bike back to the pavement. When Ida pushes off down the street, she whoops loudly, with a joy she can't quite identify. Somewhere up above, a seagull calls back.

She should stop somewhere and ask somebody for directions back, even though she believes that she can find her way home on her own. She'll follow the shore road and then the access road until she gets back to the outskirts of Fort Starlight. When she gets home, she will grab her bank card and ride out to Karr's and grab something special to make herself for dinner. A steak or a piece of salmon. She has been cooking for herself lately, real dinners; the stove and refrigerator give her something to look forward to.

Even though the road looks flat, she finds herself coasting. It is so effortless. Her clothes begin to dry as the air hits them. She passes the tree that drips with purple flowers. She looks down at her forearms, how they are stretched over the handlebars. The veins on the backs of her hands are prominent, full of her blood.

She can still feel the ocean water moving across her legs, the push and pull of the tide.

FIFTEEN

IDA HEARS ANOTHER BICYCLE'S wheels behind her. Peter flies past her before slowing down enough that she catches up with him without trying.

He grins at her. "You found it by yourself. Good girl."

"I did," she says.

"Don't get huffy, now."

"Huffy. Huh," she says. She considers the situation. She knows that she is supposed to be angry with him. For whatever reason, that's what he wants. He left her behind. But the only anger she can attach to it is weak, and what is there is dreamlike, faraway, and underwater.

What she does feel is clean, perfect exhaustion.

"You'll get over it. Look what you accomplished!" Behind his sunglasses, he is beaming.

"Yep."

"You really have no reason to complain. It's a flat course."

"I don't remember the part where I complained."

He shrugs. "I had a feeling you could do it on your own."

"You're tons of fun," Ida says. "Anyone ever tell you that?" She pushes past him. No cars are coming, so she moves to the center of the road. An ice cream cone would be perfect. She may have to make the choice between that and a bottle of water. Maybe the ice cream place will give her a few cups of tap water for free.

He passes her again. "You hungry?"

She says nothing, and he floats along next to her, waiting for her to answer. She is so hungry. So empty. The only thing she has eaten so far today is a walnut brownie in the middle of her morning shift. She offers a vague nod.

"Why don't we get you something to eat?" He points to May Belle's Crab Shack, its wooden sign giving a faux ramshackle impression. "This is a decent spot, right here."

"I don't have any money on me," she says.

"I'll take care of it," he says, and glides ahead of her before turning into the drive.

They are seated outside on a wooden deck. The view is of the inlet, of the boats moving along it. The tables and chairs are made of a thin plastic that, on a windy day, if they weren't chained to the wood and to each other, could easily blow right into the water. The sun has moved to the far side of the sky.

"I'll pay you back," she says. "Though I'd have to go to the bank."

"It's on me."

"Okay," Ida shrugs. It's his money. If he wants to spend it on her, she will let him.

She leans back against the chair, wondering if she should stand up and tell him never mind, she isn't hungry after all, because if she stays here much longer, it will start to get dark before she can get home. There are no street lights on the roads that lead to Fort Starlight, and there is no way she will be able to remember, in the dark, the way she came. Enough challenges for one day.

He has his mirrored sunglasses on. When she looks at him, she stares at her own face.

"The only thing is that if I stay," she says to her reflection, "you have to help me find home. I don't know the way. Not in the dark."

"Fine," he says, "That's not a problem." He opens his menu. "I'll ride with you all the way back."

"All the way? Without taking off on me? I'm tired. I want to ride back slow."

"I said I would."

"You'd better," she says, opening hers.

May Belle's fare is simple: fish, hamburgers, steaks. Ida can't find crab anywhere on the menu. The waitress comes by to let them know that the special is gator, marinated, dipped in sourdough batter, deep-fried, and served with a garlic sauce.

"She'll take that."

"No, I won't," she says. "I'll take the fish and chips."

He holds his hand out, to keep the waitress from taking her seriously enough to write it down. "You don't want that. The cod isn't even from around here. Get the gator. At least it's native. It'll go down nicely with a glass of white."

"Are you telling me what I should order?" says Ida. "Don't you think that's a little weird?"

"I've had it. It's the best thing here," he says.

"Is it?"

The waitress writes it down. "And what would *you* like?"

"Bring a couple glasses of Chardonnay. I won't be eating." He waves her away.

Ida turns to him. "You won't be eating?"

He shakes his head. "I ate this morning."

"It's almost nighttime," she says.

The waitress sets down two cups of water and two glasses of white wine.

Ida watches the inlet. On the far side, there is a thick ripple on the surface, but this side is smooth as glass.

"Why do you care what I have to eat anyway?" she says. "Why do you care if I order the worst thing here?"

"Listen," he says. "It's an alligator. You need to do your part to make them extinct. I don't know why people put so much energy into saving predators. Where's the logic in that? If you can get rid of them, do it. They would never be so patronizing with us if they had opposable thumbs. Or if they could use technology."

She shrugs in reluctant agreement.

"I sure hope it tastes like chicken." She is having lizard for dinner.

She drinks her water in two chugs and is still thirsty.

"*Alligator mississippiensis.* It's a beautiful animal, from an engineering standpoint. Miserable, though. Hungry and lazy and irritable. I suppose there's nothing else to be in a swamp." He takes a sip of the wine, swishes it around his mouth. His Adam's apple bobs as he swallows.

She lifts her wine glass to her lips and it is so cool and wet that she drinks all of it down in a few seconds.

"That was probably stupid of me," she says.

A small fishing boat putters by. One man drives, and two others sit at the back, their bare feet skimming the surface of the water.

"So you know those kids, the ones I was with that day?" she says. "You see them around a lot?"

"I know them enough," he says. "I know that they're up in my tree house every chance they get. If they fall, and they definitely will, eventually, I'll get sued. That's the world we live in. I don't have the patience for a couple of uneducated parents who hope their kids get hurt just enough that they can finally call one of those TV lawyers and have a big payday."

"I feel sort of bad for them," she says. "Their folks don't take care of them." The wind blows her hair into her eyes. From far off somewhere, she hears the soft clang of wind chimes.

"I've always thought that parents shouldn't name their children. They should leave them nameless, make them earn them. See how they turn out, first."

"If that was how it worked," she says "your name would be something like…oh, I dunno," she closes her eyes, as though she needs to concentrate, "…*flatulence.*"

She opens her eyes and laughs at her own joke. He doesn't laugh back, and this makes her laugh harder. And harder. She throws her head back and cackles at the pale sky.

The gator is cut into strips. She holds a piece with her fingers, blows on it, thinking of the one she saw in the canal with the bird it caught in its jaws. She takes a bite and it is pungent and ropy. Not quite delicious, but still good.

"Didn't I tell you? In the meat, you can taste the swamp, and you can taste that it was furious about getting caught. If you pay attention. If you're the kind of person who can pay attention."

"This one doesn't taste surprised," she says. "It tastes like it had a headache and a Charlie-horse and was tired of how its life was going anyway."

She smiles. He doesn't. Of course not. The sun is low, turning the water to gold. Ida looks down at her arms, how her skin is bathed in that golden light.

"Also, like he really wants to get out of the swamp and do something different with his life."

The waitress comes out to check on them.

"How about a bottle this time?" Ida says to the waitress.

To him, "If people can change, so can alligators."

He shakes his head, irritated. "People can't change. For a day. Or maybe even a few weeks, but then, it's right back to being who they really are."

The sun isn't touching him; he is just out of its range.

"I've changed," she says, picturing herself in a sleek white blouse, walking down the New York City street with a bag of peaches under her arm, her wrists dripping with thin metal bangles, the chunky Doc Marten boots on her feet, off to make her pies. It feels real now.

He shakes his head. "Permanent change is the only change that counts. And the only way you can count on permanent change happening is if you have a few thousand years to spare. Only if you can wait around for evolution. Otherwise, you're stuck. Be glad you got to be around to experience your opposable thumbs."

"Didn't you just say something about opposable thumbs?" says Ida. "Just a few minutes ago?"

"Did I?" he frowns.

"You need some new lines." Ida reaches out and pats him on the elbow.

Since he is paying, Ida wants dessert. She thinks of dark chocolate and whether or not there is any way to get the sharp, bitter, midnight taste of it to come across in an actual cake. Not the frosting, but the heart of it, the whole thing. Other than mixing in chunks of it in, she can't think how. It seems that the necessary butter and milk and eggs would leach out that essence. Maybe if she cuts the sugar by half.

He taps the table with his fingertips. "What we consider a genius nowadays will someday be a person of average intelligence. Someone like me will be, well, someone like her."

"You're a genius?" she says. "Why didn't you just tell me that sooner? I would have been using bigger words."

The waitress places a laminated dessert menu between them. She is sleepy. She could put her head in her arms and fall asleep right here.

"Where did you grow up?" he says.

"I could tell you anything right now," she says, gesturing grandly with one arm. "But I've had too much wine to think up a good lie. I came from a faraway land, in a shitty place with awful people for parents. And I don't mean the kind of awful that is actually pretty good."

"What sort of awful do you mean?" he says.

She catches herself about to say it all, to tell her story. He doesn't really want to know anything more about her. He asked, though.

"I'm all alone in the world." She spits out a short laugh. "That sounded dramatic, but I guess…it is."

Peter looks at his hands.

She sniffs hard; she isn't going to cry. Things are great now, so there is no reason.

"You'll die alone. So will everyone. There is no way around that. And so will I. Just think of it this way: if you're already alone, you are better prepared for it."

"Thanks," she says. "You can always count on a guy who lives in a tree house to make you feel better." She lifts her glass in a toast and takes a sip.

He starts to say something, but he stops, turning his head toward the water.

Ida closes her eyes. Dying alone. She sees it as if it really happened, if it had gone differently here: her dead body, found in that unfinished house of hers. It could have happened that way. Maybe it almost had. Months would have gone by before she was found—because who would realize she was missing, and who would know to look for her?—and then, once the police had figured out who she was, her mother would be notified. She can see them, knocking at the door, the rotten porch wood almost giving way, her mother ignoring the sound at first, thinking it was a bill collector.

But they would keep knocking, just as that policeman had, and Josie Overdorff would eventually let them in. And this would cause a definite blip in her mother's otherwise shapeless day, but really would just give Josie one more reason to feel sorry for herself, how unlucky she had been her whole life, except for the occasional scratch-off win. Poor thing.

Kids are a chance to change; there is the swell of the belly, the anticipation, right? How come that didn't change her?

Her father would find out through some grapevine and it would be just another push toward some ratty country road liquor store's off-brand gin.

And Robert, the only one who would care, would never even know.

The waitress walks over, the sky pink behind her. Dusk is moving in.

"What's good?" says Ida.

"Key Lime pie," the waitress says. "You'll definitely want a piece of that. We get it from a place on Key West. It's won all sorts of awards."

Ida nods. "Two forks," she says. "Hey," she turns to Peter. "You with the shades. Einstein, there isn't any sun anymore."

He takes the sunglasses off, raises his eyebrows exaggeratedly. His eyes are an ordinary blue and slightly slanted, a hint of an occipital fold. The skin around them is very white, not tan like the rest of him. His eyes are naked.

The waitress sets the pie down on the table between them. It is yellow instead of the green she expected. Thick, with a dollop of cream on top.

"To tell you the truth, I think it's a little weird that you talk about all that natural selection stuff and what the future world will be like in a few thousand years. What do you care? I mean, it's not like you'll ever know for sure." She was going to keep going, but she feels guilty. Here he is, naked-eyed, paying for her meal.

She reaches over and grabs a fork, spears the point of the pie and pops it into her mouth. The tartness moves along her tongue and to her brain, waking her up.

"I like this place," she says, taking another bite.

"It isn't the very worst view on earth," he says. "But there are much better ones."

"You're not going to have any?"

He looks at her.

Ida takes a forkful of pie and holds the fork in front of him, wondering if he'll push it away. She is in his personal space and she knows that he isn't comfortable with it.

He looks at her warily, opens his mouth, clamps his lips down and pulls his head back from the fork, leaving it clean. His nostrils are neat slits. She locks eyes with him as he moves his jaw, swallows. He nods for a second before shaking his head.

Fairy lights come on; the patio grows festive. It is almost dark now. She looks around and notices a dozen or so people. When had they all sat down?

Conversations are going on at the tables around them.

Couldn't stand him anyway. I always knew that something like this was going to happen. And a girl of fifteen!

I never loved her like she loved me.

I had good legs when I was a girl.

"The guy who owns this place," says Peter, folding and unfolding the arms of his sunglasses. "His name is Chuck. He's a treasure hunter. He's trying to find gold at the site of some old wreck off the Dominican Republic. A few years ago, an old millionaire set up this contest to find an heir, and Chuck won it. He worked on a map, and had these cryptic clues in Greek, Mandarin, Old English. Chuck went from one university language department to the next, trying to figure them out. Two months later, he found himself on a riverboat on the Mississippi River. There, in the bottom deck, was a small door, a curtain, and behind that, a tiny key on a glass table."

"I didn't know things like that existed," Ida says. "Is Chuck a genius, too?" She regrets her tone. He had been so tight when they first sat down, so sharp-angled and trying to be dominant, and now, in comparison, he looks a little worn out.

"Not quite. But he wanted to get rich and he did it. He's about to open a resort. It's being built a couple of miles from here. Almost done, from what I've seen."

When the waitress sets down the bill, Peter takes it. He hands the waitress five or six twenty-dollar bills. "I don't need change." The waitress smiles at him. It must have been a good tip.

In the parking lot, he says, "Are you ready?"

"Yep," she says.

They get on their bicycles and pedal off.

It is getting dark. She concentrates on moving forward. The sound of Peter's bicycle, just ahead of her, is steady. He isn't going to leave her behind. He slows down so that they are even.

"It really is a fantastic stretch of beach," he says. "So many drop offs that trap all sorts of good things. In the tidal pools, at night, there are these microscopic creatures that give off an incredible light. When you move your hands to part the water, it's like you're parting the heavens."

Holding the handlebar steady with one hand, she puts her other one up. The stars are bright enough that she can see the outline of her fingertips against them.

She rides on. She is floating. It is a different world here when the sky is dark and quiet, when she can't feel her body. She could turn on the flashlight still tied to her handlebar, but she doesn't quite need it yet.

When she is moving over roads with fresh asphalt, the ones that she knows lead nearer to her house, Peter says, "We don't need creature comforts, you and I. We can survive with whatever we have."

She almost forgot that she isn't alone.

"I like creature comforts," she says. "You've got me wrong."

"But you can do without. You have discipline."

She chuckles. "Discipline sure as hell isn't the reason I've been stuck in the middle of nowhere."

He says, "Just…neither of us are the kind of people who need others to tell us who we are."

She doesn't answer because she is thinking again of the day Robert left. She can still see him there, sitting on his bed and not meeting her eye. *Did I ever tell you about how they gave me away?* Robert had said, chewing his forefinger.

This upset her. He had never said *me* before. It had always been *us*.

It was in the summer. They pulled me out of bed in the middle of the night and they drove me to that orphanage in Cahill. This nun took me to this room full of beds and I went to sleep there. The next day, they changed their minds and came back and got me.

This isn't the way he usually told the story.

She always tried to believe everything Robert said, no matter what. She believed every iteration of his story of them at the orphanage. Always, she had been right there with him, given away, too. When it happened, it was just after a blizzard; it was the end of August; it was the ides of March. It was for a few hours or for a few days. She had reconciled the differences by creating an image in her head of trees full of apples and dark leaves, surrounded by knee-deep piles of snow, a nun holding her brother by the hand, and her watching all of it happen from a window. The nun said to Robert, *Take one for your sister*, and hoisted him up to a branch so that he could pluck another. For a long time, she even was able to conjure up a memory of biting into the apple, and felt the juice moving through the spaces between her teeth.

Of course he wanted to believe he could fly, that he had flown, that he had seen something as perfectly reassuring as a unicorn munching muddy Overdorff grass at the bottom of Door Hill.

The whole orphanage story had likely been a fuzzy dream that Robert made real by repetition; he needed bigger villains for parents than the apathetic ones they'd gotten. It had been so easy to believe him; there was always a little bit of truth to the stories. There really had been hoof prints in the yard, though likely just deer. And there really had been an orphanage in Cahill, but maybe he'd just looked at the orphanage's sign as they drove by, and projected everything he wanted onto it. And maybe, once he made up his mind to get out, he turned on her the way he had because he needed to see her as part of the problem. Otherwise, he wouldn't have been able to leave.

"I knew that about me," Peter says, bringing her back to the darkness. "I didn't know that about you."

"Didn't know what?" She flips on the flashlight.

He doesn't answer.

There is her house. The moon shines brightly enough that she can make out the gleam on the tarp as it breathes. Ida stops pedaling and drags her sneaker on the ground to stop.

"Peter," she says, remembering to thank him for buying her dinner, to tell him that maybe he isn't quite the sociopath she thought, but she can already hear the soft whiz of the gears on his bicycle as he rides away. His voice, his profile, all of him became soft once the sun disappeared. What had happened? Something. A warm wind touches her cheek.

SIXTEEN

RYAN AND LLOYD'S HOUSE seems miles away. She holds a cake in her aching, outstretched forearms. Walking was a terrible idea. She moves as quickly as she can because the frosting is all butter.

Bad timing. The clouds are already rolling in.

"Hurry up, you guys," she yells.

Carter and Donnie, dressed in the short sets and sneakers Ida bought them, follow behind her. From time to time, they slow down or stop, looking at a bug or a rock, and the next moment, they run to catch up with her, surprising her each time, making the cake's balance on her arms even more precarious.

The cake is a surprise for Lloyd, and she is extraordinarily proud of it. She ordered the pan from Karr's with the sole purpose of using it to make this cake. She bought herself a hand mixer for fifteen dollars, though she knows that once she gets settled in New York City, she will have to buy a real mixer, one that will take up too much space on the kitchen counter and cost a few hundred bucks.

Yesterday, Ida invited the boys, right after she walked out into the field where they were playing to give them the sneakers and clothes.

"You have to ask permission," she told them. "Don't just pretend to ask. I don't want to get in trouble with your folks."

The boys were filthier than she had ever seen them. "And you have to take a bath, first. It's the rule of the party. Not just you two. Everyone who's coming has to take one. Okay? And in your house. Not mine."

They didn't answer. Donnie had green boogers caked in his nostrils.

It was a mistake. Something had taken over her brain when she made the offer, but she was too afraid of their disappointment to take it back. What would Ryan and Lloyd do when she showed up with them?

The boys opened her door just after ten that morning.

"They said we could come," said Carter, his hand on the door. "And we could stay as long as we want."

"They said we could sleep over, too," said Donnie.

"Well, you can't sleep over," she said, wiping her hand on the front of her shorts. "And it's way too early to be here. I told you that the party doesn't start until three. Don't you have that watch?"

"I don't know how to use it," said Carter.

"I'm busy making a cake. Come back when your watch says 2:30." She pointed to the face of his watch. "That means a two there, and then a three and a zero here. And weren't you supposed to get cleaned up?"

Ida shooed them away and closed the door. She pulled the cake out of the oven. It needed to cool enough for her to frost it, and it wouldn't fit in the refrigerator. The cake pan was shaped like an enormous fish, and she was going to decorate it with stripes in dark blue, light blue, and yellow gum paste. Crushed dark chocolate flakes where the fins fanned out. A marzipan eye with a licorice pupil.

The sweet, light smell filled the rooms of the house. Baking here had changed the house, made it friendlier.

When the cake was ready and it was almost time to think about leaving, she opened her door again and there the boys were, sitting in silence on the concrete step.

She quit Karr's a week and a half ago, giving J.B. just two weeks' notice. When she told him that she needed to speak to him in his office, he looked squarely at her and clasped his hands together.

"I know what you're going to say and I just want you to know that I am already disappointed beyond belief."

"I can give you two weeks," she said.

"Well thank you very much for that great kindness."

"I'm really sorry."

"I thought I finally had somebody who would stick around. Now it's back to square one." He tugged at his collar and started to walk off.

"I know that this stinks for you," she said. "I need to move on."

"That's alright," he sighed. "I suppose this job isn't the be-all and end-all for anyone who can actually do it."

"STAY HERE A SECOND," she says, walking inside the house, past the boys. Obediently, they stand on the welcome mat and wait.

She leans in toward Ryan. "I did something stupid," she whispers. "I should have asked you, first. Just…can they have some cake? I'll take them home after."

"Don't worry," he says, shaking his head and opening the door wide.

Empty balloons are scattered on the kitchen counter. Several are blown up and are floating along the floor, bobbing gently on the tile.

"They're killing our cheeks," says Ryan. "These are the toughest balloons I've ever encountered."

"Oh God, you made this?" Lloyd says. He takes the cake and sets it on the counter. "Of course you did. How did you even get it here? I would have picked you up."

"It's too big," she says, smiling proudly at it. "I'm embarrassed. I don't know where you're going to put it all."

"Too much cake is not a bad problem to have," says Ryan.

"We're great cake eaters," says Carter, his hands on his hips, and Ida thinks he looks like a tiny business man, the rough-shaven, scotch-drinking kind.

"What flavor is it?" Ryan asks.

"Don't worry. It's not fish flavored," says Donnie. "It's vanilla. And lemon inside."

Carter had asked on the way, and when Ida told him, he nodded slowly, like she had chosen well.

"Great news about your show, Lloyd. I'm happy for you."

"Thanks," he says. "I doubt I'll sell any, but still. It feels good to be part of the world again."

Carter leans back against the counter, his arms crossed over his front as though he is one of the grown-ups, too. Donnie pulls at their silverware drawer, opening and closing it, slowly, without any banging. Just a slow, gentle sliding. They had cleaned themselves up. A little bit.

Ryan picks up an un-inflated balloon and takes a deep breath before starting to blow it up. He gets a few breaths in before his cheeks give out. He pinches the end with his finger, trapping the little bit of air inside. "This is really hard. Maybe you two can help me? Please?" The boys move forward, their hands reaching out for balloons.

Lloyd comes back with the camera and a blue gift bag with a white ribbon tied onto the handle. Tissue paper peeks out over the top.

"It's nothing big," he grins. "Don't get too excited."

"You guys are too much," Ida says.

Inside, a silver bracelet, plain and small. She puts it on her left wrist and it looks at home, like something she's had for years.

Another thing: a bag of plastic wedding cake figurines. There are separate men and women in tuxedos and dresses, black, white, Latino, and Asian brides and grooms.

"Where did you get these?" she giggles.

"A flea market," says Lloyd. "When are you leaving, anyway? It's really soon, right?"

"Thursday in the afternoon. Tomorrow's my last day of work."

"I'll drive you to the bus," says Lloyd. "I'm off. We were going to go to the beach, but it's supposed to pour all day."

"Mona and Al made it," Ryan says, peeking out the window. "He must have picked her up. Her car's not here."

There are plates of sliced fruit and cheese, bowls of olives, tortilla chips, guacamole. The boys head right for it all.

"Don't go crazy," she says.

They look up at her. Donnie has a stack of chips sticking out of his mouth. He blinks at her, crunches down and shards of them fall to the floor at his feet.

"Maybe grab a napkin," she says.

Ida crouches down and picks up the crumbs. In just a few days, she will be stepping off the bus in New York. Linda is going to meet her because the subways out of Port Authority are too confusing. Her first weekend is already planned: an Italian restaurant, Linda's friends' band playing at some cramped club, and then a beer garden that just opened up right in their neighborhood.

"Oh," Mona says to Ida. "I didn't realize you had children! They look just like you."

"No," she says, shaking her head, horrified. "They're not mine. They just live nearby." Her own kids wouldn't be dirty. They wouldn't be moochers and they wouldn't be dirty. They wouldn't have to be.

"She's not our mom," says Carter.

"She's our friend!" says Donnie.

"Yes," says Ida. "I'm your friend."

"No she's not," says Carter.

"Sure I am." Ida frowns.

"Sort of," he concedes.

Lloyd cuts into her cake. Right across its middle.

It looks a little better than it tastes. As it should always be.

"I saw three surveyors out yesterday," Ryan says. "In the field over by you, Ida. Something is finally going to start to happen, I think. I was getting nervous for a little bit."

"Let's hope," says Lloyd. "Let's hope it doesn't happen like the shopping center happened. All the stores went belly up in three months."

"Bad retail choices," says Ryan. "They'll be replaced by better things. I mean, a Fashion Bug? Come on."

"I just saw this show about how someday, people won't be able to build new towns anymore," says Mona, licking her fork. "Just another fifty years or so and a few more million people and all the land will be used up already. Town building will be obsolete."

"Lots of things will be obsolete. Like televisions," says Ryan. "Someday, everyone will just watch TV on their computers."

"I'll wait 'til then to buy one of those big TVs," says Al. "I'm waiting for the obsolete sale."

"Record stores," says Ryan. "Gasoline, cash, libraries."

"I don't like the future," Carter huffs.

"Why?" Ida asks. "The future is good."

Carter turns his body away from the conversation; his dark eyes are narrowed.

"When you're a grown-up," Lloyd says to him, "It will be so cool. You'll probably have a *flying* car."

"I can't have one," he yells, face reddening. "They're gonna be too expensive!"

"Of course you can," says Ryan. "Relax. You'll have plenty of money when you're older."

"I'll never have that much money," he says, and stomps off. "They cost a thousand dollars and I don't even got a job!"

Ryan looks at Ida and shrugs.

Mona has a book of photos of a trip she just took to St. Augustine. An old monastery, a fort, a lighthouse. Ida stands, looking over Mona's shoulder. Mona is in the center of every one. She'd gone alone and asked other tourists to take her picture.

"I would have gone with you," says Al. "If I had known you were going to be all pathetic like that."

"I wanted to go alone," says Mona. "I never mind it. I'm alone a lot of the time."

"I think that's cool," says Ida. "It's brave."

"Thank you," says Mona, and gives Ida's cheek a gentle pinch. "I like myself these days."

When Mona lets go, Ida looks around the room. Where are Carter and Donnie? She peeks behind the couch, in the corners of the room. She stands up and peeks in the kitchen. Empty.

She walks down the hall and hears banging in the bathroom.

"Who's in there?" she says.

"Leave me lone," says Carter. "I'm just going to the bathroom." She can hear him rummaging around in the medicine cabinet.

"What are you doing?" she whispers. "If you're in their stuff, cut it out!"

Donnie is in Ryan and Lloyd's bedroom, sitting on the floor. His back is turned to her.

"What are you doing?" she asks.

He jumps. "Muffing," he says.

"Do you have something in your mouth?"

He shakes his head.

"Open your mouth," she says. "Let me see."

His tongue pushes forward and out pops a coin. It falls on the floor.

She reaches down and picks it up. A woman/angel's flowing silhouette on one side, a fern on the other. A French franc.

"Where'd you get this?" she says.

Donnie hesitates before pointing a fist toward the silver piggy bank on the shelf.

"What's in your hands?" she asks. He opens them both and dozens of coins drop to the carpet.

"Give me those," she says. She scoops them up and puts them on the shelf. "Stand up," she says. She takes him by the hand and walks to the bathroom. She knocks on the door, "Carter, are you still in there?"

"Leave me alone," he says.

"Let me in."

Nothing.

"I won't tell on you if you let me in now."

After a second, he opens the door and tries to scoot out past her. She grabs his hand and pulls him and Donnie into the bathroom.

"Sit down," she says to Donnie. She points to the edge of the bathtub.

"That," she says, pointing to Carter's shirt. Something is underneath the shirt. "Take it out."

He reaches under his shirt and hands her the maneki neko cat. She opens the medicine cabinet and puts it back where she knows it goes.

"Aren't you having fun?"

"A little bit," he says.

"I don't get it. You go to someone's house and they feed you nice food and nice cake. The one thing you do not do is steal something from someone who is just being nice to you."

Carter is holding his hand over the side of his shorts.

"OK, what's that?"

Carter reaches into his waistband and gets it. A razor.

"What were you going to do with this?"

"Shave," he says.

Ida sighs. "I think I made a mistake. You guys have to go home now."

Donnie starts to cry.

"Please don't cry," she says. "It's my fault. Not yours. I'm not going to tell them you were messing with their stuff."

Ryan drives the boys home. They sit in the back seat with thick, Saran-Wrapped squares of cake in their laps. Ida is going to go back to his house with him after they drop them off.

Quietly, Donnie says, "Carter, you can have a flying car someday. We can save up and buy one."

"OK," Carter says. He sighs, laying the drama on thick.

"Where do you two live?" asks Ida. She turns and looks at Carter. "What's your *exact* address? I know where you don't live. I know you don't live in that house you told me was yours."

"Hm," says Donnie, under his breath.

"Nine-ten Bell," says Carter, sounding more bored than busted.

"I think it has to be that way, Ryan," says Ida, pointing. She turns her head. "Is it that way, guys?"

Carter nods.

They pass the woman's house, its soft, precious lawn. Seven Bell Lane. The bracelet. Jeez. She still has it. Tomorrow, on the way to work.

She can't picture another house on the street, but they follow it a full mile and then even longer as it curves around canals and becomes an all-dirt road.

"Keep going," says Carter. Ida watches the odometer as they ride a slow and bumpy mile. Finally, the dirt road ends and there is a house there, exactly like all the other houses, with dark curtains or sheets covering the windows. The blue bed of a rusted truck peeks out from the back of the house. A broken chest of drawers is on the front lawn, its side bashed in.

"This is it?" she says.

The boys nod.

"What weird numbers," says Ryan. "Why bother making a nine-ten if there are only two houses on the whole street?"

She gets out of the car to walk them to the door. She steps over a pair of men's underwear, covered in mud. She steps over an empty plastic package of no-frills hot dogs. Beer cans everywhere. Disgusting. It is like Door Hill, except for the tall trees behind that house, and those tall trees hid so many shameful things. The summonses her father got, balled up and thrown hard between upper branches. The bad report cards that nobody was going to look at anyway. The bucketsful of piss and shit that winter the oil company stopped making deliveries and the pipes froze and burst.

And the smell of rot. She thinks she is going be sick.

"You can't come in!" snaps Carter. He glares at her.

"Fine," she says. "I definitely wasn't going to."

She gets back in the car, and watches them walk to the door.

"Wait for a second," she says. "I want to make sure they go inside. They wander around all day long."

She turns around in her seat. The boys move so slowly. When they walk up to the door, they stand still, watching her over their shoulders. Finally, Carter opens the door and they go inside.

"Do you think I should knock on the door? Try to talk to their parents?"

"What would you say?"

"I don't know. They'd probably open the door with a shotgun in their hands."

"It looks like a tornado ripped through here," Ryan says, turning the car around.

SEVENTEEN

O N HER LAST MORNING in Fort Starlight, the air tastes salty and clean, just like it did in Erne City. With the windows open, the Atlantic's essence blows from the east into her nose and mouth and stings her sinuses. The rain, which started the afternoon before, is coming down so hard. She's never seen rain like this.

This storm is real. With its wind and rain and intransient personality, it is a different creature altogether. Not a twenty-minute shower that will leave the earth thirsty. The weather is sending her off with a bang.

Ida will have to go out into it, though. She promised to call Linda and confirm to her that she is really on her way. She is planning to leave for the bus station in five hours, and just over thirty-seven hours after that, her bus will finally pull into Port Authority, right in the middle of Manhattan. She has enough money for first and last month's rent and a few hundred dollars before she gets a first paycheck. She has an interview scheduled at Accountemps on Monday morning at nine. Linda will lend her something to wear. Ida can't type beyond hunting and pecking. She hopes that isn't a problem. *Everybody who walks in gets hired*, Linda said. *You can pick your nose during the interview and still walk out with a job.*

There is a lot to do. When she got up that morning and took stock, what she thought was going to be easy and small is neither. It doesn't help that on her last day of work, J.B. let go of his prickliness with her and told her that the clearance sale on the kitchen goods, not scheduled until the next week, could start early just for her, if she wanted to take advantage of it. Ida bought four non-stick pans, stainless steel measuring cups, a candy thermometer, a rolling pin and a pastry cloth. She can't fit all of her things into the duffel bag. After she calls Linda, she will have to ride to Karr's to buy another. In the rain.

She can't bring everything with her. The chair cushions she once slept on, the cooler, the drinking glasses. She wants to treat this house kindly. Anything she can't take, she will stack neatly in the corner.

Ryan gave her his navy blue University of Connecticut hooded sweatshirt because buses are always freezing.

She starts with emptying the little refrigerator. Her chicken burrito from the day before can be eaten that afternoon. There is also a half pint of cream, butter, two apples, a block of cheddar cheese, three eggs, vanilla extract, a bagel, sugar, and a smattering of flour at the bottom of the bag. Ida takes out the cheese and cuts it into chunks, chewing them, her hand on her hip, thinking about a recipe she read about that could put to use some of these things. Apple clafoutis. No decorating necessary. She remembers thinking, when she read it, that it was so much simpler than she ever would have imagined, so simple she shouldn't even have to write it down. It comes to her now, and she is so inspired by the coincidence of having almost all of the ingredients, save for apple brandy, that she has to make it, and let it bake while she packs. She will leave it in there in the refrigerator so that when Donnie and Carter come by and find her gone, they will then open the refrigerator and find this and know, she hopes, that it is meant for them. They would eat it anyway.

She turns the oven on to 375°, butters a single small cake pan, pours a few spoonfuls of sugar into it, and moves the pan back and forth so that the grains can form a whispery crust.

She washes the apples, peels their skin away with a paring knife, cores, halves, and slices them thin. She arranges the slices in a fan pattern at the bottom of the pan.

Maybe she should write them a note, she thinks, and put it next to the clafoutis, telling them she thinks they are very nice boys and she hopes that they like this special treat, that it is something that boys in France like to eat after school. Maybe it would make them want to go there someday, do something with themselves someday. You never know how some tiny thing you say or do could change somebody.

Ida mixes the eggs, sugar, and cream with the hand mixer. She can hear the wind over the noise. She looks out the kitchen window and sees that the rain is falling even harder, sheets of water against the glass. The blue tarp sucks all the way in and all the way out again, straining the thick duct tape. Last week, when she noticed that some of the tape had lost its stick, she bought a new roll and reattached it.

Ida pours the mixture on top of the apples, lifts the pan, careful not to spill, and places it on the center rack of the oven.

After just a few minutes, a sweet smell fills the room.

She sits on the floor, trying to stuff all that she can into her one duffel. She packs it tightly, and has to squeeze the top together to get it zipped. She can smell the clafoutis turning golden. As it finishes baking, she empties the bag again, wondering if there is anything she can leave behind so that she won't have to go out in the rain for another bag. No such luck.

IDA GRUNTS AS SHE pedals, but the sound is lost in the wind. Once she buys a duffel bag, she will go back to the house, take a bath, relax, and enjoy watching the storm from there. She can finish packing and wait for Ryan and Lloyd.

The rain pelts against her eyelids and ears. Ida has to put her head down to get a full breath. It is taxing just to keep the bike steady or even moving forward; the wind pushes her no matter how hard she resists, away from the pavement and into the grass. If she let it, it would blow her right into the canals.

The bike. What will she do with it? She should have thought of that sooner. If she leaves it in her house, the boys will take it. And probably get hurt. She pictures Carter riding it, Donnie sitting on the handlebars. The two of them falling, a tangle of little limbs, right down into the canal where that alligator waits.

A wall of wind pushes against her and Ida doesn't have the presence of mind to try to resist it. She hits the pavement. She notices the blood on her elbow first, but her stinging calf got the worst of it, scraped on the pavement on the outside and cut by the gear shaft on the inner. Her calf bleeds in surges. She stands up. The wind rushes at her again, but she manages to pick the bike up and slowly, one steady, pissed off step at a time, wheel it toward home. She'll call Linda from a payphone on one of the Greyhound stops.

Her hair whips around her face. The rain gutter that was so recently attached to the front eave of the house now lays in the middle of the street. The wind lifts it up and moves it a few inches at a time, the aluminum clanging as it touches down on the pavement.

She sees a dark flash out of the corner of her eye. Another. The tar shingles on the roof fly off in chunks of two and three, sailing up into the dark sky, headed elsewhere. Ida moves faster, reaching the house and quickly closing the door behind her, leaning against it, catching her breath. The rain drips from her body and onto the concrete.

The kitchen light, which she knows she left on, is off. She flips the switch back and forth, but it stays dark. She opens the refrigerator and it is quiet inside. The power is out.

Ida watches the blue tarp suck out, in, and out again with such force that she worries it won't hold.

As if her thinking it made it come true, first one side pulls away and then the other and she watches the whole big thing detach from the house and fly across the sky.

The rain comes right in, like it has been invited.

Her things. She grabs her duffel, the plastic bags from Karr's, and brings them into the white, chalky bedroom. She goes back for the clafoutis, which is still warm.

Ida watches the storm from the bedroom window, her hands on the glass. So much rain has fallen by now that the field across the street from the house is flooding and the wind pushes the water forward rhythmically onto the asphalt. Waves. It looks like the ocean, expanding itself over the land. Fort Starlight wants her to know that it is as done with her as she is with it.

A car pulls up outside. It is Ryan, dripping in a rain poncho. She waves at him.

"You're early!" Still more than three hours to go.

"Get your stuff!" he yells. "Come with me!" He runs back to the car. The wind rocks it gently, back and forth. She'll have to leave some things behind, or wrap them up in a t-shirt and just hold it in her lap. She grabs her bag and opens the bedroom door.

The floor is drenched. Something else is on the cement, enormous and diseased looking. Gnarled, desiccated, brown. The severed head of a lion.

No. It is the dried out, dead top of a palm tree.

And something else. She doesn't see it at first. Near the front door stands a blackbird, silent, shaking the rain from its feathers, taking short back and forth steps on its stick legs. It shakes itself again.

"Go," she says.

She tries to shoo it further down the hall, away from her, away from the wind. It blinks its black eyes and hops backward.

She tugs hard on the car door to get it to close.

Ryan is livid. "You should see our house!" He bangs the steering wheel with his hand. "Christ, it's like they were put together with Popsicle sticks and Elmer's glue! I can't believe Allstate insured it."

"Where are we going?" she says. His anger makes her jumpy. It has taken until now for her to see that the weather is serious, that any house but the one she has lived in, which doesn't matter to her anymore anyway, might be falling apart.

"Karr's," he says, spreading his hand and turning the wheel. "I'm driving to a supermarket while my house is dissolving in a tropical storm."

"God," she says. "This is terrible." The rain is so hard that the windshield wipers are useless.

"Can you imagine if this were an actual hurricane? That old woman who lives on Bell Lane closed her door in my face. I told her it was dangerous."

"I don't get it. Why would a house just fall apart?" she says.

"Because I'm an idiot. It's a demo house. Apparently it was never meant to be lived in."

"Do you think they're all like that?"

"Maybe. Maybe not."

"Ryan," she says. "I think we have to go and check on those boys. Make sure Carter and Donnie are okay. Make sure they aren't out walking around or something."

"Make sure they're okay," Ryan repeats. He nods and sits up straight, glad to have a task. He makes the turn onto Bell and the rain fans upward on both sides of the car, like wings.

Ida scans the fields on both sides as they drive, worried she will see them out there, Donnie picked up by the wind and sailing across the sky. There is the blue bed of the rusted truck, the busted chest of drawers in the front yard.

She gets out of the car and runs to their front door, bangs on it.

Who's at the door? she hears from inside. It's Carter's voice, though she can see Donnie watching her.

"Get away from the window!" Carter yells, and Donnie's face disappears.

She bangs on the door, the rain streaming down her forehead and into her eyes. They don't answer. She tries the knob and it opens.

She puts her hand up to cover her nose and mouth. The stench is unreal. The room is covered in dirty plates and dishes and piles of rot and garbage.

"Hello? Donnie and Carter, are your parents here?" she says, her hand over her nose.

"Hi!" It's Donnie's voice. Then Donnie says, "Ow!" And then the sound of Donnie's muffled cry.

She hears Carter's voice, a loud whisper, "I told you to stay shut up!"

"Listen," she says, "I know you guys are here. I can hear you talking."

"Don't go out there!" Carter shouts at Donnie, and this is followed by the sound of bare feet, running. Donnie barrels into the living room and stops in front of her.

"He pinched me!" says Donnie. He reaches out and touches her arm. "Guess what? Speedy came back," he says, smiling and pointing to an orange cat, curled up on the couch.

"Carter, please come out here," she calls.

"We already ate up all the cake those two guys gave us."

Carter comes out. His lips are pursed and his arms are crossed in front of him, as if to say, *This had better be important.*

"Where are your parents?" she says.

"Mom is in the bathroom and our pop is in their room," says Donnie, taking her hand.

The bathroom is in the same place as in her house. She walks toward it, covering her mouth and nose with the crook of her arm.

The bathroom door is open. "Hello?" she says. She can see the figure sitting on the floor, leaning against the wall, legs splayed out. She can see the mouth, open and dark. The eye hollows stare out at her. One hand is on the floor, the fingers bent. Deader than deader than dead.

"Oh, Jesus," she whispers, and backs out.

She takes both boys by the arms and pulls them outside and into the rain.

"Speedy!" Donnie screams.

"I'll get him," she says.

She opens the car doors and nudges them into the back seat, lifting Donnie by one flank so that she can buckle him in.

"What's going on?" says Ryan.

Ida closes the door. She runs back into the house, kneels down at the entrance, and slaps at her lap until the cat slinks out from behind the couch and walks over to her. She tucks him under her arm. When she gets into the passenger seat, she tries to tell Ryan, tries to whisper it, but she sits and shakes, the tears falling from her eyes and into her own unbuckled lap. The cat climbs up her shoulder, swipes its tail across her face, and jumps into the back seat.

"Where are we going?" says Carter.

Ryan turns around. "We're going to the supermarket."

She closes her eyes and sees that body—what had once been their mother—sitting on the bathroom floor and staring out at Donnie and Carter for all this time. Ida sees it as it happened: them, looking back at her, for weeks and weeks and weeks, opening the door, closing the door, using that single bathroom, closing their eyes.

"Why are *you* crying?" says Carter.

She bites her lip, sniffs. "How did this happen?"

"You mean why'd they die?"

She nods.

"She gave him a can of beer and he drank some of it and he died. Then she started crying and she drank the rest of it and she died, too. It was poison beer. She didn't even tell us she was gonna die," he says, still stung by the unfairness of that particular part.

"You didn't drink any of that beer, did you?" she sputters, turning back to look at them.

They stare back at her. Ryan drives slowly

"Why would we do that?" says Carter, like she is crazy. "I don't want to be dead."

Ida squeezes her eyes shut. All the times she told them to go home, to get lost. She knew. She knew something was wrong.

She sobs into her open hands.

Donnie's fingertips reach over and pat her shoulder.

Inside Karr's, the lights are bright. The rain pours sideways down the glass windows at the front of the store, but inside is serene. It is dry and bright. A Muzak version of *Hey Jude* plays.

"Hey, look who's here," a strawberry blonde cashier calls, haughtily. "I thought you flew the coop." She started just around the time Ida gave notice. Alice or something.

J.B. set up a patio table display at the front of the store, with collapsible umbrellas. $300 for a table, umbrella, and six chairs made of heavy plastic. Lloyd sits in one of the chairs, waiting for them.

"Finally," he says, his hands clasped together. "How bad did it get?"

Ryan's hand goes to Lloyd's shoulder. He leans in to Lloyd's ear and speaks in a voice so low that Ida can only hear a single whispered word. *Police.*

The boys eye the endless food.

"We're hungry," says Donnie, tugging on her hand.

"What do you want?" she says. "Whatever you want, I'll get you. Do you want fried chicken? Sandwiches?"

Carter looks at the gleaming floor. "I want cereal. With milk."

"It's cold in here!" says Donnie, pulling his arms inside of his t-shirt and hugging himself.

"Okay," she says, so brightly, like she's only ever invited them in, told them to stay as long as they wanted, only ever wanted them safe and happy and clean and well-fed.

She will feed them. She will fill them up and buy them cozy sweatshirts with hoods. "What kind of cereal?"

"What kind do they got here?" says Carter.

Ida leads them to the cereal aisle and tells them to pick out whatever they want. She'll be right back. She walks purposefully through the store, rounding up the sweatshirts, ceramic bowls, milk, spoons from the soup counter by the deli.

There is J.B.

"Bradford's my new guy," he says, gesturing toward the bakery. "So far, he's not too terrible. We'll see. This rain. Wasn't so bad when I left this morning. I was just listening to the news and it's supposed to die out in an hour or two. Hey, aren't you out of here today?"

"I'm supposed to take a bus in a few hours," she says, "but I don't know. This weather."

"This is nothing," he says, gesturing toward the window.

When Ida returns, Donnie is seated on the floor and Carter is studying the rows of cereal boxes. He sidesteps as he scans them, his hands behind his back. A box of Honeycomb is already picked out. So is Fruity Pebbles. He reaches out his hand and grabs the Count Chocula.

Carter isn't fat anymore. Not at all, really. Not skinny like Donnie, but not the tubby kid he once was, with the shaky little belly, fat fingers, puffy arms. He is hardly even husky anymore.

"Here," she says, holding a sweatshirt over his head. He puts his arms up and through the sleeves. She does the same for Donnie, and yanks the price tags off.

"I'll go pay." She bends down to get the cereal boxes, and puts them in the cart with everything else.

"Your bus is in two hours?" says Lloyd.

She nods and pours the milk over Donnie and Carter's cereal.

"Yeah. That's when it leaves Erne City."

"We'll make it," he says.

"Your poor house," she says.

"We have an insurance policy," Lloyd says. "That's what they're for."

She leans into him, feels his rough cheek against her own.

"It's not as bad as Ryan thinks," he says. "The house is mostly concrete. It'll be OK."

Ida nods. She is lucky. Nothing has been taken from her. She tries to picture the bus, the cold bottles of soda she'll get at each stop, New York City, the subway, Linda's big kitchen with the window that opens over that park.

A woman is walking toward them, clutching a tiny girl by the hand. Even from far away, Ida recognizes the woman's eyes, huge and unblinking behind her glasses. The woman whose bracelet Ida still has somewhere. Where? She can't remember.

"You took my advice," says Ryan.

"Yes, I left," she says, her voice shaking. "I heard something outside. Something flew off the house. I don't know what it was."

The woman collapses into the lounge chair, landing with a thud, the legs of the chair scraping across the floor.

"Why are we at the supermarket?" says the little girl, looking around at everyone. Her blue eyes peek out under the rim of a tiny baseball hat.

The boys take her in, studying her little face, her pink skin and the blue veins so close to the surface. Ida saw a boy like this on TV once. The girl's nose is pointed and small, pressing downward. Her ears stick out. Her cheeks, though, look soft, with fat under the skin. Almost like a kid's cheeks should look.

"What are you?" says Donnie.

"I'm a girl," she says. "I'm Madeline."

"Oh. We seen you before."

Nancy clutches at the neck of her blouse. "I'm almost afraid to go back."

"We won't go back yet," says Ryan. "We'll go later. Once this is over."

They can hear the wind over the Muzak, a subtle high-frequency whistle. The rain still rushes against the glass, but it has gotten weaker.

"You know what?" says Carter, talking with his mouth full and dripping milk on the sweatshirt. "Everybody here right now is everybody who lives in our whole neighborhood."

"Not that tree house guy," says Donnie. "He's not here. 'Member him?"

"He don't live here anymore so that's different," says Carter, munching. "He moved away. And now we're gonna move into his tree house." He reaches for the box of Honeycomb and pours more into Donnie's bowl and his own. "It's better than where we live."

EIGHTEEN

IT IS AFTERNOON, LATE December. The male North American blackbird hops from one branch of the massive live oak to the next, poking around for insects. The house that had been built around its trunk was taken away, piece by piece, and the tree, save for a few busted branches, is no worse for wear. It won't be here much longer.

He has lost his mate. She flew away, farther south. She will find a new mate on Marathon Key, and the two will make the trip back north together, and then back to Marathon Key, where they will hatch more chicks. But he will not. He is stuck here. Hopping a few feet at a time is all that he can manage.

At the bottom of the one last tributary of the Starlight River, scheduled for dredging in a few days, is a rusty and almost unreadable red plastic and tin pin, which had once been loosely attached to the front pocket of Mitchell Healy's jean shorts. The pin, which floated several miles before getting stuck in slimy mud, says *The Spiders*. Mitchell found it early on the day he died, lying on the ground near the wooden gates of his development. He wondered how it ended up in this stupid place and what it meant, and felt as though it had to be something important. The pin represented strangeness, hipness, chaos, a license to drive a car and being old enough to get a punk rock haircut. Someone cool had been there and Mitchell pretended that the someone cool was simply himself, in the future, leaving a souvenir of what was to come. *Take it.*

You'll know when the time is right to use it. And so he had.

Mitchell's remains were found in early October in a different canal, far away from the Starlight River Park. Dental records matched up. They never knew for sure how he died, but there is some consolation in the fact that there was no evidence of foul play. The Healys left Fort Starlight and buried what was left of their son at home, in Providence, and Mrs. Healy will have many nights during which she wonders whether he would still be alive if they'd never left Providence. Maybe not. She feels like she was singled out for this particular pain, that it had started heading in her direction the moment she was born.

PETER IS IN A white Jaguar, driving away from what was once the town of Fort Starlight. The only thing left of it is Karr's. The nature trails and wooden docks and platforms that lined Starlight River Park are gone. The houses of Starlight Estates are gone.

A few hours ago, Peter pulled the car over when he saw a lone temporary office, buzzing with its window-box air conditioner. The sign on the door said Stengel Incorporated. Peter opened the door. Inside, five men stood around a conference table. They turned to look at him.

"Who are you?" one asked.

"Peter Haggenden," he said.

"You aren't…"

"Yes. Byron Haggenden's son."

"Your father was an investor on one of our earlier projects. Not this one, though. I think he would have wanted to invest in this one."

Peter nodded, noncommittal.

A young man took him aside.

"I'm just…I can't believe you walked in here." His face was flushed, his eyes, to Peter, too vibrant. "This is an amazing coincidence. I *won* a Haggenden scholarship at the end of high school. It paid for my room and board for the whole four years."

He went on. He hadn't been the best student, and the Haggenden application, geared toward those who needed a second chance, was the toughest essay he'd ever written. He threw himself into it, and winning the scholarship made him see himself in a new way, as someone capable, someone with a fresh start. And it had really changed everything. Peter nodded, smiled just enough to show he was glad to hear it, which he was.

He was still talking when one of the other men gestured for Peter to come over the conference table. "Forgive him," he said. "We've been working out of this trailer here for a month with nobody but each other to talk to."

"Those houses sure disappeared fast," said Peter.

"It's good it happened when it did. Better than later. It never would have worked out. You can't just build a town wherever there happens to be land. It's not realistic."

"It's predatory development is what it is," said another.

Peter nodded. "No jobs," he said. "Where would everyone work?"

"Jobs. Now we'll have some of those. Here, take a look at this," the man pointed to the table. They were in phase four of the plans. The Starlight River has already been redirected to two new, large canals, instead of the dozens and dozens of small ones. That would make room for a monorail system to take shoppers from the stores to their cars or tour buses. It will be impressive: the people-carrying monorail cars will be in the front, and the cargo-carrying cars will follow them and go directly to the parking areas, with porters and frequent stops. No one will have to walk more than four minutes to their cars. It will all keep moving efficiently, not slowing anybody down. Shiny-white, space-aged, civilized shopping.

The five Stengel men said they were proud to be working on this. *It is incredibly exciting,* they said. *Nothing like this exists anywhere.* The land hasn't even all been razed yet, and already they have a contract for a similar project in Texas. They pointed to the map on the table, showing Peter where the actual complex will be. They handed him a shiny pamphlet, which is just a prototype. Fortune Springs will be a mammoth shopping Mecca, the likes of which have never been seen before. The investors are pouring money in so that Fortune Springs can be finished and functioning by the end of next summer. Quarter mile strips made up of dozens of stores that will be grouped according to merchandise. Clothing, Shoes, Sporting Goods, Housewares, Consumer Electronics, Linens, Toys, Books. Superstores and specialty shops alike are anxious to get in on the action, while they can ensure themselves a place.

And amidst all of that, there will be nearly a quarter mile strip made up of only dining, with mass-pleasing favorites like Cracker Barrel and Applebee's. But there will also be an original microbrewery. There will be an international food bazaar for the more sophisticated palates. Middle Eastern, Vietnamese, Greek, Spanish tapas, a French creperie, a German bratwurst haus, an Ethiopian restaurant with tables low to the floor, food ladled onto spongy bread and eaten with fingers. Three areas to leave your children, fully licensed and insured. The Pre-School-Fun-and-Learning-Space will have a ratio of one caregiver per four children. Toddlers can learn the alphabet and the pledge of allegiance while their parents shop. Kid-Zone is for grade-schoolers, and there will be arts and crafts, face-painting, kickball games, a carousel. Teenville will be less obvious about the supervision, but the teenagers will be no less supervised. They will have a wave pool, a climbing rock, access to French fries.

Everyone goes home happy. Disney World for serious shoppers. There will be a lot of Japanese, according to the research, so that will be factored in.

Peter said, "Well, that's certainly something." Then, he got back into the car and drove away and into the streets that led to where his tree house had been, but much of the woods had been razed.

He wasn't sure why he'd come back here. Seeing the change was both disorienting and a relief at the same time. He turned the car around and drove to town.

Peter stands up and stretches on this sunny strip of sand at the very bottom edge of Erne City, where the dunes and softness are beginning to appear as low tide fully sets in. It is a dangerous place during high tide. Even the intrepid surfers—who come scouring the shore, early in the morning, looking for the right height and the right amount of glassiness—don't want to risk bashing their skulls or breaking their boards here. There is no direct path to this beach; people who want to come to this spot have to make the choice to walk from far away.

He has just finished spending a few weeks alone in the empty, fifteen-room Haggenden house in Miami, one of a half dozen Haggenden homes on the east coast. He still thinks of them as his father's houses, though now they are all his.

The key was under the mat in front of the gardening cottage. The house was airy and the bathtubs were deep and wide, made of white-grey marble. There was no dust on anything, as the cleaning people come even when there is no one to clean up after. It was a house Peter had never lived in. The house his father died in.

Among the three cars in the garage was the old and perfect Jaguar, its keys in the glove box. Also in the glove box were photographs of this same car, in various stages of restoration. One of just the chassis, the headlights missing. The pictures told the story. One his father obviously took of himself, holding a box, a small smile on his mouth. Inside was a rear-view mirror, packed in bubble-wrap.

He can't picture his father, leaned over, tinkering with anything, or taking something apart and putting it together so that it would work. But he had done it.

Peter tried the key and it started right up. The gas tank was full. He pulled out of the garage and driveway and drove toward downtown Miami. People looked at the car and at him at stoplights.

He tried to enjoy himself those weeks. He sat on the veranda, sipping rum as the ice melted in the glass. One night, he even ventured out to hear Cuban jazz, but after the first set, he drove back to the house, and back at the house, he watched the jacaranda's leaves bounce in the sea breeze. He missed his father.

He wasn't enjoying himself at all. Sleep wasn't restorative. Showers didn't make him feel cleaner. Coffee didn't rouse him at all. He shaved his moustache, but nothing changed. He left the next morning.

Peter spent nine thousand dollars on his music project in paying the engineer, and four thousand more getting to Los Angeles, staying in a hotel, and leaving Los Angeles again. The wasting of money, though he has always been slow to spend it, has nothing to do with this feeling of pure failure. The disappointment was the music. The distress hit him by surprise when he was sitting down on the white couch at the studio, hearing the end product after it had been mixed and mixed again by a man Peter trusted knew exactly what he was doing. Someone who did his very best with what he had been given. Someone who could probably make something out of nothing.

Banal, New-age garbage. When his carefully selected and recorded sounds came together, they created nothing. The first time he heard it, he was hopeful; he strained his ears and his mind to hear what wasn't there. It didn't tug at his brain in any way, or make him feel like he was privy to any secrets. It would tug at no one's brain, except for the biggest of fools. No one needed to be evolved to appreciate it. It was music for now, and not even particularly good in that respect. It might be played in yoga classes, or in environmentally conscious retail stores, if he cared to try to make such a thing happen, which he did not. He sat with his head in his hands.

The engineer sat on a couch facing him, waiting for Peter to say something, but Peter didn't have anything to say.

"Let me know what you want to do with this," the engineer finally said. "It's your money."

He went to his hotel and he cried. Not only about the music, but also because there was nothing left inside of him. He felt used up, and for no good reason. As the night went on, his heart beat out of control. He could hear it in his ears like a drum. He thought that he was dying; hearts weren't supposed to beat like that. When he woke up at sunrise, alive and even rested, he felt betrayed. He was not only still alive, but felt calmer than ever before. Why?

He is hungry, and the coals are already hot. He walks beyond the seaweed, far out over the sandbars, and sits down in one of the tidal pools. He spears three smallish crabs through their middles (one on top of the other, a squirming shish-kebab, clawing at air). Before going back to the sand, he walks out farther, to see how big the waves are breaking in the distance. On the way, he notices a stingray caught in a bigger pool. Enormous and smooth, its fins like good Italian leather. It's the size of a coffee table. If it wants to get out before full low tide, it needs to go immediately. Only a few moments before it's too late, before it gets trapped for a few hours, but the ray doesn't seem to care.

Back on the sand, Peter cooks the crabs over hot coals. When they are done, he cracks and peels them to get to the flesh, but there isn't enough and there is no taste anyway. He feels hungrier than he can remember ever feeling. He stands up and starts to head back to the water, thinking that he will go in and find another tide pool, maybe find a lobster this time. He walks out and sees the stingray, totally stuck. There are a few big crabs in other tide pools, but he doesn't bother going in for them. There is nothing to season anything with. He wants to experience flavor more than he wants to satisfy his hunger. He gathers his few things and heads up the shoreline.

AT THE NORTHERN END of Erne City, right up on the shore, Ryan and Lloyd are cleaning their rented glass and stucco house. The ocean is their backyard. The rental house is a splurge. Stengel Incorporated offered them fifty thousand dollars for their house and land, provided they could vacate it immediately, and when they hesitated for three days, out of disbelief, the offer went up to seventy-five. The money is in their bank account. They are in no rush to spend it on real estate.

Ryan has the vacuum and Lloyd is washing the dishes. They are hoping to leave in half an hour, but Carter and Donnie are dragging their feet on their chores. They have been home from school for half an hour and all that Carter has done is dust the television set with four half-hearted swipes. He is sitting on the floor with the dust rag in his hand, scowling. He doesn't care enough that on the other side of the dusting and making his bed is something that he wants to do. Donnie is slightly more cooperative.

Lloyd jingles the keys to entice Carter, and this gets him moving faster. He has figured this out in a way that Ryan has not: they respond to rewards but they rebel against the threat of punishment. After the chores are done, they are going to Gatorburg in Valponia for the last show of the day.

This experiment has been a disaster. Thank God it is almost over.

No matter how many times they tell Carter that he can come into the kitchen for a snack whenever he wants, that no food is allowed in the boys' bedroom, Ryan and Lloyd continue to find food hidden under Carter's bed. He eats in the middle of the night. And once, he knocked over the fern on purpose, spilling dirt all over the floor, and wouldn't clean it up. There was an embarrassing *you're not my father* tantrum in the middle of a shoe store when Ryan refused to buy him soccer cleats for school shoes.

Donnie is destructive, wiping his nose on the sofa, the curtains, writing his name on the wall in Sharpie, jumping off of a chair and onto a glass table (somehow not breaking it).

Both of them lie at nearly every opportunity.

It's to the point where Ryan has to remind himself that they went through something awful, and will probably never be okay. Ryan is embarrassed that Lloyd turned out to be the patient one. Lloyd doesn't take any of it personally.

There was one good moment: Carter didn't know until recently that the moon was a real thing that other people knew about and not just something he sometimes thought he saw in the sky. He hadn't known that people had walked on it. They spent a few hours in the library in Erne City, turning pages in their stacks of heavy books, looking for photographic proof.

Last week, a woman at the DSS called Ryan; she'd located the estranged sister of the boys' mother—a single, professional woman who seemed to have her act together—but she had been traveling for the past few months and no one had been able to contact her until last week. She hadn't even known the boys existed. She is arriving next week to meet them and it looks very likely that she will take them in. Hallelujah.

Lloyd calls into the living room. "Hurry up," he says. "Or we'll go without you." He walks out, to show that he means it. He smokes again. Three cigarettes a day, enjoyed far from home, and with lots of tooth-brushing and mouth-washing directly afterward. It is worth this amount of trouble, and he doubts that three cigarettes a day, over the course of a lifetime, can do him much harm.

Carter runs the dust-rag along the stereo. He puts the rag on the table, turns, and runs out of the room, runs out the front door. Donnie is already seated in the car, and belted in.

A HALF MILE DOWN the same ocean drive, on the tiny terrace of her two-bedroom rental apartment, Nancy stands and looks out at the water, thinking about the boutique in town, near the café, with a shawl in the window that she likes the looks of. Lavender with mauve fringe. The nights are getting cooler and she can wear it while she sits out here, looking out at the ocean. It is beautiful here, and she is lonelier than ever before.

She quit her job when she sold her house and land, for slightly more than she paid for it, to Stengel. She found her grand-nephew by calling his trucking company. She made the choice of humiliating him to his company, and insisted that he send money to help care for his child. He complied, but still has not visited.

He will not manage to visit in time. Madeline will die just under a year from now of a heart attack while she is in the West Palm Beach waiting room of her pediatric cardiologist's office, following complaints of feeling dizzy after a trip to Disney World.

But right now, Madeline is taking a nap, dreaming of winter, which she vaguely remembers.

Nancy goes inside and picks up the phone. She is finally going to call Corinne back, and instead of putting her off like she usually does, she will invite her over. Tonight. Corinne won't have any other plans. They can go for a slow walk into town, stop off at the grocery, make a nice dinner for themselves, and watch a movie. With the way Nancy naturally is—melancholy, stuck in her own head, always feeling a little sorry for herself—she knows she is lucky to have a friend at all.

❖

Claudia Zuluaga

THE WINDSONG RESORT IS brand new and close to the southern part of Erne City. It is all-inclusive, and most of the guests are European. There is windsurfing, tennis, yoga, a babysitting service, a nighttime discotheque. The guests come for a week or two, at most, and go home sunburned and a little heavier. The workers in the resort, from the kitchen staff to the bartenders, are all of college age. Many are European, but all speak perfect English. They live together in small dormitories in groups of three. The pay is not impressive, but they have no expenses at all. Whatever the guests get, they get, too.

In the dining hall, every component of every meal is presented on silver chafing dishes, served by men and women in gloves and starched uniforms. The ceilings are high and white; the walls are mostly tempered glass to let in the sun and the full view of the waves as they lap against the shore. There is food available at all times, but dinnertime is when all the stops are pulled out. For non-resort guests, the meals are prix-fixe of twenty-five dollars for lunch and sixty for dinner, but those prices have not stopped the curious and well-heeled residents of Erne City.

There are themes for every meal: chiaroscuro, Japanese, fruits-du-mer, high-end American barbecue. The desserts, though, are mostly the same no matter what was served for dinner: a classic Viennese table and hand-made ice cream for the children. The pastry chefs come in early each day, making the same intricate Napoleons, Operas, and mille-feuilles.

There is another dining hall: Paradis. It opens only on Saturdays and Sundays and is not available to the resort guests. Ida works for the main hall three mornings a week, making pastries. She works all weekend in Paradis, where the business is exclusively American weddings. Windsong is the only such well-situated wedding venue within an hour in any direction.

Part of her job is spent talking to nervous, irritable future brides, grinning mothers, and detached grooms-to-be about cake. She takes a binder of wedding cake pictures to inspire them. And since the wedding catering fee starts at a hundred twenty-five per plate, the cake, though included, is always custom-designed and custom-made. She is in charge of making the cake for every wedding held here and she learns more with every single one.

Ida has finally learned how to work with fondant. She has to be quick but gentle. It breaks easily if it gets a chance to harden. When she was hired, Ida knew that she was under-skilled. Once again. Worse off, even. The cakes she made at Karr's now seem embarrassing, childlike. She is learning everything there is to know about cakes. A year or so of this is what she needs. Then, she'll probably be able to get a job as a pastry chef anywhere. Maybe even in New York. She is in no rush to be out on her own; Ida is now aware that she doesn't know a thing about running a business. She can see how easy it would be to lose everything.

When Ida had gotten a five thousand dollar check from Stengel, she deposited it in the national bank in Erne City, where it still is. Her piece of land turned out not to be the one with the house on it, but the empty lot directly behind it. But it is a lot of money, supplemented with every paycheck. She needs very little spending money; everything she might need is here. Sometimes, she imagines Robert finding her, and coming for a visit, how all of this finery will reflect so well on her.

Ida is done with work for the day. It is just past lunchtime. All morning long, she rolled croissants and hasn't had anything to eat other than the few flubs that happen invariably, accidentally on purpose, in any pastry kitchen. Most of the lunch guests are long gone, but the buffet is still set up, and several servers stand at the ready.

She takes a plate and asks for slices of tenderloin, roasted red bliss potatoes, Caesar salad. Her skin is tawny from afternoons spent in the waves. She doesn't swim alone because she has friends at Windsong; they are probably not the kind she will keep forever, but she is grateful for them anyway. After her shifts end, she has girls to sit next to in the white beach chairs, to stretch her legs with and talk about the winters they remember. They hand magazines back and forth and take turns going to get cold cans of Coke. This is what she's planning on doing today.

Ida sits down alone at a table, unfolds a cloth napkin and spreads it over her lap. She spears a potato with her fork and pops it into her mouth.

A man approaches her table and points to the chair.

"Do you mind?" he says, sitting down.

Ida shakes her head; her mouth is too full to respond. She stares at her plate.

He is eating the same thing that she is eating. Before he takes a single bite, he cuts the tenderloin in small pieces, cuts the potatoes in half.

"Hi there," he says. His fork spears a bite of potato.

"Hi," she answers.

"Good to see you," he says.

He is a guest, and there are rules about how to interact, even if they are flirty or confrontational or just plain weird. Smile once, she tells herself. Don't make eye contact. Focus on the food and eat quickly. Her fork clangs against her plate.

Something flashes and she looks up. He is pointing a butter knife in her direction.

"You look taller or something," he says. "Or maybe a little shorter."

"Look, I don't think I know you."

"Sure you do," he says, stuffing a fork full of romaine lettuce into his mouth.

"Excuse me," she says. But she does know him. In her head, she adds the moustache and sunglasses. It's Peter.

"Oh boy," she laughs, and rolls her eyes. "I didn't recognize you. You know, I wanted to get a crème brûlée but I decided it wouldn't be worth sitting with this wacko any longer."

"Forget the crème brûlée," he says. "Let's go for a walk. I want to show you something."

She follows him as he exits the restaurant and moves past the swimming pools toward the shore. He only walks a little bit faster than she does. They pass the bungalows of the resort, and dozens of houses. There are intermittent sunbathers, squinting, rubbing on lotion. They walk on and on. He is quiet, but he does not walk ahead of her. The houses thin out until there aren't any more.

The trees close in, cutting off the view of the road on the right. The strip of sand narrows, and rough, black rocks spring up in the water. She has never been here.

"This way," he finally says. She rolls her pants up above her knees and follows him in. The waves are low, free of foam. The water rushes in over her calves and then her knees. She rolls her pants up higher and they walk a fair way out. The water never gets any deeper, except in the tide pools, which both of them avoid.

He stops and so does she. "It must have gotten out," he says.

"What?"

"A great big stingray." He holds his arms out to show the size. "It seemed like something you would have liked to see."

"Oh," she says. She looks at him. Without the moustache, he looks delicate, even with his tight muscles. He is not a big man.

"No. It couldn't have gotten out," he says. "Let's go out a little bit more."

They keep going forward, scanning the tide pools on both sides. The water is so clear that Ida can see to the bottom of all of them. Small fishes, sand, bits of seaweed, scallop shells, whole and cracked.

There is the stingray in the last tidal pool, just before the sand bars end and the open ocean begins. It looks like the ones she's seen in pictures, only she didn't know they were this big. A brown-black diamond. Enormous. She stands very still as she watches it, its wings lifting softly, creating a current where there isn't one.

"You found it," he says. "Reach on down. Put your hand on its wing."

She looks at him and says, "I'm not going to touch it." It will bite or sting; the name has to come from somewhere. But he crouches down and reaches out to it. She watches, his fingers and palm gently stroking. She crouches down, too. First, just her fingertips. The ray is soft. She opens her whole hand over the top of the right wing. And the ray offers itself to Ida, nudging itself more fully into her hand. So soft. She laughs to herself and pulls her hand away and the ray stays there fluttering, waiting for more. She reaches out and pats it again.

"They're friendly," she says.

"That's because they know they're not all that delicious."

They stand up.

The water level is rising. It won't be long before the ray will be able to glide over the sandbar. Slowly, it turns its entire body around and faces the open ocean, like a car stopped at an intersection, waiting for the light to change.

ACKNOWLEDGMENTS

I would like to thank super-editor and force of nature, Victoria Barrett, whose sharp and thoughtful edits helped *Fort Starlight* become its clearest self. I feel so grateful and lucky to have had the experience of working with you.

I'd like to thank Katrina Roberts, stellar teacher of my first creative writing workshop, who was so enthusiastically encouraging. Thank you, my incredible teachers at Sarah Lawrence College's MFA program, who taught me to take reading and writing seriously: Mary LaChappelle, Brook Stevens, Peter Cameron, Lucy Rosenthal, and especially Sheila Kohler and Mary Morris.

Thank you to my most patient and insightful reader-friends, who offered help and encouragement along the way: Hope Chernov, Michelle Wildgen, Yasmin Dalisay, Jane Young, Maia Rossini, and Lucy Neave, and to my family, especially Alicia and Lauriana, who read the earliest drafts and gave me the confidence to write many more.

Thank you to my mother and father, for having had the guts to give pioneering a try.

Thank you, Jeanne Uhl, for generously watching my children and giving me space and time to both draft and revise.

For your friendship and encouragement, thank you to my colleagues at CUNY and in the English Department at John Jay College of Criminal Justice.

Thank you to both the Hall Farm Center for Arts and the Bread Loaf Writers Conference, for giving me the time and inspiration I sorely needed.

Thank you, E.A.B.

An extreme, heartfelt thank you to Sarah Yaw, my fabulous writing partner and friend, for our many drafting getaways and telephone marathons. May we always find a place and time to recharge each other and figure out we need to get to the next part.

Thank you, sweet Pilar, for my daily dose of joy, and for your superior knowledge of the finesse of dragonflies.

And thank you, most of all, to my wonderful husband, Christian Uhl, for your bottomless love and support over these many years.

ABOUT THE AUTHOR

 Claudia Zuluaga was born in White Plains, New York, grew up both there and Port St. Lucie, Florida, and now lives in New Jersey. She earned an MFA from Sarah Lawrence College. Her fiction has appeared in *Narrative Magazine, JMWW,* and *Lost Magazine,* and was included in Dzanc Books' *Best of the Web* series. She has been nominated for the Pushcart Prize and Best American Short Stories. Claudia is a full time Lecturer in the English department at John Jay College of Criminal Justice in New York City.